THE GERANIUM WOMAN

HAZEL MANUEL

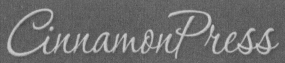

INDEPENDENT INNOVATIVE INTERNATIONAL

Published by Cinnamon Press
Meirion House
Tanygrisiau
Blaenau Ffestiniog
Gwynedd LL41 3SU
www.cinnamonpress.com
The right of Hazel Manuel to be identified as author of this work has
been asserted by her in accordance with the Copyright, Designs and
Patent Act, 1988. © 2016 Hazel Manuel
ISBN 978-1-910836-11-8
British Library Cataloguing in Publication Data. A CIP record for this
book can be obtained from the British Library.
Designed and typeset in Garamond by Cinnamon Press. Cover design
by Adam Craig © Adam Craig.
Cinnamon Press is represented by Inpress and by the Welsh Books
Council in Wales.
Printed in Poland
The publisher gratefully acknowledges the support of the Welsh Books
Council.

Hazel Manuel is a CEO turned full time novelist whose writing
follows a rewarding career in education, first as a teacher/
lecturer and after as a business leader within the education
sector. She now lives and writes in Paris.

Also by Hazel Manuel and available from Cinnamon Press:
Kanyakumari
Whether you label yourself 'traveller', 'tourist', 'adventurer' or
'spiritual explorer', you should read this before you leave the
front door. ... The mysteries of what really happened on the
. beach (will) keep you enthralled until the book's final
revelations."

Gary Botrill

Learn more about Hazel and her work at www.hazelmanuel.net

THE GERANIUM WOMAN

The Geranium Woman is dedicated to the world's business-women who, by the very fact of their achievement bring about positive change.

Prologue — Troyes

T-P. The letters sat there black, bold and resolute, as though the mere fact that I'd written them validated their power and the effect they had on my life. I handed him the sheet. I watched him stare at it for a long moment as firelight flickered over his face, carving deep shadows in the hollows of his cheeks. A log shifted and we both watched a spray of orange sparks fly up the chimney. He folded the sheet, kissed it and handed it back to me. I spoke quietly. 'You know what this means?'

I went to Troyes because I had to change my life. And by coincidence—or not—it was the time that people say the Mayans predicted the end of the world. Certainly, the end of T-P ended a world for me. I'd watched him that night through the kitchen window as he collected wood from beneath the trees. As he bent to pick up the logs, I saw his violent honesty etched into the lines of his face and the set of his eyes. Later, by the fire, he opened a bottle of Argentinean Malbec. It was called *Fin del Mundo* and I smiled thinly at the irony. He remained unsmiling. I watched the veins on his forearms bulge as he tightened the corkscrew, his eyes fixed on mine, and slowly withdrew the cork.

'Burn the old to make way for the new.' The words came to me silently from across the years and I murmured them into the flames. He proposed a toast to the end of the world and clinked my glass more firmly than he needed to, his eyes narrowed, never leaving mine. We talked about trust and risk and freedom. And fear. We both knew that we were talking about the end of T-P and what that would mean.

Mumbai

I like to think he came from a dream…a dream I had in a hotel room in Mumbai. In spite of the ceaseless traffic-noise and the drone of the air-conditioning, I was sleeping soundly until something—I don't know what—woke me or half woke me in the early hours. Lights from passing cars cavorted through the half-light of the room and something that wasn't quite him, his shade perhaps, stroked the edges of my consciousness as tendrils of his essence lured me back into sleep. I woke later with a feeling of anticipation that had nothing to do with my reason for being in Mumbai.

When I met him I can't say I connected him with the dream. That came after. But I had the feeling that something at the root of me recognised him. He was standing by the double doors of the conference hall, a tall Indian man, apart from the other suited delegates crowding into the atrium, a linen jacket slung over one shoulder. I noted that he wasn't wearing a tie and that his rolled up shirt sleeves revealed taut, brown forearms. I noted too his naked ring-finger. Savouring the fascination, I watched him, my eyes moving up the length of his body, lingering at his firm thighs, a leather belt, the hint of stubble on his face, before coming to rest at his eyes. I put my water-bottle to my lips and took a long, slow sip.

He neither spoke with nor acknowledged the other delegates and he didn't look at me either, his eyes resting instead on something indeterminate in the middle distance. He gave the impression of encompassing all his gaze passed through, as though his mind had left the confines of his body and swept ahead of him into a future that only he could own.

After some minutes watching, I walked over and introduced myself, shaking his hand firmly. He looked at me for a long moment before I let go. He told me nothing more than his name. Ardash.

I didn't sit by him, but throughout the morning session I watched, noting the straightness of his back, the intensity in his eyes. He made no notes and didn't open his delegate pack. Afterwards, I followed him out of the hall at a distance. He lingered in the atrium and I wondered whether he'd noticed me watching him. Before I left, I walked up to him once more. I gave him my business card and before turning to leave told him: 'I hope we meet again.'

Paris, Montparnasse Tower and Les Halles

'A business that makes nothing but money is a poor business. Didn't someone famous say that?'

'Making more money wouldn't be the worst idea. Besides, you know what he'll say if you quote *that* at him!'

I cursed the fact that we'd coincided on the platform, but as we pushed our way through the mass of suits streaming out of the metro-station, the gargantuan erection of Montparnasse Tower bearing down on us, Marine at least had time to air her views about our impending meeting. More particularly about one of its participants.

'He'll have made sure he gets here before you,' she said, elbowing her way ahead of me.

'You give him too much power,' I replied.

'Well the meeting should be fairly routine.'

'*Business meetings are never routine.*' I smiled as I quoted my old mentor. No doubt this morning would see me running the usual gauntlet of egos and ambitions.

'Taxi!' a man with an American accent yelled, cursing when it failed to stop. *We're all hunters.*

'*Eh, regarde où tu vas!*' I accepted a woman's shrugged apology as she shoved past us.

'I'll bet you anything he's already got to Jean. That guy needs to grow a pair.'

I glanced at Marine but she merely raised an eyebrow.

At the entrance to the tower, the uniformed security man winked and stood aside to let us pass and we entered the fray, joining the rest of the suits hurrying across the lobby.

'I don't see why he should get his own way on this,' Marine said. 'It makes no sense to focus solely on Europe, India is an excellent market for us. He's just digging in.'

'Don't worry about that,' I answered. 'We'll get our expansion.'

The lift arrived just as we did and once inside we looked straight ahead as twelve or so others crammed in and we all began the familiar ritual of shuffling backwards, pressing our arms to our sides, trying and failing not to touch our neighbours. 'Hold it!' a woman's voice called just as the doors closed and the lift jolted upwards. 'Not her day,' a man muttered. No one responded.

'I'm in the mood for a fight,' Marine murmured. I didn't answer her but kept my eyes fixed on the floor-indicator which raced past ten, thirteen, twenty-seven, continuing upward.

A little over three years before, I'd sat in the bar of the Les Halles Novotel sipping gin and watching the late afternoon light filter prettily through the glass walls of the courtyard garden. A man in a white suit was playing something soothing on the grand piano and François' voice, slow and deliberate, punctuated the music. He'd just put a proposition to me.

'I need to think this through,' I answered him, wondering immediately why I'd said that. *Be careful*, I thought, *slow down*.

François smiled at me in a way that made me think of my father. 'What's to think about?' he replied. 'I'm offering you the post of CEO.'

He was right of course, what was there to think about? A great swell of emotion rose in my stomach but I forced myself not to respond other than to shake my head at a prim waiter who had sidled up to the table. François cupped the back of his neck and massaged it for a moment.

'I'm getting too old for this game,' he said. 'I don't have the energy for it any more. You've all seen that I've become less involved in the day-to-day running of the business and I don't mind admitting that these days I think more about the golf course than I do about board meetings.' He chuckled and tinkled the ice in his glass before draining it.

'No, it's time for me to step aside and let some fresh blood take the helm.'

I held my tongue and looked at him for a long moment. The pianist began a more up-beat tune and I took a sip of gin to hide my excitement.

'Are you actually stepping down,' I asked eventually, forcing myself to speak slowly, 'or just taking a back seat?'

François smiled, clicked his fingers at the waiter and pointed at our glasses. 'I think we can stand another couple of these, don't you?' He turned back to me. 'You're a shrewd player. You want to know whether you'll be given full rein.'

'I want to know exactly what it is I'd be agreeing to,' I said. 'I know how important the business is to you. Don't take this the wrong way François, but I wouldn't want to be a puppet.'

François' eyes followed a woman in a tight red dress as she walked past us to where some American tourists were having difficulty making themselves understood. '*Coffee*, I want a *coffee*,' a man said, his New York accent turning it into 'kaw-ah-fi'. I smoothed my hemline as François turned back to me. Our drinks arrived along with a little dish of olives.

'I won't deny it,' he said, 'I'd be lying to myself if I thought I could just hand it over. I started this business in a back room, with nothing but a phone and a file-o-fax.' He chuckled. 'Now...a board of directors, international clients, offices in the Paris Montparnasse Tower...' He shook his head. 'Corporate events management... who'd have thought it...?' His eyes snapped back to me. 'You know what I think, when I walk through those doors and see all those people working away at their desks? Power. That's what I think. I built all this. Me.'

I breathed in slowly and took a sip of my gin. *He's offering it to me because of what happened in Troyes.*

'In answer to your question,' François continued, 'obviously I'll retain my shareholding and a directorship, non-exec of course. And I'll put in an appearance at the board every now and then. But I want to hand over the running of it to you.'

I began to speak, careful to modulate my voice. 'I have another question before I accept. What about—'

But François cut me off. 'Don't think I haven't given this a great deal of thought.' He popped an olive into his mouth. 'You've served your time on the board. You know the business. You know the market. To a greater or lesser extent the same can be said of all four of you, you make a strong board.' We both nodded. 'Marine, Jean... No. Neither have been on the board as long as you have and Jean's too young, as keen as he is.' François leant back in his chair and watched as the Americans bustled past in a loud stream of chatter. 'Boy, that French *mill-fool* sure is good,' one of them said. I smiled. François turned back to me and put his glass down on the table. His jaw tightened and he looked at me intently, but I spoke before he did:

'Have you told Tristan that I'm to be CEO?'

Three years later. A typical weekday morning and in the lift, the scent of recent sweat fought with 'Clive Christian' and 'Chanel.' I held my breath until we lurched to a halt. Five of us pushed our way out, three turning right, Marine and I turning left, and we walked in silence along the carpeted corridor before reaching the long, oblong window to our offices. We both stopped and looked inside at the open-plan which was already occupied by a dozen shirt-sleeved inhabitants silently talking into handsets, typing, staring at screens. *The hive.*

'He's here,' Marine said nodding towards a glass-walled side-office.

'Good,' I replied, pushing open the door to a rush of noise. 'Let's get this meeting started.'

A hospice in Levallois, Paris

'Father, please, must we talk about this now? You need to rest.' The awkwardness of his movements intensified my father's helplessness as he strained to lift himself in his white-sheeted hospice bed. I took his elbow and eased him up, wincing inwardly at how fragile his bony shoulders were beneath my hands.

'I'll be resting in perpetuity soon enough, girl,' he rasped, clutching at my arm. 'I have things to say to you while I still can. Important things.' The seat of the small leatherette armchair by the side of his bed stuck to my thighs and I stood once more to straighten my skirt as a nurse wrote something on the chart at the foot of the bed. Evening was falling and a rosy light filtered through the trees outside. I watched a bird silhouetted against the sky as it flew and marvelled that beauty could still exist when death was so near. 'Okay Father,' I said, sitting back down. 'I'm listening.'

He glanced at the nurse. 'I've had time to think, lying here hour after hour. I need to know that when I'm gone, you'll be okay.' He was still clutching my arm and I stared down at his knuckly fingers, his yellow finger nails. I went to speak but my father half raised a liver-spotted hand to stop me. 'If only you had married, I could have died content, knowing you'd be looked after.' The nurse made eye contact with me and gave me a sympathetic half smile.

'Come on now,' she said in a no-nonsense voice, replacing the chart at the foot of his bed. 'Let's get you a little more comfortable.'

'I'm comfortable enough, silly thing, leave me alone,' my father tutted. The nurse ignored him and made little humming sounds as she gently lifted him to re-arrange the pillows. He scowled at her but let himself be eased forward.

'I don't understand,' he wheezed as the nurse and I helped him to lie back down, 'what you have against marriage.'

'Father, really,' I said, trying to sound soothing. 'You know full well I don't have anything against marriage. It isn't as though you've encouraged it in the past, is it?' I picked up my paper cup of weak machine-coffee, took a sip and squeezed my father's hand.

'Well girl, you should have brought home someone more worthy,' he grumbled. 'Not one of those 'Jean-Something's' was suitable.' He started to cough and the nurse and I both made shushing sounds. The nurse said, 'Now, now.'

'I don't know,' my father said with a little less agitation once his coughing had subsided. 'You young things. You don't know what's good for you.'

'Father, I'm hardly a young thing, am I?' I smiled at him.

'Exactly!' He broke into another rasping cough that lasted for some seconds. The nurse placed a damp flannel on his sweating brow and said 'Now, now,' again, as if calming a fractious baby.

'Father, you are a mass of contradictions,' I said gently once he was settled. 'You tell me that you want me to marry, but no one is ever good enough.' I smiled at him again. 'I promise you, if I meet the right man—and I really do mean the *right* man, then I will marry him. Is that a good enough compromise?' I sat back in my chair and took another sip of lukewarm coffee.

'I don't know why you talk about compromise. It's only natural to want to get married. But not to any old waster!' He wagged a bony finger at me. 'Besides...' he sighed and I heard his breath rattle wetly in his chest. 'I'd have loved to see you in a white dress... walked you down the aisle...'

'I'm not sure that would have happened anyhow, Father,' I said. 'I'm not the 'white-dress' kind.'

'More's the pity.' He smiled back at me and shook his head before closing his eyes.

'That's good,' the nurse said, drawing up his blanket, 'you get some rest.' My father's eyes snapped open.

'I've said already, haven't I?' he barked. 'I'll have all the rest in the world soon enough. Leave me alone to talk to my daughter.' The nurse patted me on the shoulder as she walked to the door.

'You know where I'll be if you need anything,' she said. 'I'll pop back presently.' My father's eyes drooped and I watched his face, waxy against the pillow. It was hard not to see the shallow rise and fall of the sheet as counting down the moments. I looked away.

Outside, some birds twittered loudly. I stood and walked to the window, parted the blinds and looked outside. My jaw ached from forcing myself not to cry and I choked back a sob as I watched the trees, black against the darkening sky. I turned as I heard my father stir. His lips began to move and I went to him, bending forward to hear. '...things to say...' I caught. '...important things...'

Achille De Quincy—Before my death

I am an old man but that is not the point. The point is that I am dying. There is a sickness incubating inside me that will not abate. I imagine it multiplying, cloning, colonising more and more of my body and as I watch the nurses coming and going it seems ironic that in spite of a lifetime spent ministering to the sick, I have ended up sicker than I have the power to heal. They call me 'Doctor.' They fuss around me, checking their machines, writing on their charts. They say what they hope are comforting things and they are kind enough. But I know and they know that soon the sickness inside me will begin to shut my body down, organ by organ. It is only a matter of days before those machines, this bed, this room will be the last material things I see.

For now my mind is functioning and I have been granted some small period of time in which I am able to think. What consumes me, alone in this bed as my life approaches its final moments, is not my impending death. Whatever it is that waits for me to draw my final breath is irrelevant. I am not religious; I have no wish or desire to confess my sins. These drugs, these machines will ensure that I will breathe my last peacefully, and I will slip away into whatever awaits me beyond. No, I do not fear death.

The weightier concern by far is the inscrutability of life. Of my life. The life I have lived, have finished living and can do no more to influence or change. What I leave behind me is pressing far more urgently upon my final resources than what lies ahead. "What I have done and what I have left undone." That I have lived these seventy eight years and still large tracts of my life remain an enigma to me is what my mind now returns to again and again. The same theme, the same questions dog me and trying to make sense of them is ultimately as ungraspable as the wind. But still shall I try. For her sake, I must.

Luxembourg City

Of course I'm on a train and of course I'm going to a meeting. It's an annoyingly sunny day and I look up tetchily from my laptop to squint into the early morning glare as Paris' northern suburbs flash by. I rub my temples and look back at the rows and columns of my spreadsheet, willing myself to concentrate. But the numbers all run together and I swear inaudibly.

'Cancel it!' he'd said. 'Luxembourg is *my* baby, it's *me* they want!'

'No, Tristan,' I'd replied, 'this project is far too important to let your plumbing emergencies hold things up. I'll go myself.'

It hadn't been easy re-arranging my own appointments to make the trip to Luxembourg City, and Tristan had remained resolutely thankless when, an hour after his call, I'd managed to clear my diary, book my tickets and confirm with our contacts that I'd be attending in his place. *Damn him.* I force myself not to dwell on it. Outside, the urban sprawl has given way to fresh green fields, and I let my mind wander away from Tristan to my father...and to Ardash.

Ardash, his dark eyes staring off into the distance... Ardash, linen trousers across taut thighs...his hand hot and hard in mine...and more. But not enough perhaps. I lean back in my seat. He doesn't know whether I have other lovers. I turn this fact around in my mind, picturing myself shutting it away from him in a room he has yet to access. I'm glad I still count the days before I'm with him. 'Twenty,' I say out loud. The man opposite raises an eyebrow at me. I ignore him. 'I wish you'd met him, Father,' I say silently. But turning to stare once more at the Champagne vines as they rush past in a blur of green, a part of me is glad he didn't.

16

The train slows to a halt and I strain to listen to a tinny announcement over the tannoy system. A barely audible voice informs us that there's a problem on the line and the train will be delayed. There is a collective groan in the carriage and a general flicking of glances at watches. The man opposite rolls his eyes at me and I feel an odd sense of disconnected community as I think how many of us will be late for meetings. The thought doesn't comfort me though and I mutter and frown as I fumble with my phone.

'Yes, probably at least half an hour, maybe more…

I appreciate that, but it's out of my control, there's a problem on the line…

Indeed, and I'll do my utmost to get there as soon as possible.'

The whining tone of my contact irritates me and after the call I sit back in my seat gazing out of the window at the vineyards. The thought occurs that a lot of the doubt and uncertainty of a new relationship is absent for me. I don't have to wonder whether Ardash is having sex with other women because I know that he is. I consider this, as a bird of prey—a Kite I think—arcs its solitary way over the field towards the forest beyond. The fact of Ardash's freedom makes me sharply aware of my own and I wonder whether or not this is a good thing.

He once talked about a trinity of him, me and us. I remember it clearly, we were dining at Lutetia, close to my apartment. It was late spring and we were sitting beneath the red awning on the little corner terrace enjoying the evening sun as it cast a reddening glow across the Seine. I remember watching Ardash, his face sharply profiled as he sipped his glass of Bourgogne Aligote and gazed past me across the cobbled Quai de Bourbon, its tall, black street lamps standing sentinel, to the shifting water beyond. 'We must look after all three parts of the trinity,' he'd said without turning back. 'That way we won't lose ourselves in each other.' At the time I loved him for it. I consider his words now and wonder, as the train begins to lurch forward, what my father would have thought. Outside, I watch the Kite swoop to catch its prey.

I see the men I'm meeting seated at a window-table of the Hotel Europa as I arrive, and I raise my hand in greeting and hurry over. The men all stand as I approach and they say cordial things and tut over the delayed train. 'I'm so sorry, I got here as soon as I could,' I say with what I hope is a mixture of graciousness and authority and I shake each of their hands decisively. As I take off my jacket and place my laptop case by my seat, one of the men hands me a thick wedge of papers.

There you are,' he says with a laugh. 'A small rain-forest for you!'

I feel the thing I'd feared. None of the men notice, but it alarms me nonetheless. I know that what I'm feeling isn't about Tristan, as much as I'd like to blame him. I place my laptop on the table in readiness and look around. Three pairs of eyes meet mine and I sigh inaudibly and force a smile.

'Let's make a start shall we?'

Where once a meeting like this would have stimulated me, today the men all blur into one and although I've met them before, I feel something inside me sink as I try to hold on to the differences between them. It's just tiredness I tell myself, and I invoke my father's voice telling me how proud he is of me. I find with relief that putting my feelings to one side isn't too difficult and I manage to hide behind a veil of professionalism as I settle into the meeting.

I'd spoken to Theo-Paul about my concern on the phone last night.

'I'm not looking forward to tomorrow,' I told him.

'Why not?' he answered 'I thought you loved dashing around the planet being Miss Big Exec.'

I laughed. 'I do,' I replied. 'Well, I like aspects of it. But to be honest, it's beginning to bore me. It's the same conversations each time. The only reason we meet is to work out strategies for making even more money.'

'Well yes,' Theo-Paul laughed. 'That *is* your job.'

I sighed. 'Well, yes of course, but not exclusively. It's starting to seem like a game to me, Theo-Paul. One with a matching set of players. They're like a great white army.'

'They?' he answered. 'Don't you mean 'we'? You're part of that army, if you want to look at it like that. And you certainly knew the rules from the start.'

'Yes, okay. But the game's just not as interesting any more. You know, I've never thought that making money is enough.'

'Oh come off it,' Theo-Paul scoffed. 'The size of your dividend is as important to you as it is to the rest of your shareholders.'

Now, as I sit in this bland hotel restaurant picking at a salad and discussing the finer points of our fledgling partnership, I watch myself watching the men. I allow myself to smile as they prowl around like cats, tacitly trying to divine where the real sources of power lie. But through my amusement, I feel the weight of expectation bearing down on me and whereas once this would have motivated me, today I feel only half here. I try hard not to laugh as one particularly vacuous Londoner with a Freudian obsession for growth says, 'Why not aim to be five times the size we are now within three years!' Ten minutes ago he was talking about the inevitability of redundancies if the economy doesn't pick up. I hold his gaze for a fraction longer than I should whilst the others fawn around him, attempting—and failing —to ingratiate themselves by loudly buying into this unexamined assumption of what constitutes success.

'This fixation on growth at any cost seems so juvenile,' I'd said to Theo-Paul.

19

'Have you considered,' he'd replied, 'that it is precisely this passion for growth that makes our species so successful?'

So, we are the successful ones. I look around the table at the fine silk ties, expensively manicured hands, statement watches. We are the ones with the city-centre apartments, tailored suits clinging to gym-honed bodies, or else straining against over-fed stomachs. 'Money is the key,' Theo-Paul often says. 'Not for its own sake, but for the freedom it buys.' But the shadows beneath their eyes betray their fear, and when they speak, there is a hint of desperation behind what they say. Something Henry Thoreau once wrote flashes into my mind, something about an 'unconscious despair concealed under the games and amusements of mankind.' As I inch the fortunes of our two companies together though, in spite of the hope that we will now make even bigger profits, I have no doubt that having more money will not make a single one of us happier. But of course that isn't the point I tell myself, and I realise that it isn't happiness or freedom that these men get from the size of their profit margins, but self-esteem and a feeling of power. I glance at the Londoner's crotch and wonder about negative correlations.

Insomnia

12.17. Curled up in the warm duvet it feels as though sleep should be easy. Turning this way and that, I seek out with my legs first the cooler parts of the bed, then the warmer. Irritated, I punch the pillow, drag the duvet tighter around me. I clamp my eyes shut, try to empty my mind but his absence fills the whole of the blackness ... I don't have the words to comprehend that he no longer exists.

1.02 ...and minutes march by. And sleep won't come. I count the cars on the bridge. I listen to some late night revellers singing as they leave a bar. This is stupid. I bury my head under the pillow. *I must sleep!*

2.26 *Use the hours resourcefully.* Check-lists, tasks that need to be done present themselves to me but I end up mumbling silent nonsense. I fight against tears. I compel myself to be practical. I watch the things I need to do stumble over one another. The funeral. His apartment. His will. Each new task tears itself out of my grief and feels like a betrayal. They take me further and further away from him, assaulting me over and again with the fact that he is gone.

2.31 ...*He is gone.* All returns to this one, final, immutable fact. I soak my pillow silently. *Merde!* I yell as an inevitable siren wails in the distance. Even so, I hold onto its sound for as long as I can, hoping that it will pull me into some deeper place. It doesn't.

3.00 The darkest of hours. Father is dead.

Paris, Ile St Louis

The day my father died, I returned to my apartment so full of feeling that I felt nothing. I paced around, my feet silent on the parquet, trying to inhabit the rooms as I used to, but instead of comfort in my familiar things, I found only estrangement. The dark wood bookshelves with their rows of antiquarian books, the bronze statues of Cupid and Psyche and Diana the hunter, the delicately painted Japanese vase all stood resolutely separate from me, as though the adornments I'd bought with love and care had become alien and hostile.

As I wandered from room to room all the things I had to do crashed in at me like waves, one behind the other. But the disjointed thoughts I had about organising the funeral, the death certificate, telling the people who needed to know, sorting out my father's apartment, his affairs, all broke against the shoreline of my consciousness and rolled out again, and I couldn't catch hold of anything long enough to separate it into meaningful action. Even the most straightforward of tasks—phoning my aunts for example, seemed baffling in their complexity. Confusion welled up, bringing with it yet more tears, and obscured the simplicity of the act.

Was there some protocol about who to inform first? What ought I to say? Must I plan a date for the funeral before calling? I closed my eyes. 'What do I do, Father?' I whispered. I almost thought I heard his voice in response; *a list.*

Yes, I must make a list. Taking a piece of paper and a pen from the bureau, I sat down to write. But as I stared the sheet in front of me seemed to deepen into a vast, blank void and the words I might have found sank into the white before I could capture them. Instead of words, tears appeared on the page in front of me. I put down my pen and rubbed my temples. *Maybe Father, I just need to get some sleep.* I got up and went to the kitchen for some painkillers.

His last night replayed itself over and again in my mind and I tried to fix in my memory every detail, every word he said, each squeeze of his hand. I'd sat with him as dusk faded to darkness and I stroked his hand and watched his shallow, rattling breaths in the dim half-light of the hospice room. He'd woken at around ten o' clock and looked up at me for a long moment, a frown playing around his forehead as though he was struggling to remember who I was.

'It's me, Father,' I said, putting my warm hand into his clammy one. Nightfall had obscured all but the dark shapes of the trees, and silence, punctuated by the digital bleeping of the Morphine auto-injector permeated the room. My father stretched his lips as though he was trying to smile.

'...thinking such a lot...' he wheezed. '...things to say...' With some difficulty he laid his free hand on mine. '...listen girl...'

I drew closer to him, my chest tight, my jaw aching from forcing back the tears.

'I'm listening Father,' I whispered.

'I...I'm proud of you girl... you know that don't you..?'

'Father...'

'...love...strong...' It was clear from his wheezing that he was struggling not to cough and I laid my free hand on his chest. Bending, I kissed his brow.

'...so much to say...proud of you, girl...' We squeezed one another's hands.

'I love you, Father.'

From time to time I stood to relieve the tension in my back, and paced the room, occasionally standing for some moments by the window to stare out into the shadows of the hospice grounds. I spent a long time gazing at my father's face, committing every detail, every line and curve to my mind, as though my knowledge of his face alone could will him to stay like that forever, dozing peacefully in this bed. I couldn't grasp the fact that I was watching a dying man. His occasional murmurings punctuated the night and I thought I heard him say my mother's name, 'Pauline'. I squeezed his hand gently.

As the night wore on, his murmurings stopped and time seemed to gain a specious quality. I looked at his face in the darkness and began to feel as though I was grasping to comprehend something of meaning that was suspended between the hours, between life and death, just beyond my reach. The hours and what was between them stretched long and silent into the night and although I felt their urgency, I willed them to endure and for this night not to end.

The nurse put her head round the door and crept in to take my father's pulse or bring me more coffee. Just before three o clock she bent close to me and whispered, 'You know, it won't be long now.' My father's breathing had slowed almost to nothing and I looked in alarm at his fingertips which had begun to turn grey. 'It's normal,' the nurse said gently. 'His body is beginning to switch off.'

After he died, a flash of comprehension illuminated a fraction of the moment. His breathing had slowed still further until he was scarcely breathing at all, then after a final rattling out-breath, he didn't breathe in any more.

And I... I just stared into his stillness in that most shocking of silences, the thing that had been hiding between the hours crashing into my consciousness, in racing slow motion, naked and pure; a knowledge that was beyond knowledge, so profoundly simple but monstrous and monstrously exposed. It retreated immediately back through the spaces between time, taking my father with it before the spaces themselves closed and I lost it and my father completely. A great howl rose up in me, a primordial keening which, had I been able to give it voice, might have ripped a way into whatever tunnels and darkness had claimed my father, dragged him back to the light, back to me.

But instead... instead I sat by the bed, the howl frozen inside me. My father was gone and I couldn't comprehend this aberration that was left behind on the bed. A silence darker than solitude crystallised around it and me. I swallowed hard and stroked my father's hand which was no longer his hand and watched as my tears dropped onto it.

Luxembourg City

After the meeting, I decide to take the long route back to my hotel in the Place D'Armes, and I listen absently to the city birds chirruping in the linden trees as a warm breeze softens the late afternoon light. Something inside me is still struggling and I feel ill at ease. It seems to me, as my heels ring on the hard pavement, that loss robs one of a sense of meaning in the things that were previously significant. *Father, is this what grief feels like?* Trying to grasp at what it was that used to excite me about such meetings, my sadness slides from my father to François and the discussions we'd had when I'd accepted the CEO's role.

'What I want to achieve,' I'd told him, 'is a sustainable company, steady growth that contributes to the wellbeing of all our stakeholders, not just shareholders.'

'As long as you protect our profits,' François had replied, 'you have my blessing.'

In Rue des Capucins I stop at a boutique window and look, vaguely interested at a display of expensive shoes; subtle suedes and calf-leathers tip their toes, stylish and proud in their elegantly-dressed window. But I'm distracted by my own reflection. I'm staring at one of the 'great white army' in my neat, fawn-coloured business suit, carrying my Italian laptop case. I turn away and notice a homeless man curled in a sleeping-bag in a doorway. *"J'ai faim,"* reads a stained scrap of cardboard. *How naive I am*, I think, as I toss a two Euro coin into his paper cup, *to imagine that I'm any different from the men at my meeting.*

At my hotel I slip off my shoes and rub my stockinged feet. I call Tristan to update him, and after listening to his answering-machine, flick through the TV news channels noting with annoyance the perfectly groomed replicas of the men I lunched with. I flop on the bed and think back to my first business meeting as a young intern, smiling at how eager I was and how keen to prove myself worthy to my mentor. Before the meeting he'd sat me down in his office.

'Now listen well,' he'd said. 'As progressive as you think the world now is, making it in business is tough, especially for a woman. If you're ambitious you're going to need more than just the letters after your name and a good CV. You're going to have to learn how the corporate world works. And by that I don't meant what they taught you on your MBA. No. These are carnivorous animals you're dealing with. And if you're going to succeed you need to learn their behaviours, desires, their fears. You need to know them better than they know themselves.'

I smile at that young woman of almost twenty years ago, so intoxicated by her first introduction to the world of business politics. But I sigh too. My thoughts flick to Ardash as I first met him, tie-less in his light suit and shirt-sleeves. I switch off the TV decisively and snatch up my mobile phone.

'So quit,' Ardash says.

'Don't be ridiculous,' I answer, 'it isn't as simple as that.'

'Then don't complain,' he replies.

After a shower and a gin and tonic from the mini-bar I head out into the twilight streets of Luxembourg. I don't know the town but Jean has given me a restaurant recommendation and I use my phone-app to find the Aka Cité in rue Genistre.

'A table for one please,' I say to the Japanese waiter, and I think I detect a touch of sympathy in his expression as he guides me to a table in the corner. One of my associates from the meeting had invited me for dinner and I feel pleased I declined, giving the waiter a bright smile as he hands me the menu. Sitting back in my chair, I glance around the brightly lit restaurant with its polished floor tiles and glass tables. The place is almost full and as I look at its occupants, I notice the women, the wives, elegantly coiffured in their stylish linens and silks, smart handbags resting discreetly by their designer-shod feet. During the working day the wives don't exist and I wonder which world is more real. I watch the mostly silent couples eating their way through their sushi. There are never silences during the working day. Not this type anyhow. The men don't look vacantly around as they do here with the wives. It seems to me that these men are magpies at work and cows at home. Both prospects repel me.

In the morning, as I shower in the white hotel bathroom I think about last night. After dinner, back in my room and in spite of my efforts at distraction, I couldn't stop myself returning again and again to my father and I was suddenly overwhelmed by tears and panic, my thoughts crazy, flowing from haunted things into shadows, through tunnels to sinister places.

I step out of the shower and as I towel myself dry I consider the day ahead; a client to meet, a report to write, emails to send. But the tasks seem ethereal and oblique and they fade away from me. I set about making coffee. As the kettle boils I look at my body in the mirror, my curls hanging in wet strands over my breasts and I realise that growing hair marks the passage of time; that today I am minutely different from the person I was last night. Still naked, I take my coffee to the window and as the sky lightens over the rooftops and the last stars disappear from the blue, I think about my dream.

I was at a race. I ran a warm up lap and then, needing to rest, I changed my clothes and shoes. When it was time for the real race, I found that my father had locked my sports clothes away and although I had a key, I couldn't find them. I stole some running shoes but they didn't fit me. Theo-Paul was there and we were sitting together on a couch. He came close to me and hugged me but I was worried about missing the race. I realised that I was holding the strings of a puppet. It was a girl dressed in running clothes and shoes.

Mumbai

The conference sponsors had organised an art tour for a select group of delegates, and I'd been pleased to be among them. Despite my loose cotton tunic, I was perspiring in the intense heat as I waited outside my hotel for the coach that would take us around the galleries. The forecourt was attractive and orderly, its newly washed marble steps gleaming in the early-morning sunlight. A man in white trousers was watering the many pots full of glorious purple flowers. 'What are they?' I asked. He simply wobbled his head at me and continued with his work. I looked outside for the bus and saw that beyond the gates, despite the exclusiveness of the neighbourhood, rubbish had accumulated in the broken gutters of the wide street, rotting fruit and old plastic-bags routinely ignored by all but a hungry-looking dog. A man in a smart business suit tossed an empty plastic water-bottle into the road as he hurried past. I looked away.

A big white coach arrived and shuddered to a halt by the hotel gate. I noted with pleasure the orange garlands and tassels strung up in the driver-space. A guide stepped down to welcome me, wobbling his head as he spoke. 'We are very pleased you could join us,' he said, bringing his hands together. He pronounced 'we' as 'vee'. 'Vee have a very enjoyable day planned for your liking and entertainment.' A glance inside the plastic bag he handed me revealed a programme, some gallery brochures, a branded pen and a bottle of water. On board, my eyes flicked expectantly among the faces, but I didn't see Ardash and I put my disappointment to one side and took a seat next to a large Indian woman.

'This heat!' she exclaimed, fanning herself vigorously with her programme. I smiled in reply. 'I hope the air conditioning in the bus starts working,' she said. 'I am simply melting here.'

We plunged into the traffic amid a cacophony of hooting and swerving, and the woman and I looked out of the window as we nudged our way out of our road and into three lanes of resounding mayhem. Cars and push-bikes fought for space with equal zeal, and colourfully painted trucks implored us with signs at their rear to 'Okay Horn Please.' Everyone obeyed. 'The mantra of Mumbai,' the woman said without turning around. 'The cars might be newer but the chaos hasn't changed.'

At Galerie Mirchandani we filed out of the coach and gathered on the pavement. I felt a jolt of pleasure as I saw Ardash moving along the aisle from one of the rear seats. I noted his raw-silk shirt and good leather shoes as he jumped down the steps. As he looked up we made the briefest of eye contact, he nodding his head in recognition. Inside the gallery I watched him as he moved alone around the bright, airy space from one art-work to the next, lingering by some, only glancing at others. He paused at the painting next to the one I was looking at, a large abstract piece, all geometric shapes and curved lines which the plaque proclaimed was supposed to represent 'the predictability of chaos.' As I stood looking at it, the Indian woman bustled over.

'So good to be out of that heat,' she said. 'The air conditioning in this place is just glorious. I can't say the same for this so-called art though!' Her bracelets tinkled as she flung a carefully manicured hand at the painting in front of us. I turned to reply.

'I guess it's meant to be meaningful in its own way,' I said. When I looked back, Ardash had moved on.

I walked with the woman to the next piece which was an installation of bricks and pieces of wood stacked in a corner with what looked like dismembered body parts in between.

'Shocking,' the woman said as we looked at it. She shook her head. 'This is not art. Real art doesn't shock but astonishes. Real art makes you want to want to kneel down before it.'

'Don't you think,' said Ardash from behind us, making us both jump, 'that perhaps we are not as literate in the modern visual arts as we are, for example, in literature? Perhaps we simply aren't used to understanding this kind of art?' It was the most I'd heard him speak and his perfect English accent surprised me.

'Understanding art is an oxymoron,' the woman retorted. 'Some place far too much emphasis on analysis. What is important is our emotional response.'

'And doesn't this piece evoke an emotional response?' Ardash replied, smiling.

'Yes of course,' the woman railed, 'but not of any positive sort.'

'Must art always evoke a positive response?' asked Ardash. 'Is not whatever we feel, valid?'

'What is the point in art that doesn't raise us up?' the woman asked. 'I want to be augmented by great art, not brought down to baseness by the likes of this!' She thrust a hand at the pile of wood and bricks.

'Wasn't it Nietzsche who said something like "we have art in order not to die of the truth"?' I said. Both Ardash and the woman looked at me.

'Ha! Exactly!' the woman exclaimed.

I smiled at Ardash and moved on, liking the fact that his replies opened doors rather than closed them.

Our next stop was in another part of the city and back in the coach the woman and I sat side by side once more.

'Do you know that man?' she asked me. 'Our friend the art critic.'

'No, I met him at the conference,' I replied.

'Be careful with him,' the woman said. 'He knows what he wants. And I'll guarantee he's used to getting it.'

31

Chemould Gallery was bursting with people and I managed to position myself so that Ardash and I wandered together through the hordes of giggling school children and elderly tourists.

'You seem quite knowledgeable about art,' I said as we walked. 'Is it your line of work?'

'Not at all,' Ardash replied, pausing at a colourful oil painting called 'Kite Race.' 'Was it Picasso who said, 'Art washes away from the soul the dust of everyday life'? I'm simply drawn to anything that can help me to live a little better.' I nodded but didn't speak.

'Perhaps art is a conduit,' he continued. 'A way in which we can deduce something that has meaning only for us.'

'So you think art has no intrinsic value?' I replied.

'I'm something of a relativist,' he answered. 'Some of the time.' We both laughed.

'The Beguiling of Merlin' was on loan from a gallery in England and I was pleased because I hadn't seen it before. I stood for a long time looking at the deep, dark eyes of Merlin fixed on Morgana who returns his gaze with equal intensity. Morgana holds a book away from him and as I gazed at her I imagined she had secrets that she knew he wanted.

Ardash interrupted my reverie when, without moving his eyes from the painting, he said: 'In fact her book is empty. She's taunting him with her secrets but what she really wants is to fill her book with his. She will seduce him to get them.'

'Really?' I answered, turning to him with a raised eyebrow. Ardash winked.

'No' he said. I think they both have secrets. Maybe they will seduce each other.'

Achille De Quincy—Before my death

The fact of her birth remains as unfathomable to me now as it did then. Pauline, lying sweating and bloody in a bed not unlike this one, exhausted and triumphant from the struggle that is birth, handed me a sticky, grey bundle with the words, 'Voilà ta fille.' *My daughter.* I couldn't comprehend the fact of her. Suddenly she was here, alive. A life. A girl. A daughter. Had I thought for a thousand years, it wouldn't have been enough to explain that profoundly inexplicable truth. With this tiny girl that we'd created was the advent of my manhood, confronting and challenging me with its being, howling the fact of its fledgling reality into an alien world.

So I became father to this fragile thing, this daughter with her big dark eyes and her bouncing brown curls. She never was what you might call a gregarious child. Serious. That's how you'd describe her. Solemn. She was that kind of girl; quiet, and with a certain effect on people. They wanted to look after her. To protect her. Maybe even to save her. At first.

Even as a child, it was hard for outsiders to know what was going on inside that head of hers. But as quiet as she was, timid she wasn't. Many confuse quietness for shyness. Many are mistaken. My girl had a particular way of looking at people, a way of regarding them that...how shall I say it? That *unnerved* them. She had a look that didn't waver. Piercing you might declare. As though she was looking right into the heart of you, scrutinising. I'd watch her with her Aunts, scolding her for some misdemeanour or other, a toy left on the table, crayon on the parquet. She, silent, staring right up into them, eyes like lasers as though she were trying to work out what manner of creatures were these. Yes, those eyes... I'd say it was those that made people nervous around her. She's like that even now. I like it. I always did. It keeps unwelcome types at bay.

She hardly had friends. Even as a child, she never asked to bring anyone home to play. I might have welcomed it, seeing her with a little friend, playing games together. But no, a loner, that's what she was and she seemed none the worse for it. I remember old Madame Emaux from the école maternelle phoning me one evening after surgery. Said she'd been watching my girl at playtime, seen her wandering around the yard all by herself, looking like she was in a daze, not playing with the other children. And daydreaming in class too. Said she was worried for her. 'Daydreaming?' said I. 'Isn't that just another word for 'thinking'? And why not prefer your own company when your sensibilities are so much finer than those loutish brutes flinging themselves around the playground like they don't have brains in their heads?' She didn't phone again.

Paris, Ile St Louis

The day after my father died, I woke from a fretful sleep early in the evening and glancing at my bedside clock, was surprised to see that I'd dozed for more than three hours. I blinked around me as I sat up, fuzzy headed and clumsy and was baffled that everything was still the same; there was my pale oak dressing-table, neatly laid with silver and black make-up bottles, there was the wardrobe, standing stoutly against its wall exactly as it had done the night before, its oval mirrors reflecting the image of some shadow-eyed wraith-like thing in my bed. I turned away and tried to ignore the frightful fact of the world's indifference to death.

Forcing myself to throw back the covers, I stood, and yawning and stretching padded bare-foot across the cool parquet to the kitchen. I opened the fridge door but gagged at the sight of food. '*Oui, je sais,* I know I should eat, father, but I can't,' I said, and I closed the fridge door quickly and turned instead to pour a glass of water. I swallowed two painkillers and went through to the salon. Picking up the remote control from a side table and still standing, I clicked on the television but after flicking through a few channels, clicked it off again. I ran my hands through my hair and sat down heavily on the sofa. Gazing around the room, the inert symbols of my success remained mute observers, perhaps even mocking the fact they are unceasing and we are not. Everywhere I looked I was confronted by another tasteful statue, some expensive piece of furniture, a rare book... I decided to call Theo-Paul.

'I'm so sorry,' he said. 'Was it a good end?'

'That's an odd phrase,' I replied, comforted to hear his familiar voice. 'It was peaceful, sort of. He was in and out of consciousness for much of the last day but we managed to talk a little. And eventually, first thing this morning he just slipped away. I'm not sure if that counts as a good end or not.'

'I'd say it does,' Theo-Paul said. 'When's the funeral?'

'I don't know, I haven't been able to think about it,' I said, swinging my legs up onto the sofa and pulling a cashmere throw around my shoulders. 'Soon I suppose. You will come, won't you? If not it'll just be me and a handful of aged aunts plus a cousin or two. I haven't seen any of them for years.'

'You know...' Theo-Paul faltered, 'I'm just not sure I can...I don't really... I don't do funerals...'

'Okay, okay,' I cut him off. 'No need for explanations.'

'Thanks.' Theo-Paul was silent for a moment. 'You're holding up though.' It was a statement rather than a question.

'It's strange,' I said. 'I suppose it doesn't seem real yet. I'm incredibly tired. I think I'll probably just try to sleep for most of the weekend and get down to the practicalities next week.'

'Not a bad plan.' I pictured him nodding.

I stood and took the phone with me to where my Japanese vase stood on its dark wood plinth, and, stretching out my free hand, ran my fingers along its elegant curve.

'Theo-Paul,' I said, 'do you think I've achieved anything in my life?'

'Christ, this has hit you hard hasn't it?'

'I suppose losing someone makes you think.'

'Well, you could've done a lot worse. Not many women your age have achieved your position. I'm sure your father was very proud of you, if that's what you're getting at.'

'Hmmm. Yes he was, he told me that. But even so...'

'Okay, look,' Theo-Paul cut in. 'You're grieving. Worrying about what you have or haven't achieved can be put down to that. It isn't your style, you know that, you're a do-er not a worrier. And besides, *your* life isn't over, you still have time to do whatever it is you think you haven't done.' I nodded silently. 'Give it time,' Theo-Paul continued. 'You'll be back on form.'

I smiled into the phone. 'I think what you are telling me,' I said, 'is to keep my chin up and to keep my angst to myself?'

Theo-Paul laughed gently. 'You might have me there,' he said.

I went back to bed at nine after flicking aimlessly around the television. I hoped that perhaps a news programme would distract me, but my mind seemed only able to grab at the odd word and I couldn't follow the stories. In bed though, in spite of my exhaustion I couldn't sleep. Instead I lay there thinking about my father, his life, my own. A sense of dissatisfaction was playing around the edges of my mind, making me feel as though what I'd done with my life was irrelevant, superficial even. '*Est-ce que c'est normal*, Father?' I asked. I told myself that it was; that this was simple grief, as Theo-Paul had said, and that it would change in time. But my feelings about my life and my father had somehow turned into a thick knot of intertwined threads and later, as I half slept and half dreamt, I felt as though I was caught in an exhausting, repetitive loop, trying to separate one thread from the others. In the early hours I finally pulled myself out of this half-conscious state and, without switching on my lamp, sat on the edge of my bed. The familiar drone of the Paris traffic beyond my bedroom window eased me into full wakefulness and after a while I stood up, groped for my slippers and pulled on my dressing gown.

Walking from room to room in the pre-dawn darkness, I gazed around my elegant apartment. I stroked the back of the wool-covered sofa, a cashmere throw hanging over one arm. Turning, I regarded my furniture, less solid in the shadows, and, walking from piece to piece, I ran my fingers along the lines of antiquarian books I hadn't read, the ornate statues from countries I'd never visited.

My eyes came to rest on the Japanese vase, and I looked at it for some moments before picking it up and turning it around in my hands. It was the first time I'd really looked at its design properly and I stared at its turquoise, hand-painted birds and delicate foliage. The man at the antiques fair where I'd bought it had told me that it couldn't be precisely dated but that it was at least 400 years old. I pictured the long dead Japanese potter working intently, squinting as he bent over his work, sitting back to scrutinise whether he had the shape, the design, the colours exactly as he wanted them. I imagined how proud he would have been to see the exquisite thing he was creating. But now it was just a thing, one among many whose worth was not in its beauty but in its perceived value. I stared at it and tried in vain to evoke the spirit of its maker, the love and passion he'd put into it.

Still clutching the vase, I turned, walked to the balcony, opened the patio doors, and stepped shivering into the chilly, pre-dawn air. Traffic hummed in the milky darkness and I could hear revellers laughing and talking on the other side of the bridge. The merest hint of dawn was creeping pinky-yellow into the corners of the apartment windows but the water of the Seine was restless and dark. I stepped up to the railings and looked down. The street below was deserted apart from a homeless man sleeping in a doorway.

I held the vase out over the balcony railings, and looked at it suspended there, beautiful and fragile between the ground and the sky. I closed my eyes, aware of the cool porcelain beneath my fingers. I loosened them, already hearing the crash of china on stone. I raised my head, and opening my eyes, found myself staring straight ahead at the geraniums on the balcony opposite, black in the moonless night. A curtain twitched. I gripped the vase, turned and went inside.

Achille De Quincy—Before my death

My girl was strong. By god was she strong. She had reason to be. She's still strong now and it makes me proud to see it. I've always told her that. 'Be brave,' I'd say to her when she fell and skinned her knee or when some neighbourhood lads taunted her. 'Don't cry like a baby, be strong, make your father proud.' I remember one time, she must have been what? Five years old perhaps, certainly no older than six. We'd gone to visit her Aunt Constance in Reims and we were sitting in the garden at the back of the house. I remember it being unseasonably hot and Constance and I were drinking lemon tea on the terrace while the girl and her two cousins played on the grass; him, a rough, burly boy, destined for a career in the military, much against my advice, the other a slip of a thing with a wide, rangy face, beautiful, like she had oriental blood in her. Both a good few years older than my girl they were, but you'd never guess it from their frolicking and showing off.

They found a spider in the woodpile. Or more likely the boy found it, and his mother and I watched him flick and prod at it with a stick. Big hairy brute it was, I went over to look. 'Leave it be, Jacques,' I said, 'it has a right to live as much as you or I.' But leave it be he didn't. Called the girls over to look, and when they arrived, flicked it at 'em with the stick, laughing like a monkey. Constance's girl, Annie, started squawking and acting out fit to get her legs slapped, in spite of her years. The boy threatened to kill the poor beast and hovered his stick over it, and the flapping of arms and bawling of eyes that created in Annie was a sight to behold. I shook my head and sighed. 'Annie, don't make such a fuss,' I said, but the girl blubbered all the more, yelling and pleading with her brother to spare the creature's life. And Constance, that lazy sister of mine, just sitting there in her sun chair, doing nothing but fanning herself

39

with her hat and calling over, 'Leave it Jacques, don't taunt the girls.'

As for my girl... my girl stood silently by the woodpile, not interested in the spider or its fate. Instead, I watched her staring first at Jacques, then at Annie, all the while a shadow of a frown furrowing her brow. She was...what? *Impassive*, that's the word. Like she was more fascinated by the carrying-on of her two cousins than in what was happening to the poor wretched spider. And then Jacques set to squishing the thing dead with his stick and Annie launched into wailing and ran to her mother, not before receiving a sharp pinch on her leg from her brother. And my girl just stood there not moving a limb, staring up at Jacques full in the face till he sauntered off, twirling his stick, a look of feigned nonchalance on his face as though he was trying and failing to convince himself of his victory. My girl turned and regarded the poor, mangled creature for a second or two before scooping it up and tossing it over the hedge. We watched her dust her hands off on her frock. Constance shook her head. 'Ay, she's a fey one, that girl of yours.'

Mumbai

After the art tour, we'd cooked in the stuffy bus, whose air-conditioning never did work, as it crawled its way through the cacophonous Mumbai traffic. At the first hotel-stop, I was grateful to take the opportunity to stretch my legs and I filed out with a weary group of fellow delegates and stood, savouring the slight breeze that only mildly relieved the relentless heat.

'Well, this is me,' Ardash said. His jacket was slung over his shoulder and a thin breeze flicked his hair across his eyes. 'Do you have plans? How about joining me for a cup of chai?'

A little girl in a ragged dress sidled up to us and tugged at my sleeve. Before I could respond, Ardash winked at her, pulled something wrapped in tissue from out of his pocket and placed it into a dirty hand, before the tour guide shooed her away.

'Not a bad use for hotel biscuits,' he said. 'I'm meeting a client this evening or I'd suggest dinner.'

I was about to speak when the Indian woman from the tour bustled up to us.

'Still so hot,' she said, fanning herself with a brochure. 'I want to thank you.' She turned to Ardash, laying a plump hand on his arm. Her bangles flashed gold in the sun. 'Most insightful, your comments on modern art, very thought provoking.' She levelled a look at me. 'A very interesting man,' she said.

'Indeed,' I replied. 'I'm sorry,' I said to Ardash. 'I have a lot of work to do. But let me have your card. I'll call you if I get a window.'

The Indian woman smiled.

Back at my hotel, I spent the rest of the afternoon and most of the evening working. At eight Marine called.

'*Bonsoir*, I hope I'm not interrupting your evening,' she said. 'It's only three o' clock here. I thought I'd give you a quick call before my next meeting. How's it going there?'

'You're not interrupting me,' I answered, leaning back in my chair with a wide stretch. 'I was just catching up with my emails. So far so good here, although the heat is unbearable. I've got a pretty good idea of what the market could be, but the most interesting speakers are tomorrow.'

'Okay great, well I won't keep you,' Marine said. 'I'm in the office tomorrow so I'll give you a quick ring around lunch time.'

'That's fine,' I replied. 'Is Tristan in tomorrow? There's something I'd like to discuss with him.'

'India? Are you crazy?' Tristan had said when I'd mooted my plan to scope the market here. I was keen to get him on side by making him feel included.

'No, he's meeting François,' Martine said.

'Is he? Why?'

'Your guess is as good as mine, but I don't like it.' There was obvious mistrust in her voice. 'He said he'd fill me in after, but I won't hold my breath.'

Two hours later exhaustion forced me to bed but not before wondering what Tristan was up to. As I lay there beneath the cool white sheet listening to the sound of the air-conditioning, I considered phoning him but thought better of it. I wondered whether to call François but decided against that as well, telling myself that there was no reason they shouldn't meet.

I woke early the next morning and as I showered, dried my hair and drank a coffee, made a conscious effort not to think about Tristan but to focus on the day ahead. I wondered, as I dressed for the final day of the conference, whether to invite Ardash out for dinner. *Why not*, I thought as I stood in front of the full length mirror adjusting my dress.

The crawl though the mêlée of Mumbai traffic made me feel, by the time we arrived, like I'd done a day's work already. 'Why do the drivers hoot all the time?' I'd asked the taxi-driver. He simply wobbled his head. At the Conference Centre, I squinted into the heat-haze shimmering between the sky-scrapers, before straightening my suit and walking through the big glass doors to register my attendance. I glanced around the lobby as I walked, but didn't see Ardash. Nor was he at the tea station, where an immaculately dressed Indian man served me a glass of sweet chai. 'A biscuit miss?' he said in his lilting English. 'No thank you,' I replied, but then, 'Actually, I will.' I took two and folded them into a paper napkin. Turning to sip my tea, I surveyed the arriving delegates. Still no Ardash. I went into the auditorium feeling disappointed.

As I'd hoped, the speakers were more inspiring today and as he spoke, I noted down the name of a man I particularly wanted to speak with. I hadn't seen Ardash all morning but I put thoughts of him out of my mind as, at lunchtime I hurried through my lentil salad before leaving the dining hall. I found Roshan Naik talking animatedly with a group of Americans in the lobby. He didn't pause as I walked over to join them but shook my hand for the briefest of moments after the Americans held out theirs.

'I was very interested in what you had to tell us today,' I said. Have you been working with foreign businesses for long?'

'Many years,' Roshan replied. I chose to overlook the fact that he directed his answer at the men. He looked as though he was about to resume his conversation with them but I spoke first.

'Would you be free to talk more after the conference?' I asked. Roshan barely made eye-contact with me.

'Of course, of course,' he snapped. 'It's what I am here for, it's all about contacts.' I ignored his irritability.

My flight was due to leave early the following morning and as I headed back to the auditorium, I weighed up the likelihood of being able to meet with Roshan and then take Ardash for dinner. *It's perfectly possible*, I thought, retrieving his business card from my laptop case. My phone rang just as I was about to dial, making me jump. What a coincidence I thought, smiling. It wasn't him though and I answered my phone with a trace of disappointment.

'Much better today,' I said in response to Marine's question. 'I've got a meeting with one of the speakers from this morning. He seems stand-offish, but I'm sure I can soften him up. From what he said, it's possible he could be interested in acting as a local partner. Look Marine, I'll fill you in when I get back, there's something I need to do.'

Ardash didn't sound surprised to hear from me.

'Love to,' he shouted in answer to my dinner invitation. 'But I won't be back until later.'

'Sorry, can you repeat that,' I replied. 'It sounds as though you're in a noisy place.'

'I'm dirt-bike racing,' he yelled above the scream of engines. 'Does nine o' clock work for you? I can meet you at your hotel.'

'Nine is perfect,' I replied. 'You're doing what?'

'Dirt-bike racing. I have to go now, but I'll tell you about it later.'

After the final speaker, I waited for Roshan in the lobby, considering the best way to 'soften him up' as I'd said to Marine. He emerged from the conference hall a few minutes later, his eyes darting around as he walked. He spotted a man he clearly knew, and, holding a palm up to me, stopped to speak with him. I watched him greet the man warmly, shaking his hand for a long time. Once more I pushed my annoyance aside. *It is what it is*, I told myself.

'We'll find a table through here,' Roshan mumbled once he'd finished with his colleague. He started walking before I could shake his hand, leaving me to follow him into the delegates' lounge where a number of people were sitting in pairs and small groups.

'Can I offer you something to eat or drink?' he asked as we sat down at a corner table. I wondered how it was that his perfect civility sounded so disdainful.

'Just a coffee will be fine thank you,' I replied.

Roshan motioned to a waiter and without making eye-contact with him demanded two coffees. The waiter nodded and scurried off.

'I was very interested indeed in what you had to say this afternoon,' I said. 'My company is keen to expand into India, and it seems to me that our interests may well be similar.' As I spoke, Roshan continually glanced over my shoulder and I resisted the urge to ask him why.

'It can be complicated for foreign businesses to establish themselves here. But with the right connections, the opportunities are ripe.' He spoke without enthusiasm and glanced at his watch.

'I haven't fully introduced myself,' I said. 'Let me give you my card.' I retrieved the little silver business-card holder from my bag, took out a card and held it just far enough that Roshan had to lean forward to take it. He flicked a glance at the formal lettering declaring me as CEO and looked up with renewed interest.

'I'll tell you about my business,' I said. 'We organise corporate events and functions—from private soirées right through to international symposiums. We take care of everything, from venue sourcing and catering to booking specialist speakers, arranging the publicity, transport, accommodation, everything. We even arrange private jets if that's what our clients want. We're a small company, but we work with some *very* major clients.' All the while Roshan looked at me intently through narrowed eyes. 'I'm confident,' I continued, 'that what we can offer will be of great benefit to our clients who want top-end event management in India.'

Our coffees arrived and having poured our cups, Roshan dismissed the waiter with a curt nod of his head.

'I think that given Mumbai's importance as a major business hub, what we can provide here is very timely indeed,' I said, maintaining eye contact with him. 'But it's clear we'd need a good regional partner to advise us and to get us in front of the right people.'

Roshan regarded me for a long moment. 'Well it seems that our meeting was fortuitous,' he said at last. 'Let me tell you more about what I do here.'

As I listened to him and sipped my coffee, I allowed myself to savour a little thrill of victory.

Paris, a quiet café close to the Boulevard Saint Germain, and an office in the Montparnasse Tower

With less than a week to go before the funeral, I still hadn't written my father's eulogy. Sleep had continued to evade me since his death, and last night was no different. I'd tossed and turned and only half slept and finally, hot and restless, sat up at 5.30, with the thought that we are all equidistant from the unknown. I got out of bed and ten minutes later sat down in front of my laptop with a cup of coffee. Still the words refused to come. *My book of secrets is well and truly empty*, I thought as I snapped shut the lid of the computer. Frustration followed me into the bathroom and made me clumsy and I knocked a bottle of shampoo into the shower, spilling most of its contents. *Useless!* I muttered out loud.

Now, at a quiet café close to the Boulevard Saint Germain I listen, as I wait for the company accountant, to the chatter on the terrace, and I marvel that people have so much to say. I glance around and notice a man in a striped shirt whose wild hair makes him look vaguely insane debating something with a waitress. An attractive young woman in a bright red jacket is telling her companion in a shrill voice that the bank is understaffed. 'Speak quietly,' I want to say to her, as my aunt Constance used to say to my cousins. Instead I turn to watch two old men with beards amble out of the café. One of them sees me without a drink and says to me, '*C'est toujours très long ici, n'est ce pas?*' before shuffling off into the street, grumbling to his friend. All around me, I hear the murmur and babble of conversation, from inside the café, from the terrace, from the street and I feel baffled. All these words, I think, all these sentences flung around with such casual abandon and I cannot find a way to translate my father's life into some combination of them that feels in any way meaningful.

The accountant arrives, puffing and out of breath and apologises for being late, although he isn't.

'*Bonjour*, Luc,' I say, standing to greet him, 'good to see you.' He kisses me on each cheek.

'*Bonjour*,' he replies, glancing around the terrace. 'Lovely idea to meet here, so much more pleasant than in the office.' I don't believe him and watch as he wrestles his laptop out of its case, elbowing a heavily-perfumed woman who is leaving the café. She tuts audibly.

'I like getting out of the office when the weather's like this,' I say, indicating with an upturned hand the glorious sunshine. 'Plus, I think people are more creative when they're in unfamiliar surroundings.'

'I'm sure they are,' Luc replies, 'but can we discuss this here?' He scrapes his chair loudly from under the table.

'We can if we're discreet,' I answer. 'That's why I chose this corner. Coffee?' I hail a waiter.

'Where would we be without coffee?' Luc says. I smile in agreement and order two *allongés*.

'Okay,' I say. 'Now, I know you've been discussing elements of this with Jean. It's a shame he has a prior commitment, I would have liked to have fully updated him before I take this to the board.'

'I think you and he are in general agreement about the elements he's seen,' Luc says. 'He and I have been over the figures thoroughly.'

'That's good,' I answer. 'I have too. I'm not going to say I'm not worried, Luc. The economy is on its knees but we're achieving steady growth and making a reasonable profit.'

'Yes, you're managing to stay above water,' Luc says. 'No mean feat in these conditions.' The waiter arrives with our coffee and we both make space on the table with our laptops.

'There's no room for complacency though,' I say, once the waiter has left. 'And in any case, as you know I'm far more interested in long term sustainability than in short term profit.'

'Well,' says Luc. 'I've never been a great believer in the value of short term profiteering. Tends to lead to short term goals in my opinion. But tell that to your average shareholder.' I nod and flip up the lid of my laptop.

Three years before, I'd sat alone at the boardroom table of our newly decorated offices in the Montparnasse Tower, my laptop and papers set out neatly in front of me. I was early and wanted time to gather my thoughts before the others arrived. I looked up and watched two pigeons flap past the window, the Eiffel Tower in the middle distance standing proud in the morning sun. The door opened and the musky scent of Marine's perfume wafted through the room as she bustled in, carrying her laptop like a tray.

'All set?' she said as she seated herself at the long boardroom table. A little jewelled ear-ring flashed in the sun.

'Indeed I am,' I answered. She smiled at me.

'Nervous?'

'No,' I said. 'Just keen to make a good start.'

She gave a little laugh. 'Does nothing scare you?'

Jean and Tristan came into the room together, Jean beaming, Tristan nodding first at Marine, then at me. Jean took off his jacket and hung it over the back of his chair, pulling down the white cuffs of an immaculately pressed blue shirt. 'This view…' he said, turning from the window to settle himself.

'Right,' I said when everyone was seated, pens, paper and laptops at the ready. 'Let's make a start.' Marine smiled at me once more and Jean nodded and picked up his pen. Tristan leant back in his seat and crossed his arms. *This isn't going to be an easy ride.* Nonetheless, I noted with familiar pleasure my heart beating hard in my chest, smiled, took a deep breath and began.

'Well then, welcome to what isn't my first board meeting, but *is* my first board meeting as CEO.' Congratulatory noises were made around the table. 'As you know, François will only be attending board meetings intermittently and has elected not to be present today but has asked me to convey his support for what I'm about to outline to you, as long as we have majority backing around this table.'

'Yes,' Marine said, 'he sent an email to that effect.'

'Good,' I replied. 'What I'm going to offer is a vision of what our company could be. It's very much a vision at this stage rather than a strategy and you will see why shortly.' I flicked a glance at Tristan. 'We have a great business which offers a valuable service, and in spite of mounting economic difficulties, we've been resilient. It's clear that in order to remain buoyant, we must maintain growth and continue to add value to the bottom line.' There were nods of agreement all round. 'However, I see that as only part of the vision.'

I paused and looked up. Spread out below us, the white-cream stone of the buildings of Paris and the wooded hills of Mont Valerien and the Bois de Boulogne all bathed in sunshine looked so permanent, so immutable that I felt even more keenly the sense of purpose that I wanted to convey. I looked back to the expectant faces before me with something approaching a maternal feeling.

'I believe strongly,' I continued, conviction welling into my voice, 'that if we have the will for it, we can create and maintain strong and principled long-term values. I want to move away from an exclusive focus on annual profit and revenue to a more broadly-based approach. What I mean by that is creating a company whereby we actively take care not only of our profit, but our people and our planet as well.' I breathed in slowly and looked around. Tristan made a strange noise and coughed loudly.

'Firstly, let's consider people,' I said, ignoring him. 'Traditional business is about rewarding shareholders in the form of share value and dividends. Yes, we can say that we are providing jobs and a useful service for our clients, but those tend to become secondary concerns because as a responsible board of directors, we all understand that profit and growth are paramount.'

As I was speaking, Tristan took off his jacket and turned to hang it on the back of his chair. Two patches of sweat sat damply beneath his armpits and I had to force myself to look away from them.

'Because business today is so focused on the value of the shareholding,' I went on, 'this often shapes the kinds of strategies and timeframes we're willing to deploy. What I want is to create a company which benefits and rewards all its stakeholders. To develop a set of principles and practices which considers not only our shareholders but our employees, their families, our clients, suppliers, the local economy and community and the broader, global community. I want us to be more than simply a corporate events company, but a business that actively works to improve all that it affects.'

I paused and looked around. All eyes remained on me and I purposely didn't look at Tristan but he began to speak, shaking his head.

'Surely,' he said, 'you can't be expecting...' but I raised my hand and cut him short.

'Tristan, please hear me out.'

Jean looked from Tristan to me and the words of my old mentor flashed into my mind. '...*work out who has the real power...*'

'There'll be time for discussion later,' I said. Tristan leaned back in his chair and held up his palms in mock surrender. I maintained eye contact with him for a moment before continuing:

'Now clearly, what I want to achieve is a major undertaking, which requires a root and branch scrutiny of the way we currently do things. And by its very nature, this kind of re-focus can't work with a top-down approach. I want an inclusive approach which encourages and draws on the talent and ideas of our broader stakeholder community to develop the kinds of practices which will embody our new vision.'

I paused once more and let my words sink in for a moment. Marine was smiling broadly. She gave a little nod. Tristan re-crossed his arms and glared at Jean who began writing something on his notepad. *Good*, I thought, *with Marine in support, I have fifty percent of the board.* I looked straight at Jean and continued.

'Let's now consider the second leg of our vision, the planet.' Tristan's eyebrows shot up.

'What I want to develop is a proactive approach to ensuring that all our operations consider the impact of our business practices on the environment. This is not about tree-hugging.' I glanced at Tristan, who rolled his eyes. 'This is about taking responsible steps to ensure our environmental footprint is minimal and that wise use of resources is integral and fundamental.'

I looked around. Marine was nodding her approval, both elbows on the table in front of her. Jean shot a look at Tristan who had started writing something. *It's like that then, is it?* I thought, looking away from them. Outside little puffs of cloud were scudding overhead, their shadows sending dark shapes across the buildings below. Tristan's spreading sweat patches flashed into my mind and I suppressed a smile. Turning back to the table, I made eye contact with all three in turn, ending with Jean.

'I began by saying that what I would outline is not a strategy, but a vision. I hope it's clear that in order to develop the strategies that will enable us to achieve this vision, we must engage energy and commitment beyond those of us around this table. I also made it clear that we cannot as a business lose sight of the fact that unless we achieve steady growth and a healthy bottom line, our vision will be in vain. I've left talking about profit and growth until last, not because these are the least important, but in order to finish by emphasising my 100% commitment to the fact that as a business, our vision must not be at the expense of these clear commercial imperatives but must run through and alongside them. Each of the three legs of our vision: profit, people and planet must support the others. I want a company where this culture is so deeply embedded that one cannot stand without the other two. In this way I want to create something of genuine and lasting value that we can all be proud of because what we are doing is intrinsically good.' I looked straight at Jean. 'François and I are counting on your support.' Jean nodded vigorously. Marine smiled. Tristan made a strange noise but otherwise remained silent. I suppressed a smile. Seventy five percent. I had my majority.

Now, a little over three years later, sitting with Luc in this quiet corner of the café terrace, I think about how eager I was then at the prospect of creating something different with the business, something of worth. I sigh and glance around, glad that the few people seated at the far end are paying no attention to us.

'Okay,' I say to Luc quietly. 'We've had a *reasonable* year.' I move my chair closer to his and turn my laptop around. Luc moves his to one side and I lean forward, speaking more quietly still. 'This is the percentage our turnover has increased by—it's not huge, but at least it's growth.' I point to a cell in the spreadsheet on my screen. 'And this is the gross profit we've made. Again, not huge but profit nonetheless.'

'Ok...' Luc says, scrutinising my spreadsheet. He makes little 'uh huh' noises as he traces his finger along the rows and the columns on the screen. After a minute or so, he pulls his own lap top back in front of him and checks my figures against his own. 'Yes,' he says at last, nodding. 'Yes, okay, what you have here is pretty much spot on with mine.'

'Good,' I reply. 'As you'll agree, we need to exercise caution here. Theoretically speaking, this is what I think we could pay in shareholder dividends.' I lean across and click into another sheet. 'Would you say that's reasonable?'

Luc lifts his glasses and squints at the screen.

'Let's have a look at this,' he says more to himself than to me. I sit back and sip my coffee while Luc does some calculations. 'Yes, okay,' he says, looking up. 'Not unreasonable at all.'

'Excellent. But I'm going to put it to the board that in fact we don't pay all that in dividends. I have a different strategy to outline.'

Luc replaces his glasses and looks at me, a small frown playing around his brow. He raises his eyebrows and I know what he is going to say next.

'Whatever your reasoning or your strategy,' he replies, 'you must know the others will have done their sums too. If you propose a smaller dividend than expected, failing economy or not, certain parties will give you one hell of a fight.'

Mumbai

Ardash arrived at my hotel at 8.55 where a taxi was waiting to take us the short distance to the restaurant I'd booked. I came down the steps, enjoying the warm heat of the evening when I noticed him leaning against the hotel gate. He sauntered over.

'How long were you there for?' I asked.

'Long enough,' he smiled. 'That's beautiful.' He indicated my blue silk scarf. 'Did you buy it here?'

'Yes, there's a boutique just here in the hotel,' I said, shaking his outstretched hand. The driver hopped out and opened the back doors of the waiting taxi.

'I see. Not yet braved the streets of Mumbai?'

I ignored the question and climbed into the car. 'The Lotus Dancers please,' I said to the driver.

'Very nice,' said Ardash. He draped his arm along the back of the seat behind me.

Mumbai was no calmer by night than it was by day and we lurched and crawled the short distance to the restaurant amid the ubiquitous cacophony of hooting.

'I'm guessing this is your first time in India,' Ardash said, watching me as I took in the scene outside.

'I'm not sure whether to be irritated by that assumption,' I replied, smiling.

Ardash followed my gaze to the wide street lined with chai bars where groups of men stood chewing paan and chatting, oblivious to the plastic bags, used cups and rotting vegetables which filled the gutters. We watched a man spit his chewed paan leaves into a slew of garbage.

'I don't understand why they do that,' I said. 'I feel bad saying it but Mumbai is already filthy.'

'The cities in India have expanded hugely in a relatively short space of time,' Ardash said. 'People still behave as though whatever they toss away will biodegrade quickly like it would have in the villages not so long ago.'

'It's a shame,' I replied. 'Especially because so much of the rubbish is plastic.'

'Mumbai isn't an easy city if you're not used to it,' he said. 'But it has its charms.'

'Are you from here?' I asked.

'Originally yes. I live in London now. I'm an NRI.'

'NRI?'

'Non-resident Indian.' Ardash smiled. 'It'll be Gandhi's 150th birthday in 2019,' he continued. There's a Government initiative to clean up India's cities by then. The idea is not without opposition, believe it or not, but it's a start.'

The restaurant was fresh and modern and a smartly dressed doorman rushed down its marble steps to usher us inside. The aroma of spicy food assailed us as we entered and, breathing in deeply, I took in the candle-lit purple and silver décor, the wrought iron and glass tables, noting with satisfaction that most of them were occupied.

'Always a good sign,' I said as a waiter helped me out of my jacket. 'And the food smells wonderful.' Another waiter arrived almost immediately we'd sat down, to take our drinks order.

'Have you tried any of the Indian wines?' Ardash asked, taking the proffered wine-list.

'I haven't,' I replied. 'But I'd like to. Are they good?'

'Sula are making some rather interesting whites,' he said, and without waiting for my response ordered a bottle of Dindori Reserve Viognier. As the waiter nodded and left, an image of Roshan Naik flashed into my mind, which I shoved away. We sat in silence for a moment.

'I'm glad you could come,' I said eventually. Ardash didn't answer, so I busied myself looking at my menu. 'The food here is excellent, apparently,' I continued.

The waiter returned with our bottle and an ice-bucket, telling us in a hushed voice that he recommended the Kaju Mattar Khumb. I smiled my thanks at him as he unscrewed the lid and poured a drop of wine into Ardash's glass. Ardash swirled it, sniffed the wine deeply and nodded his head. The waiter poured our glasses and placed the bottle in the ice-bucket, carefully laying a folded napkin over it.

'Screw-top?' I whispered once he'd left.

'It's all about the wine, not the ritual,' Ardash replied. 'Although amusingly, we're still expected to sniff the wine in case it's 'corked'. Santé.' He raised his glass and we both took a sip.

'Not bad at all, I said savouring its soft peachiness.

'Praise indeed from a Parisian,' Ardash smiled. 'Have you had a productive time at the conference?' He maintained eye-contact over his glass as he took another sip.

'I met with an interesting man earlier,' I told him. 'Roshan Naik. Do you know him?'

'Not personally. I've heard him speak at a couple of events. He's well connected by all accounts.'

'He isn't an easy man to communicate with,' I said carefully. 'But he could be a useful contact.'

'As a woman you'll have a harder job establishing your credibility here. Then again, I imagine that's the case beyond India.' Ardash looked at me intently for a moment. 'You don't need to be female to be aware of male privilege. Most men probably don't even notice they treat woman as subordinates. It would be different if you had a penis.'

I liked the way he used the word 'penis' without smirking and I nodded in agreement. The waiter returned and lit a little candle and I watched the flame flicker gold in our glasses.

'Are you having a good conference?' I said at last.

'I did what I came to do.' Ardash took a sip of his wine. 'I'm not a great fan of business trips although they can on occasion have their upsides.'

'Oh?' I answered. 'And has this trip had any upsides for you?'

'I'm not sure yet,' he answered with a smile.

I looked at him, enjoying the way the candlelight exposed his skin, revealing prominent cheekbones, a dark growth of stubble which made me wonder whether he'd shaved today.

'Who do you work for?' I asked. 'Only your name was on your business card, no company details.' Ardash smiled.

'That,' he said, 'is because I work for myself.'

'I see.'

'I'm freelance. I have been for years.'

'That's interesting,' I said. 'Do you prefer freelance work?'

'I have absolutely no interest in being told when and how to work,' Ardash answered. 'My freedom is important to me.'

I nodded. 'And what is it that you do exactly?'

'I arrange fixers.'

Before I could respond, the waiter arrived to take our order.

'I'm going with your recommendation and will have the Kaju Mattar Khumb,' I said. 'With...' I hastily consulted my menu. '...with Basmati Biryani Rice. No starter, thank you.'

'Sounds perfect,' Ardash said, closing his menu. 'I'll have the same.' The waiter nodded and left.

'Fixers?' I said. 'Is that a *mot-nouveau* for some finance-industry chicanery?' Ardash smiled and reached for the wine bottle but before he could lift it, a waiter rushed over and took it from him. 'Please sir, let me,' he said, as he re-filled our glasses, one arm behind his back. Once he'd gone Ardash took a deep sip.

'I think the waiters are more formal here than they are in Paris,' I smiled. 'Anyway, fixers…?'

'Fixers. They are individuals who know a local region or a country inside-out and who assist people who need discreet and reliable know-how.'

'Really?' I sipped my wine. 'What kind of people?' Ardash looked at me for a long moment before answering.

'Industrialists, Government officials, film crews, spies.'

I raised my eyebrows. 'You're not serious?' I said, trying to interpret his inscrutable expression. 'Aren't you the mysterious one!' Ardash simply smiled.

I looked around, and seeing the tables filled with smartly dressed couples and men in business suits, wondered whether I would have preferred a more traditional restaurant. I turned back to Ardash, noting with pleasure his open topped shirt, which revealed just a hint of dark hair.

'Tell me about this bike-racing you were doing,' I said.

'Now that is far more interesting,' he replied. 'Dirt-bike racing is where you leather-up, get yourself onto an off-road motor-bike and race like crazy round a dirt track, hopefully without killing yourself.'

'Really? It sounds dangerous!'

Ardash smiled.

'There'd be no point in it otherwise.'

The Kaju Mattar Khumb was delicious, the cashews and mushrooms perfect together, the peas adding a hint of sweetness to the spice. Ardash hailed the waiter and asked him to compliment the chef. The waiter bowed in response.

'I haven't seen anything of India but Mumbai,' I said. 'I imagine the countryside is beautiful.'

'Parts of India are unimaginably beautiful,' Ardash replied. 'I spent some time living in Gujarat. There, the desert rolls away into the far horizon, the sun sets in orange fire behind the Arabian sea, while the rising moon casts strange shadows on the sand and billions of stars prick through the sky.' He took a long, slow sip of wine and spoke in a low voice. 'Can you imagine making love in a place like that?'

I stopped eating, my fork mid-way to my mouth.

'You have an interesting mind,' I said. 'And a poetic one at that.'

'Do you like the idea?' he held my gaze.

'What idea exactly?'

Ardash leant forward and spoke more quietly still and I watched twin candle-light flames dance in his eyes.

'The idea of doing something wild in a forbidden place.' We were both silent for a long moment.

'Why do you want to know?' I asked eventually.

'I'm ascertaining whether or not you're an interesting woman.'

'Oh?' I replied. 'And how will I know you're an interesting man?'

'You'll have to get to know me,' he said.

Achille De Quincy—Before my death

She was a bright little thing. She always was, but I do like to think that I helped her along the way. "It is wiser to find out than to suppose," I used to quote. She loved books of any sort, but unlike other girls her age, she preferred fact to make-believe. Maybe I steered her in that direction, I don't know, being a Doctor's daughter must count for something. She certainly did read novels when she got to be of that age, but mainly in the holidays. It was a sign of things to come, but don't misunderstand, you might take her for a Stoic at first, many have, but she was no martyr and she enjoyed life's pleasures as much as anyone, in her own way. She still does. Maybe growing up with a scientist, her way to live in this world became to learn as much as she could about what *is* knowable, and to find her own space and limits within it. I had another explanation though. Perhaps she drew knowledge around her like a shield.

School work came easily to her and over time, because one rarely exists without the other, her quest for knowledge mutated into a general respect for work. No, I don't think that's quite right. She certainly did work hard at her studies, not out of respect for the toil itself but rather out of interest in where it could lead. Work was a pathway for her and she followed it gladly. Her teachers never had any trouble with her and there was never any doubt that she would do well. I wondered whether she would follow in my footsteps and forge a career in medicine. I might have liked that for her. But I didn't try to influence her, and she took an altogether different path from mine. And it hasn't turned out badly for her.

In the wintertime, when it got too cold for walks in Père Lachaise or the Bois de Vincennes, we would spend our evenings with our noses buried in the National Geographic or the Paris Review or the New Scientist. Sunday mornings would be spent reading Liberation and later, when she was older, the Economist. She'd never tire of this and over our meals we'd tell each other about the article we'd just read, expounding its points of interest and its limitations. Often she'd ask to read the one I'd just finished and we'd swap periodicals. I'd watch her sometimes, reading or doing her homework at the table, lamplight pooling around her and her books. I watch her now sometimes, reading the Sunday papers after lunch and she's kept that same expression she had back then as a child, a slight frown, lips pursed as though she were trying to read right through the page to something more profound which lay just beyond her reach.

We devised a tradition for ourselves whereby each year on January the first, we'd light a fire, make two steaming cups of hot chocolate and sit side by side on the couch, each with a pad of note paper and a pen. We'd write on the sheets a different topic to be researched. Twenty six topics each, one for each week of the year. She'd suck the end of her pen and gaze up at the ceiling for inspiration before bending to write her topics in her neat, round little hand. I'd always try to peek at what she'd written and she'd scold me: 'Ne triche pas, papa!' We'd fold each of our sheets in half and in half again and we'd drop them into an old blue shoe box we kept especially for the purpose. It was her job to shake the box to make sure the sheets were thoroughly mixed. And throughout the year, every Sunday we would take it in turns to choose a topic, closing our eyes, dipping our hand into the box and triumphantly pulling out a sheet. We'd unfold the page carefully and read aloud what it said. 'The Kings and Queens of France and England,' she'd read slowly. Or 'The life of Sophie Blanchard.' 'Varieties of tomatoes.' 'The Chateaux of the Loire Valley.' 'Chickens.' No topic was too silly or taboo or dull and we researched each one throughout the week with equal enthusiasm, both of us delighting in our discoveries. Sometimes we'd laugh at the new topic. 'The history of the egg whisk. Seriously

Father?' Or else we'd nod sagely, congratulating one another on our depth of imagination. As she grew older, the topics changed and began to suggest the path she would follow: 'Corporate governance,' 'The Herzberg Model,' 'The Pareto Principle' But the ritual never changed, and on Sunday evenings, after our meal, we'd sit and share what each of us had found out during the preceding week. If it were wintertime, we'd sit by the fire. 'Tell me what you've learned then, girl,' I'd say. And after, we'd each kiss the sheet of paper and toss it into the flames.

'Burn the old to make way for the new.'

Insomnia plus Mumbai

3.00 Three o' clock is always the worst. Too early and too late for anything you want to do, Sartre said. He meant three o' clock in the afternoon of course, but even so... This lurching between hovering around the edges of sleep and the stark punishment of it being nowhere near. I'm not given to self-pity, but I've found a great store of it stashed away around the hour of three o'clock and I plough right into it on an almost nightly basis. Sick of being on the edge of sleep only to be thrust back into full wakefulness by some party-goers or a police siren, I've taken to wearing earplugs. I've stopped drinking coffee in the evenings. I still haven't got any medication. I still don't sleep. But tonight I am calm. Perhaps it's a good sign.

3.39 I can't help but think about Ardash. Ardash and Theo-Paul. Alike yet so different. Both honest. Both distant, neither wanting to commit, yet both needy in his own way. With Ardash I fear the unknown. With Theo-Paul I fear the mundane.

4.22 ...Mumbai...
The taxi-ride back was interrupted by Ardash telling the driver to stop, but before that, we sat in silence, watching the dirty heat of Mumbai unfold itself to the characters of the night. The lateness of the hour didn't stop drivers from blaring their horns and as we inched through the crowded streets, I watched the now familiar groups of men standing around, drinking chai, talking. I saw very few women. As we rounded a bend, I noticed the moon, high and bright, poised between a group of skyscrapers, the light from its imperfect orb duplicated in countless windows. 'A hunter's moon,' Ardash murmured.

Without warning, the car skidded and we all lurched forward. The driver said something and pointed to a skinny little dog slinking away through the traffic.

'You okay?' Ardash said. I nodded. As we settled back in our places, Ardash rested his arm on the back of my seat as he had done on the way to the restaurant. I felt certain I could feel his heat and I resisted a strong urge to lean into him and fold myself against his body. I wondered if he was contemplating touching the skin on the back of my neck, but he didn't and we passed the journey in silence until, a few blocks from my hotel, Ardash leaned forward and asked the driver to turn left.

'My hotel is that way,' I said, pointing back down the road.

'There's something I want to show you,' Ardash said. 'Trust me.'

'Trust a man I've only just met?'

Ardash simply smiled. 'Just here,' he said to the driver. We pulled up by what seemed to be a disused scrap of land between a row of small shops that were closed and shuttered for the night. I saw two beggars sleeping in a doorway, their thin, bare legs flung with abandon across the pavement.

'Wait for us here,' Ardash told the driver as he climbed out of the car. I opened my door. 'Come with me,' he said. I picked my way behind him along the uneven concrete pavement until we came to a kind of entrance into what seemed to be a little park.

'Are you sure this is safe?' I asked, glancing around. Ardash didn't reply but came to a stop just inside. A big old tree stood to one side, around which some shrubby plants were growing, their flowers black in the dark of the night. A bench made out of old planks of wood stood next to the tree and two rubber tyre swings hung from a huge branch. Ardash gave one a push and the rope creaked as it swung. I looked down at the hard-packed earth and imagined skinny urchins playing cricket here during the daytime.

'Notice anything?' Ardash said. Traffic rumbled and tooted in the background and I thought I could make out the sounds of distant drumming and chanting.

'Not really.'

'Okay, anything you don't see?'

I glanced around again, confused.

'Well, it's a nice little park,' I said. 'I guess in the daytime children play here.'

Ardash nodded. 'Take a look at that sign.'

A rectangular piece of wood was attached to the low wall at the back of the park. It bore a kind of logo made out in pastel colours, a rising sun in yellow between two words—to the left something written in Hindi lettering and to the right what I supposed was the translation. '*Saucha*,' I said out loud.

'It's Sanskrit,' Ardash said. 'In Hinduism it's seen as an important part of spiritual development. The word *Saucha* means purity.'

Underneath was something written in English. I walked closer.

'*Pure body, pure mind, pure heart, pure home*,' I read. 'Okay... but I'm still not sure...'

Ardash moved to the bench and sat down and I followed, resisting the urge to draw closer to him. A dog barked and then yelped as though in pain.

'No one knows for sure who he is,' he said. 'Some say he's the son of a Mumbai property magnate. Some say he's a holy-man. He's known in Mumbai simply as *Saucha*, which is the sign he leaves at all his sites.' I glanced at Ardash more confused than ever. Outside the park our driver climbed out of his seat and we watched him light a cigarette.

'Saucha is an environmental vigilante,' Ardash explained. 'Look around you. Normally, a piece of abandoned land

66

like this would be covered in refuse and crawling with rats and stray dogs, not just an eyesore but a hazard. Saucha shows up, clears the rubbish, plants things, installs benches, swings, and out of wasteland creates a community park. No one pays him to do it. And he gets nothing out of it except the satisfaction of creating something good. I imagine he sees it as his Karma Yoga.'

I looked around again and saw what Ardash meant. There wasn't a plastic bottle or bag to be seen.

'Karma Yoga?'

'Yoga isn't about gymnastics. Karma Yoga for example is about doing selfless acts without expecting any kind of gain or reward. It is an important part of my religion and culture.'

'Karma Yoga,' I repeated, nodding.

'The locals appreciate it,' Ardash continued. 'They've started looking after these 'Saucha Parks' as they're calling them. I saw two women litter-picking in one just this morning. Some think Saucha is a kind of urban hero. Kids are starting to copy him.'

'That's astonishing,' I said. 'And very heartening.' The drumming in the distance grew louder and I realised I was starting a headache. 'But why did you show me this?' Ardash turned and looked at me intently.

'From the little I've learned about you,' he said, 'I'm guessing you appreciate acorns.'

Paris, Montparnasse Tower

'Mais oui, the place is certainly looking different, quite a transformation.' François is looking around him at the expanse of desks arranged in circular pods, each with three or four people busy at docking stations. 'And you don't mind these glass walls to your offices?' A sweep of his hand takes in the row of glass walled offices along one side of the open plan section. He walks to the end of the row to my office. I follow him in and he crosses the floor to the plate glass window where he stands gazing out across Paris spread out below us.

'I never grow tired of this view,' he says. He chuckles. 'It's somewhat different from when I ran things from my cottage in Troyes.'

Hearing the name 'Troyes', I feel a mix of nostalgia and disquiet. I miss my weekends at the cottage, but could never have foretold the consequences of what happened there...

'François is from Troyes,' I'd explained to my father, when I'd first joined the company as a Junior Director. 'He began the business there years ago. A lot has changed since then of course, including opening the Paris office.'

'So you'll be working between both offices?' my father had asked.

'Yes,' I replied. 'I think the Troyes office will close eventually, now that François lives in Versailles. But he says that while we still have it, I can use his old cottage.'

'Well, you look after it then, girl.'

'Don't worry, Father,' I'd said, 'I'll treat it like a second home.'

Putting thoughts of Troyes and François' cottage out of my mind, I smile and follow his gaze towards the Eiffel Tower in the middle distance, the golden dome of Des Invalides. François is silent and I don't interrupt, but follow his slowly moving gaze east along the Seine to the gentle bulge of Montmartre, crowned by the twin domes of the Sacré Coeur.

'It's a real privilege seeing this each day,' I say. 'The glass walled offices were a compromise. I'd have preferred that the directors didn't have offices at all, that we all work in the open plan section along with everyone else but there was some opposition to that idea.'

'Well I can see the point,' François says. 'There are certain things that as a director you need privacy to discuss.'

'Yes, that's true,' I say. 'Although my idea was to keep as much open to the staff as possible and to have private 'hot desks' in side offices for when such discussions are absolutely necessary. And of course we have the meeting rooms. Besides,' I nod towards the open plan section. 'I didn't see why the staff shouldn't enjoy the view as well, albeit through our glass walls.' I smile at François. 'It is a little like working in a goldfish bowl, though.'

François chuckles. 'Always a new way to do things,' he says, shaking his head indulgently. 'Well, shall we go through, I expect the others will be waiting.'

We walk out of my office towards the large conference room on the opposite side of the open plan area. François greets several people as he crosses the space, patting backs and shoulders as he goes. Tristan and Jean are already waiting in the conference room when we walk in.

'No Marine?' I say, knowing what the answer will be before I'm told.

'She's making coffee,' says Tristan. I frown.

'Don't blame us,' he says, 'she offered.' At that moment Marine bustles in with a tray of cups and a plate of Madeleines. Solange follows with a coffee pot and a dish of sugar, looking apologetic.

'Lovely,' Jean says, clearing space on the table. 'I'll be mother shall I?'

Solange smiles at me. 'Let me know if you need anything else.'

'Thank you Solange,' I answer, a little too curtly. She backs out of the room closing the door behind her.

Once we're all seated with our laptops, papers and coffees in front of us, François turns to me.

'Who are we going to get to take the minutes? Shall I call Solange back?' he says.

'We don't do that anymore,' I answer, smiling at him. 'The staff have more than enough to do. Like making the coffee, we take it in turns to take the minutes ourselves.' I flash a look at Marine. 'I believe it's Tristan's turn today.' I turn and smile sweetly at Tristan and ignore the sarcasm in his return smile. He doesn't say anything.

'Novel idea,' says François without conviction. 'Right then, I'll open shall I?' We all nod and ready our pens.

'Well, this is of course my bi-annual appearance at a board meeting which I declare open and fully minuted from now.' He glances at Tristan as though dubious that notes will be taken. Tristan nods at him, pen in hand. 'Okay, well first of all, in order that we focus on the matters at hand and wrap up in a timely fashion, a few words about what this meeting is not. Firstly, we are not here to re-visit our strategic plan.' François and I both glance at Tristan but he doesn't look up from his note taking. 'Whilst we clearly need to discuss how best to weather this *worsening* economic storm, I remain satisfied with the direction in which the company is moving. The economy notwithstanding, you are all to be congratulated on steering this old ship in the right direction and indeed taking it into previously unchartered waters.' I see Tristan flick a glance at François but he continues writing. 'I will of course want a full strategic review at the appropriate time and as you are aware, this is planned for the middle of next year. Your esteemed CEO has some ideas about how she wants to conduct this.' François nods at me. 'Also, as you can see from the agenda, neither will this meeting focus on detailed operational matters. We will have high-level updates on the business sectors and I have made a note of a few brief queries I'd like to raise but as you know, as long as the cash is handled well,' he nods at Jean who nods back, 'I am more than happy to leave the day to day running of the business in your capable hands.' François picks up his coffee and takes a sip. A fly buzzes past him and I watch it land on Tristan's shoulder and rub its front legs together. Francois continues. 'What I do want to focus on are the financials. Jean will shortly take us through the Profit and Loss account and outline where we stand in terms of our annual return. We can then move onto the cash-flow projection for the next 12 months and of course the little matter of shareholder dividend payments.' He chuckles and looks around the room. 'All agreed?'

We nod our agreement and Jean prepares to go through the Profit and Loss account, handing out spreadsheets to each of us. Tristan puts down his pen and scrutinises the sheet over the top of his glasses. 'Damn fiddly little numbers Jean,' François mutters, holding the sheet at arm's length. 'A bit bigger next time please.'

'Apologies, certainly,' says Jean. We all continue to examine the sheet as he runs us through a summary. I've been through it already of course, but study it along with everyone else.

'So, we continue to show a profit,' Jean says, 'although somewhat more modest than we'd predicted.'

'Indeed,' François says eventually as Tristan puts down his spreadsheet and starts to scribble something onto his pad. 'It doesn't surprise me. As you know, De Cheverné shut up shop last month. Couldn't make it pay. Damned pity they didn't have clients suitable for us to pick up. Fortunately though, our strategy of focusing on the top-end has paid off. Clients like ours won't be tightening their belts any time soon, mark my words.' He chuckles. 'No, the downturn is temporary for us. In which case you won't be surprised to know that dividend payments are well earned and justified!' François nods his satisfaction. 'Not a bad outcome at all, all things considered.'

'François,' I say. All heads turn to me. 'Whilst not wishing to seem overly pessimistic, I have a proposal that I'd like to recommend to the board at this point. It concerns dividend payments. It think this would be a pertinent time to move onto this.'

'Certainly,' François says, picking up his agenda and tapping it with a finger. 'I for one am not aware of the detail of your proposal and I'm looking forward to hearing what you have to put to us.'

'Okay,' I say. 'Are you ready to move onto this now?' I look at François and at the expectant faces around the table. I think back to Luc saying I'll have to fight to get my proposal accepted.

'Indeed, indeed, do carry on,' François says. I press a couple of keys on my laptop and a large spreadsheet springs to life on the projector screen at the foot of the table.

'Ah now that's more like it,' François says. 'Organised as ever.' Tristan makes a strange sound but I don't look at him. Jean writes something on his pad.

'Okay,' I repeat. 'I'm asking you to hear me out before responding. My proposal is in three parts. I've been through the figures with Jean and with Luc as well and I'm confident that they stack up.' I look around the table. Everyone is looking at me intently. Tristan has his pen poised. François is steepling his fingers in front of him. I savour a familiar rush of exhilaration and suppress a smile.

'I'm sorry to say that I don't fully share François' optimism about the economy, nor our client's ability to fully weather it. We've previously identified a vulnerability—namely that we have a relatively small number of very major clients. We can't afford to lose any of them.

'No reason why we should,' Tristan interjects.

'I'll come back to this later,' I say, ignoring him. 'Now, the first part of my proposal is this: before looking at what we can realistically pay out in dividends, I want to highlight what we need to earmark for investment in our new ventures—particularly the potential India project. I know there has been some opposition to this,' I glance at Tristan, 'but we as a board are committed to the Asia expansion. Jean will take us through the detailed cash-flow projection for the coming 12 months, but prior to that, this is what I'm suggesting we budget for business development.' I highlight a figure in my spreadsheet. 'You will note that it is bigger than what we budgeted for last year. This is because although Tristan's Luxembourg project should shortly be realising revenue, the development and set-up costs of the India initiative are likely to be substantial. We're not in a position to produce a detailed cost breakdown or revenue projection for that yet, but clearly we must invest sensibly if that project is going to have a chance of succeeding.' I glance up. Everyone is looking intently at me. *So far so good,* I think. 'I've done some initial calculations for that project, which I believe are sensible. I'm assuming that none of us will object to investing some of our profits to aid our expansion plans.' There are nods of assent around the table. Tristan is writing.

'Makes perfect sense,' Jean says.

'Okay.' I pause. All eyes remain on me. Tristan is holding his pen at the ready once again and for some reason this irritates me. I look at François and continue. 'This is the second part of my proposal.' I click a button and another spreadsheet appears on the screen. 'We've already allocated this amount'—I highlight a cell—'to sales-related staff bonuses, which are clearly self-funding.' There is more nodding. *This will be interesting,* I think. 'What I want to propose is that two of our key senior managers—Gilbert and Sophie—receive an immediate one-off bonus payment of this amount'—I highlight another cell—'in respect of their contribution to our success last year.' I look around the table. 'And in addition, I would like to make this amount payable'—I click on another cell—'between them and their teams on successful delivery of certain KPIs which we will agree.' There is silence for a moment while everyone looks at the screen. Marine nods slowly. Tristan takes a fresh sheet of paper and begins to add up figures.

François takes off his glasses and leans back in his seat. 'Why these two?' he says. 'Don't they already receive a commission? Why would we pay them a double bonus?'

'They're not from the sales team,' I reply. 'Gilbert runs our Client Services Team and Sophie is Head of Operations. They don't receive a commission of any kind but without their dedication and loyalty, we certainly wouldn't be in the position we are now.'

'We have a female Head of Operations?' says François. I smile.

'Yes we do,' I say. 'You might also have noticed that we have a female CEO.' François chuckles.

'Remarkable,' he says. 'But I'm not sure why these two weren't included in the budgeted bonus scheme last year, if you want to reward them like this?'

Tristan nods decisively. 'Good point' he says, frowning.

'It is a fair point,' I say, looking at Tristan. 'I think we all agree that we were thinking more cautiously last year. I'm still urging caution but rewarding staff like this has longer term benefits and the figures show that we can afford to be a little generous.'

'Okay, okay,' François snaps. He looks around at the others. 'Well?' he says. 'Thoughts?'

'Well,' says Jean, staring at the spreadsheet on the screen for a moment longer before turning back to us. 'All it would mean in the immediate term is smaller dividend payments for us shareholders. And going forward we could make an element of their KPIs profit related so next year their bonuses would be at least partially self-funding.'

'Yes, and it would be very good for staff morale,' says Marine. 'We've worked hard to get the staff on board with the changes we've made and by and large, we've had a positive response. I for one would be willing to take a reduced dividend to reward credit where it's due.' She glances across at me and I smile at her.

'Exactly,' I say. 'Thank you Marine. And if we are all agreed I'd like Marine to work on a proposal for the on-going scheme to be presented at the next board meeting.' Marine nods her agreement.

'Tristan?' says François. We all turn to Tristan who is staring at the spreadsheet. He is silent for a moment.

'As requested, I'd like to hear the whole proposal before I respond,' he says. I nod.

'Right,' I say, steeling myself. 'The third part of my proposal.' I look around the table. Expressionless faces look back. I'm sure that no single element of what I'm suggesting would be disagreeable to them in isolation, but I'd be very surprised if any of them are willing to accept all three elements. Once more, that feeling of excitement rises from my stomach and I part my lips and make myself breathe in slowly to calm my heart thumping in my chest. *Here goes*, I think.

'My view is,' I say, 'that although we've returned a profit this year and have continued to deliver growth, we must proceed with caution. As I said before, we have some very large-spending clients, the loss of any one of which would hurt us. In addition, a not-insignificant part of our future revenue is in relation to the Luxembourg project, which although it will do very soon, has yet to generate an income. These factors, coupled with the prevailing economic conditions which still look uncertain, point firmly at our exercising caution. We must be responsible and ensure that we are able to stand on our own two feet come what may.' I click a button on my laptop and reveal a third spreadsheet. 'In the past, we've always had a contingency fund, although we've rarely used it. What I'm suggesting is that until the economy looks more certain and our new business revenue is firmly established, we retain a much larger contingency fund.' I highlight a cell in my spreadsheet. 'Whilst at this point there is no reason to suppose we'll use it, we must steel ourselves against the worst. I'm suggesting that a short term reduction in shareholder dividend payments is a reasonable price to pay for future-proofing ourselves.' I look around the table. No one is looking at me, all are staring intently at the screen. 'This, when we take into account the other elements of my proposal—new business investment and staff bonus payments—would leave a total dividend payment-pot for us five shareholders of this amount.' I highlight a final cell in my spreadsheet and hold my breath.

Paris, Montparnasse Tower
and the Jardin de Luxembourg

Two weeks after returning from Mumbai, I stood with Ardash in the Jardin de Luxembourg, watching water flowing upwards.

He'd emailed me. I'd just come out of a meeting and, back in my office, I stood talking with Jean who had followed me inside. We both gazed out at the evening sky streaked with a glorious orange-pink sunset, before I turned to my laptop and clicked a few keys.

'Stunning,' Jean murmured. He glanced at his watch. 'Right, I'm going to make a move then. There isn't time now to start anything else and anyhow, Emily and I have opera tickets.'

'Very nice,' I said. 'Yes, you get off, I won't be far behind you.' I waved to Gilbert and Solange who were also on their way out. 'I'm just going to see what I can clear from my in-box and I'll be off too.'

'Don't forget I won't be in first thing tomorrow morning,' Jean replied. 'I'm meeting Luc at his office. I'll be here for around eleven I should think.'

'Yes, fine,' I replied, running my eyes down my list of emails. Ardash's name hit me like a blow to the stomach.

'You okay?' Jean said. 'You seem a bit...flustered all of a sudden.'

'Yes, yes,' I said a little too quickly. 'I'm fine. I'd better make a start on these. Enjoy the opera.'

'Right-o.' Jean looked at me curiously. 'I'll see you tomorrow then.'

I stared at the email for a few long moments, acutely aware of my racing heart. *It's bizarre*, I thought, *how a series of zeros and ones translated into words on a screen has the power to affect my biology.* And indeed, after reading it, the power of

Ardash's email made my hands sweat and my stomach tense.

I'll be in Paris next Tuesday, would you like to spend the afternoon with me? That first message had said nothing more than that. I don't know how many times I read it, each time finding something miraculous in the words, each time looking for something more between them, and although the wait was exquisitely agonising, I forced myself not to reply until the following day. *'I'd love to.'* I said.

We met by the Fontaine de Medicis in the Jardin de Luxembourg. I arrived first, a little early, and found a place by the fountain from where I hoped I would see him arrive. I stood, fussing with my dress which I'd chosen carefully after rejecting several others. Standing in front of my mirror that morning, I'd regarded myself from one angle then another before deciding that this one was not too sexy but not too staid either, revealing, I hoped, just enough flesh to intrigue him. 'Nice dress,' Marine had said, eyeing me up and down.

The morning passed with an excruciating slowness and nothing I did held any of its usual significance, least of all my meeting with Tristan. As he entered my office, he too eyed my dress and smirked before walking to the meeting table. I wondered whether I'd chosen badly and fought to keep the irritation out of my voice.

'Take a seat Tristan.' I remained at my desk and indicated the seat opposite. 'I won't keep you long, a brief update on Luxembourg will suffice ahead of your formal report.' Tristan returned to the desk and sat down with a scowl.

His voice droned on and as he spoke of supplier issues and market testing, I allowed my thoughts to wander to Ardash. He was somewhere in Paris right now. I glanced out of the window and was pleased to see that the weather was still bright and sunny, perfect for a walk in the park. Was he too in a meeting? I imagined him in an office in one of the buildings below. What kind of meeting would someone who arranges 'fixers' have? Perhaps he was looking out of his window right now, thinking of me?

'I said, I need to delay my report.'

I snapped out of my reverie and saw that Tristan was glaring at me.

'Right, your report,' I said, annoyed with myself for the slip. 'When can you have it finished?'

'I've just told you, it'll be another couple of weeks, there are a few more details…' I was about to interject when Tristan's mobile phone rang. He glanced down at it.

'I need to get this,' he said. 'It's François. 'I think we're pretty much done here.'

Normally I'd have told him the call could wait, but today, in spite of wondering why François was calling him, I was glad to get Tristan out of my office.

As I waited by the fountain, my dress felt uncomfortably constricting and I tried unsuccessfully to adjust the neckline an inch or two higher. I squinted through the crowd, my hand shielding my eyes from the sun, and smiled at myself as I reached into my bag for my sunglasses. What is it, I wondered, putting them on, that causes this amount of eager anticipation to meet up with a man I barely know?

After a few minutes I spotted Ardash in the distance and in spite of my relief, the cool, collected persona that I wanted to project was instantly undermined by the reaction of my body, which seemed to have a relation to Ardash that had nothing at all to do with me. I took a deep, slow breath in a vain attempt to stop my heart from beating ridiculously fast in my chest. I had the strangest sensation as I watched him move through the crowd, that the other people in the park had suddenly switched into 'fast-forward' and were buzzing crazily around whilst Ardash moved slowly and deliberately towards me. I placed my hands on my hot cheeks, hoping that his pace would allow enough time for my flushed face to regain its usual pallor. I smoothed my dress and patted my chignon. I straightened my sunglasses.

Ardash hadn't yet seen me and I savoured being at the centre of this connecting moment, this point between points, to note at my leisure and with appreciation his ruffled hair, his charcoal business suit and the fact that, like the first time I'd met him, he wasn't wearing a tie. Some birds twittered loudly in a tree and took off in a shower of flight, and I saw that within this moment, its magnitude and profundity which seemed to have the power to unify my impassioned body and my pitching thoughts, were all the more acute, because I knew that as soon as our eyes met it would be over and something else would take its place, something unknown and beyond my control. As I hung there, suspended in temporal limbo, I watched him stop, take his mobile out of his pocket and read something on the screen. He smiled and tapped the phone. Was he sending a text? I grabbed my phone from my bag. Nothing. The exquisite moment crystallised, froze and shattered. I closed my eyes and turned to face the fountain.

Paris, the Bois de Vincennes

'I'm not happy at all. I made a perfectly rational case for not paying the full dividend.' Lac Daumesnil looks fresh and glassy in the mid-morning sunshine and I watch the reflection of the clouds skimming across its surface. Theo-Paul takes a long drag of his cigar.

'Well,' he answered. 'You have to admit, it was a strange decision. It's usual for payments to be made when you've made a profit. Beautiful day by the way. No idea why you decided to come here but it's nice.'

It's the first time I've been to the Bois de Vincennes since I used to come with my father, and as Theo-Paul and I stand watching a flock of Canada Geese flap and squawk after some bread, I wonder whether it was a good idea. I look up.

'Are those clouds Stratocumulus?' *Tell me what you've learned then.* The memory of my father patiently explaining to me how to recognise different clouds sends a wave of melancholy through me.

'God knows,' Theo-Paul answers without looking up. 'I can see the logic behind your proposal, but I'm not at all surprised at the response. Business just doesn't work like that.'

'What does that mean though?' I way, looking back at the geese. 'It's obvious that we need to invest in future development, or we'll stand still and stagnate. That's what the India project is about.' I turn and lean my back against the railing and face Theo-Paul. Behind him a group of runners is jogging by and I watch them, faintly amused as they scatter over the path to avoid a little white dog that is yapping around their ankles.

'And given the current economic climate,' I continue, noting with resigned tolerance that Theo-Paul is staring after the runners, 'it makes perfect sense to retain a meaningful contingency fund.' Theo-Paul turns back to me and goes to speak, but I continue. 'And why not reward the staff as well as ourselves? They deserve it for heaven's sake, they work every bit as hard as we do.' I turn back to the lake and watch a mother telling off a child for throwing stones at the geese. 'After all,' I say, 'it's not as though I was suggesting that staff bonuses be unrealistically high. What I suggested was very modest and us shareholders would have still done quite nicely with our dividends.'

'You know your problem?' Theo-Paul says. 'You're an idealist. I've told you before and I'll say it again. You'll never change the way business works. It's about profit, full stop. You want my advice, grow the business. Sell it. Make your money. Then you can do what you want.'

We move away from the railings and continue to walk along the edge of the lake, standing aside as a group of teenagers on roller-blades whizzes past. 'Have you ever done that?' I ask, indicating the roller-bladers.

'God no!' Theo-Paul retorts. 'Why the heck would I risk my neck doing a crazy thing like that?' I wonder what Ardash would say if I asked him. 'I'd be more likely to try that.' Theo-Paul chuckles as he indicates a group of old men playing Pétanque on a stretch of grass. I smile, enjoying the acrid scent of Theo-Paul's cigar as he blows smoke in front of him.

'This is the way I see it,' he continues. 'As you said before, each element of your proposal is perfectly fine in isolation, since no one part would make the dividend unacceptable in the eyes of the shareholders. But all three...come on, you know the score, it's obvious that future investors or buyers are going to want to know what level of dividend payments were made. It's a measure of how confident you are in your own future. And like it or not I'd be surprised if François didn't have that in mind.'

I shake my head. I can see we're not going to agree. It seems he senses this as well. 'Regardless,' he says, ogling a young woman jogging past us in a tight tee shirt, 'what was the outcome?' I shake my head at him and raise my eyebrows. 'What?' he says with a boyish look on his face.

'Their stances were pretty much what I expected. We had a right old fight.' I continue. 'No one wanted to accept the whole proposal. Marine fought for keeping the staff bonus element and reducing the contingency pot. François was also adamant that we don't need much of a contingency. I thought Tristan was going to burst a blood vessell. He and Marine went full head to head.'

'Good for her,' Theo-Paul says.

'Yes, I had a lot of respect for her for that. Tristan was accused me of exaggerating our financial exposure, of getting my figures wrong, and tried to argue that we won't need to invest so much in the India initiative. He's fought with me against expanding into Asia ever since I proposed it. But François is all in favour of it, and insisted the investment remains at the level I'd set.'

I sigh and look at two women walking towards us. They are laughing and talking, their heads bowed close together as they make their way to a bench and sit down. I think they must be about my age, and I watch them as one shows the other something on her mobile phone which causes both to laugh again. They seem so light and free in their closeness and in spite of Theo-Paul's presence I suddenly feel lonely. Perhaps it's just tiredness, I think as I rub my temples. I look at Theo-Paul, his weighty bulk reassuringly solid beside me and I consider taking his arm. But I think better of it. *Pull yourself together.* I yawn widely and continue speaking.

'Anyhow, Jean kept coming back to the revenue that Tristan's project will soon be bringing in and argued for keeping the dividend payments and the investment, but dramatically reducing the contingency pot and staff bonuses. That's what was agreed in the end.'

Theo-Paul nods.

'Okay, so not a bad result then,' he says, eyeing a beautiful woman with a shock of black hair riding a bicycle. 'Seriously, the talent in this park is astonishing; I should come here more often.'

'Theo-Paul!' I say in mock outrage. 'Honestly, do you think you can keep your eyes off other women for more than two minutes?'

'Jealous?' he says playfully. He taps the end of his cigar on a tree and spits on it before placing it into his top pocket. 'Anyhow, each part of your proposal was accepted, just the amount was compromised. Not a bad result,' he repeats with finality. He shields his eyes from the sun and peers around.

'Do you fancy a coffee?' he asks. 'I'm sure there's a cabin around here somewhere.'

'Yes, ok,' I reply as we continue to walk. I sigh. 'I guess you're right and I guess the others are right, we probably won't need the contingency fund. I hope not—there's hardly anything in it!' We spot the cabin at the end of the lake and make our way towards it.

'I imagine the coffee here will be foul,' Theo-Paul says 'but at least it'll be hot. Grab that bench will you?'

I walk across to the bench and sit down. In spite of my fatigue I feel some small degree of catharsis at having told Theo-Paul about the meeting. 'He's a good listener sometimes, Father,' I say to myself with a twinge of guilt and resolve not to talk about work anymore. The faint breeze isn't enough to chill me, but I pull my jacket tighter all the same and gaze across the lake to the little wooded island at its centre. I watch a group of brown mallards— females I suppose—bobbing around the bank. I wonder where the males are and this makes me think about Ardash. I imagine he's with a woman. Maybe they're roller-blading through some park in London, I think, and I almost smile in spite of the pang of hurt the thought causes. I turn and watch Theo-Paul hurrying across the grass, two paper cups in his hands and I feel a wave of gratitude towards him.

'Watch it, they're hot,' he says, settling himself on the bench.

'It's so good to be able to talk with you Theo-Paul,' I say as I take my coffee from him. 'Really, I don't talk about my work dilemmas with anyone else. I do appreciate it.' I take the lid off my coffee and blow across its dark surface.

'Steady on!' Theo-Paul says, as he eyes the ample breasts of another jogger. 'Next you'll be telling me you're ready for marriage!'

Paris, The Rodin Museum
and a café nearby

Even though I was expecting it, Ardash's touch on my shoulder felt shocking and I turned, trying hard not to smile too broadly. He leaned forward and the skin of my cheeks burned against his lips. I looked at him and he looked back. Neither of us moved or spoke.

'Look at the water,' I said eventually, turning and placing my two hands on the rail in front of us. 'It looks as though it's flowing upwards. It's an optical illusion.' We both looked, and our eyes followed the rectangular stretch of water to the stone statues of Acis and Galatea embracing at the head of the fountain.

'Things aren't always what they seem,' Ardash replied, smiling. We turned and started to walk through the park.

'So what brings you to Paris?' I asked.

'You.'

I looked at him.

'I thought you were here on business?'

'Oh, I could easily have Skyped my meeting.'

I smiled.

'Well, I am honoured.' I didn't tell him that it had taken me some considerable amount of effort to clear my afternoon diary so that I could meet him. 'Do you know Paris well?'

'I come here more or less each month so yes, I know it pretty well. It's a beautiful city. One of Europe's most elegant in my opinion.'

'And is it generally business that brings you here?'

'Not this time,' he replied.

We decided to walk the half an hour to the Rodin Museum and set off along the Rue de Fleurus, pausing for a moment at the window of Livres Anciens. A display of dark-coloured old books stared at us solemnly.

'I have a collection of antiquarian books,' I said, thinking about the dusty tomes on my shelves. 'I only read on trains though, and then only e-books. I wish I had more time for reading.'

'Then make time,' Ardash replied. I glanced around at his abruptness but he just smiled.

'Did your business in Mumbai come to anything?' I asked, continuing along the street.

'I have a major client there. Did yours?'

'I'm hoping it will.' I let myself enjoy the mystery of Ardash' elusiveness, picturing a handsome spy meeting his fixer in some dark, Mumbai bar. 'I have some ideas about how I'd like to do business in India that could be implemented across my organisation,' I continued. 'You partially inspired my thinking actually.'

'Oh?'

'Yes, I've thought a lot about this 'Saucha' chap and what he's doing in Mumbai, creating green spaces, not being defeated by the enormity of his mission, instead inspiring people. What he's doing there made me think more about the impact my business has. I thought, if Saucha can do so much for the city with so little, then certainly my business can make more of a contribution than it currently does.' I glanced around to gauge Ardash's response, hoping he wouldn't find my views ridiculous. He simply nodded.

'Good,' he said. 'In the right hands business can be a powerful force for good.'

I looked at him. 'Do you really think so?'

'Of course. I consider that business has a moral obligation to use its power to make life better for people.'

We continued for a while in silence, walking along the cobbled street past a flower seller, the yellows, purples and oranges of the blooms bursting into the afternoon sunlight, past a fromagerie where huge round Bries and Camemberts competed for space with pointy little Chêvres. As an elderly lady opened the door and bustled inside, we caught a strong whiff of cheese and I heard the cheesemonger say 'Oui madame, la tomme de savoie est excellente aujourd'hui'. We continued past a café terrace where a young couple laughed and kissed, while a smiling accordion player serenaded them.

'Now I know I'm in Paris,' Ardash laughed.

At a baker's shop, the smell of freshly baked bread wafted into the street, making me feel hungry.

'Artisan Boulanger,' Ardash read aloud, looking up at the sign, as we paused to take in a display of exquisitely decorated cakes and pastries. 'It's true, the pâtisseries in Paris are works of art in their own right.'

Turning into Boulevard Raspail, we crossed Place Boucicaut where some old men were playing Pétanque.

'Nice for the elders to have something companionable to get them out into the sunshine,' Ardash remarked. I smiled at his use of the term 'elders' and because his remark made me think of Theo-Paul.

'You're much...I don't know... *softer* than I first thought,' I said.

Ardash didn't respond.

At the Rodin Museum, we were both silent as we wandered from room to room, lingering at some of the statues, wandering past others, and I was reminded of the art tour in Mumbai. Once again, I watched Ardash as he walked. He seemed to engage with the sculptures in a way that suggested he was searching for something that only stone could reveal.

'Let's go and find The Thinker,' I said once we had toured all the rooms. Outside in the grounds, it wasn't long before we were standing in front of the famous statue.

'He has great legs,' I said, smiling. It was a comment I knew would have amused Theo-Paul. Ardash though, didn't respond but continued to gaze up at the immense sculpture.

'You know, it was originally named The Poet,' he said at last. 'I don't know why the name was changed.'

'He seems the ideal man,' I replied. 'Powerful. Intellectual. Beautiful.' Ardash looked at me.

'You like powerful men, do you?' His lips moved into a half smile.

'There's something extremely compelling about a man who knows his own power but doesn't need to demonstrate it.' Our eyes met and we stood for a long moment before moving on.

We came to a halt in front of The Gates of Hell. We both glanced up at the suddenly darkening sky. 'This is one of my favourite pieces.' Ardash didn't answer immediately, but stood staring at the sculpture.

'Entrancing,' he said eventually. 'What does it say to you?' I gazed up at the mass of writhing, twisting, naked bodies, a scaled-down version of The Thinker above them and The Three Shades above him, their hands eternally linked in their mutually damned destiny.

'I find the frenetic madness of it exhilarating,' I replied. 'It makes me feel energized. Expectant, somehow.' Ardash nodded. Something in the concentrated way he stared up at the crazed figures, the tensing and un-tensing of the veins in his neck, his jutting jaw, thrilled me.

'The souls of the damned stand above all suffering,' he murmured. He turned and fixed me with an intense look as the first fat drops of rain plopped around us. 'Let's get a glass of wine, shall we?'

The sun continued to shine as the rain got heavier and Ardash took off his jacket and held it over our heads as we ran the short distance to Café La Bonnechasse.

'I love summer showers,' Ardash said, shaking out his jacket. 'They remind me of India.'

We took a table on the terrace where we could hear the rain drumming softly on the awning, and I ordered two glasses of Sancerre.

'I know you like white wine,' I smiled.

'Cheers,' Ardash said once the waiter had brought our drinks, along with a tiny dish of charcuterie. We clinked glasses.

I sat back in my chair and looked at him, a glow of pleasure rising from my stomach as the sunlight glanced off his shades, the rich brown of his skin giving him an air of vitality. We sipped our wine in silence and I appreciated the way he didn't feel the need to fill it with small talk. Outside, the wet cobbles shimmered. Eventually Ardash took off his sunglasses and regarded me intently.

'There's something I'd like to tell you,' he said. I looked at him. He wasn't smiling and something in his tone made me apprehensive.

'Oh dear,' I said. 'Is this is the part where you tell me that in fact you're married with three children but it's okay because your wife doesn't understand you?'

Ardash laughed. 'Not quite' he answered. 'No wife—not any more anyhow. And no children.'

'Okay then...' I put down my glass.

Ardash paused. The linden tree in the street swayed in the breeze and its leaves dripped water. Ardash stared up into it for some moments and I followed his gaze. The rain was beginning to ease.

'Okay,' he said, turning back to me. 'I may be a little premature, but this is something I want to be clear about. You and I seem to be getting on well. I'd like to get to know you more, and I'd be pleased if you felt the same.' He leaned back in his chair and took a sip of his wine, all the while looking at me intently. 'But before things go any further, there is something I want to tell you. Something about myself that is likely to affect what you think about me.'

I leant back in my chair and folded my arms. *God*, I thought, *I hope he doesn't have some awful disease.* I took a gulp of wine. A waiter came to ask if we were planning on ordering food and I waved him away.

'It's only fair that you know this, before we see each other again.'

A man and a woman came laughing into the terrace and took a table close to ours. The man bent to kiss the woman and they continued to talk and laugh quietly together. *Why is it never that easy for me?* I thought, turning back to Ardash. I sighed inwardly. I wasn't sure I wanted to know what he had to tell me.

'Ardash,' I said, before he could speak. 'Look. You don't owe me anything—explanations or sincerities. We barely know each other.'

'I realise that,' he said, an edge of hardness creeping into his voice. 'But if you want to see me again—and I hope you do—this is something you need to know.'

I took a deep breath and breathed out quietly so that Ardash wouldn't notice.

'Okay,' I said. 'I'm listening.'

He seemed in no great hurry to enlighten me. He took a long, slow sip of his wine, maintaining eye-contact with me over the top of his glass. *Is he playing with me?* The rain had finally ceased and the late-afternoon sun was glancing off the windows opposite, giving the street a cosy glow that was quite at odds with how I felt. *The rumble of thunder would have been appropriate at this point,* I thought, suppressing a sardonic smile. At last Ardash spoke, but what he said wasn't at all what I'd expected.

'What I want to tell you is that I'm not exclusive in relationships. And I'm not looking to change that.'

I sat there staring, not knowing how to respond. A child in the street began to cry and I waited for her to stop before continuing. Ardash remained silent.

'I see.' I nodded slowly. 'Is that short hand for 'I can't commit and I sleep around'?'

91

Ardash smiled. 'The first part, possibly. The second part, no. I'm choosy about my lovers. I wouldn't describe myself as promiscuous.'

'Is that so?' I raised a sceptical eyebrow. 'And how many lovers do you have?'

'Until recently, two. Now I only have one.'

I snorted. 'Oh, I get it. You have a vacancy and you think I might like to apply?'

Ardash laughed and shook his head. 'Not at all.' He paused to take a sip of his wine.

'The way I choose to live is open and transparent. I'm always honest.' He replaced his glass on the table. 'At the same time, I don't want to hurt anyone either. I never discuss my lovers with any others.'

'Well. I'm not sure what to say.'

Ardash picked up his empty glass and stared into it for a long moment. 'You know,' he replied, looking straight into my eyes, 'the first thing that attracted me to you was your independence.' He lent closer and spoke quietly. 'I think you and I are not so different in what we want from our lives. And from our loves.' He turned to hail the waiter. 'Let's have another glass of wine.'

Paris, Ile St Louis

'Father,' I say, 'tell me what to say in your eulogy.' The windows across the river are reflecting what is left of a glorious flame-red sunset and a few of the balconies have their patio-doors open, suggestive of a mild evening. I'm standing on my balcony in my bare feet trying to think about the funeral. My head is thumping and I glance down and watch the traffic as it snakes across the Pont Louis Philippe, headlights on, and watch business people with briefcases, and camera-toting tourists hurrying across the bridge.

I've arranged for my father's funeral to take place at Père Lachaise and most of our few family members have responded. Theo-Paul won't come and I haven't invited Ardash. I thought about inviting François and his wife or maybe even Marine but decided not to, preferring to keep my grief away from my colleagues. I feel a morbid sense of accomplishment as I look out at the other apartments and I chide myself for it because it feels as though with everything I do, I am pushing my father further away. I sigh deeply and bite my lip.

Twenty minutes later I'm still staring down. The people crossing the bridge have begun to thin out, with only a few tourists left, dawdling over the cobbles. It's too early yet for the evening restaurant goers, who will arrive later, well-dressed and eager at L'Orangerie, and Lutetia and Le Tastevin. Most people are at home now, I imagine, settling into their easy, domestic routine. I think of them flowing through the calm of the warm night. I watch the occasional bird flying high in the blue-green sky to its nest and feel a melancholy settling on the world, as people and birds and cars retreat and leave the streets to the lost and the restless. I sigh once more and look across at the balcony opposite. It seems empty, there is no light coming from the window, but the geraniums are a rich, deep purple in the growing dusk. I've never seen the person who lives there but I am certain it's a woman. I smile as I look at her flowers and imagine her re-planting each spring-time, tending them with care until the new blooms open. They seem to me with their brazen blaze of colour to represent a kind of optimism. I think back to my father and how I can possibly find the right words to honour his life. 'Ju suis désolé, Father, I can't do it now,' I say. 'I'll write your eulogy tomorrow.' I turn to go inside to pour a glass of wine.

Five years earlier, my father and I sat on the balcony on an evening such as this one, drinking a glass of Pineau des Charentes and enjoying the twilight calm. The aroma of our Magret de Canard came wafting from the kitchen, making me feel hungry, and I took a cashew from the little crystal dish between us. 'Not bad girl, not bad at all,' my father said, swirling his wine and gazing over the railings to the river beyond. The setting sun had cast a pretty pink shimmer across the water and the street lights had just flicked on, illuminating the bridge and the quay below with warm orange light. My father nodded in fond appreciation before sitting back in his seat and turning to look at me.

'You've done well girl, it's a fine apartment, first rate,' he said, nodding once again. 'Who'd have thought that my little girl would one day have an apartment on the Ile Saint Louis?' He winked at me. 'You're a real catch you know.' He reached for a cashew and popped it into his mouth. 'You've got a solid career and a beautiful home. All you need now is a husband.' I laughed as I stood up to check on our meal.

'Father,' I said over my shoulder, 'I am perfectly content by myself.'

Now, returning to the balcony with my wine, the evening has darkened to night and I shiver as I notice a coolness in the air. I take a sip and draw thoughts of Ardash around me as though they can warm me. The days before I'm with him stretch ahead like a punishment and something deep inside me can't stop aching. I wonder as I gaze into the evening whether the emptiness I feel is for him or for my father. A bird squawks as it flies low over the river and I tell myself that I will not contact Ardash. It's another two weeks until I see him again and I will not contact him even though I long for him. 'He will have only the best of me, Father,' I say, watching the bird as it flies into the distance. I shift my gaze to the geraniums opposite. Even if he is with another woman right now, and in spite of a spike of guilt about Theo-Paul, I know that a word from Ardash, just his voice, would ease at least some part of my pain. But I know too that later, even as I cry in the dark of the night, lonely in my bed, I will not call him because I love him.

Paris, Ile St Louis
and the Montparnasse Tower

After our afternoon in Paris, I'd had a lot to think about. Having left the café, Ardash rode the metro with me and then walked the short distance across the bridge to my apartment building. I didn't invite him up.

'I'd love to see you again,' he'd said. 'But I'll understand if that doesn't happen.' He'd kissed me lightly on each cheek, his lips barely brushing my skin.

That night I went to bed early with a mug of hot chocolate, and as I stretched out in my bed, enjoying the feel of the crisp, cool linen, I replayed the conversation we'd had. A degree of admiration for Ardash crept into my thoughts. There was no denying he'd been scrupulously honest. If I wanted to take our relationship further, I simply had to choose whether or not I could accept his way of life. I blew across the hot, milky froth in my mug. The idea of honesty in un-exclusivity was certainly intriguing. Although I felt attracted to Ardash, I thought, arching my back and stretching my legs, I wasn't going to be made a fool of. If we are to be together in any way, I decided, I need to be sure I'm accepting his conditions for myself, not just for him.

I was thinking about this when working late one evening. The building was quiet and I'd intended to take advantage of this to review some supplier contracts, but as I stared at the screen in front of me, I couldn't get Ardash out of my mind. I stood up from my desk and walked to the window. The buildings below had faded from white to grey as night began to descend, and I gazed out at the lights of the cars snaking their way along the Boulevards Garibaldi and Des Invalides. Little by little, as darkness fell, the city became studded with gold, and the words 'embers' and 'ashes' flashed into my mind. I had the impression, as I stood and watched, that if I blew across it, Paris would catch fire and burn.

I was the only one left at the office, or so I'd thought, until Marine popped her head around my door.

'Still here?' she said. I turned round in surprise.

'Nearly done,' I replied. 'You're late this evening too.'

'Yes,' she said, coming to stand next to me by the window. 'I wanted to finish that report before tomorrow. I like working at this time of the day—I find I can get a lot done.' I nodded. We both stared into the deepening night. The lights of Paris were shimmering brightly now and the buildings looked almost black.

'I sometimes think,' Marine said, almost to herself, 'that the only people working at this time of the night are those interested in the dirty gold of the city.' I glanced at her, confused, but she turned away from the window. 'Will you be here much longer?' she asked.

I decided to call it a day.

'No, I'm about done,' I said, stretching my back before walking to my desk, clicking a couple of keys and snapping the lid of my laptop shut. 'I'll come down with you.'

We walked together in silence to the elevator and stood waiting at the doors, each occupied by our own thoughts.

'Do you have any plans for this evening?' Marine asked.

'No, not tonight,' I said, then cursed myself silently for not inventing some.

'Let's go for a drink.'

'Err...' I faltered, '...I'm quite tired...'

'Nonsense,' Marine said. 'You can stand to have one drink. And I could do with some company, I'm fed up with going home to an empty apartment.'

Out of the building, we walked together the short distance to a small café, where we sat inside at a table by the window and ordered two gin and tonics. I looked around. The café was almost full and a line of men in business suits was standing at the dark wood bar. I noticed that the floor was littered with sugar wrappers, and as though I'd conjured him up, a waiter with a broom appeared and started to sweep them away. I looked back at Marine and smiled again. Once more, Marine smiled back. I felt relieved when the waitress came back with our drinks and a little dish of olives. I picked up my glass.

'Cheers,' I said. We clinked our glasses together and each took a sip. I ate an olive. Neither of us said anything until we both started to speak at once.

'Did you manage to finish your report?'

'You seem to be doing well—'

'Sorry, do go on.'

Marine smiled. 'I was wondering how you are now. After the passing of your father, I mean. You seem to be coping well.'

Passing. What a strange word to describe his death.

'Yes, I'm getting there, thanks,' I replied.

'You must miss him a lot,' Marine said. 'You were close, weren't you? And an only child?'

'Yes,' I answered. 'But I'm getting there.'

'Everyone was surprised at how soon you came back to work.'

I didn't know how to reply, and didn't want to repeat myself a third time, so I took a slug of my gin instead.

'Theo-Paul tells me you're doing okay,' she said. 'That's good. But you know, it's okay to take some time if you need it.'

I looked at her. I wondered whether she had something to say about my friendship with Theo-Paul, but her concern sounded genuine. I softened a little.

'Thank you,' I said. 'There have been sleepless nights, but I'm coming to terms with it gradually.'

'That's good,' Marine repeated.

Two women in smart dresses and high heels bustled into the café and sat at the next table to ours. They ordered their drinks with barely a pause in their conversation. I imagined for a pregnant moment telling Marine about Ardash. *Could you entertain the idea of a non-exclusive relationship?* I gulped back some more gin.

'I meant to thank you,' I said, deciding to stick within safe bounds, 'for your support over the new bonuses.'

'Oh, thanks.' She sounded surprised. 'Well yes, I thought that was a really excellent suggestion, Gilbert and Sophie have both worked so hard.' She took a sip of her gin and another olive. 'Tristan was fucking awful in that board meeting though, wasn't he?'

'He has some very strong views,' I said guardedly.

'That's one way of putting it,' Marine replied. 'I found him insufferable. And it isn't the first time.' She looked as though she was going to continue but I cut her off.

'Well,' I said, 'I wouldn't go that far.'

'You must be joking. It was obvious he was determined to be as obstructive as he could. You know, I have some concerns about his attitude.' I looked at Marine for a long moment. I didn't want to offend her but I didn't like the way the conversation was going.

'Marine,' I said firmly, 'I don't want a divided board. It's important that we work well together.'

'I don't think telling you what I think is going to change the way things are,' Marine said.

'What do you mean?' I replied. 'The way things are?'

'Look, I don't want a disagreement with you,' a shade of weariness creeping into her voice. 'I just felt like some company this evening, and I thought we could talk, that's all. You know, talking openly isn't a bad thing. You might even find it helpful yourself.'

Paris, Montparnasse Tower, Marine's office

'It's a fascinating city. A great clash of developing and developed worlds, the old and the new, the archaic and the innovative, all competing for space and attention.'

Marine listened attentively from across the little meeting table, while behind her Paris sparkled, the late afternoon sunlight glinting off the Eiffel Tower, car windscreens and countless windows.

'Well, Mumbai is certainly the place to do business,' she said, picking up the cafetière to pour our coffee. 'How did you get on with your contact, didn't you say he was difficult?'

'Roshan Naik...' I paused, remembering his chilly demeanour and reluctance to engage with me until he realised I was the CEO. 'He is what he is,' I said. 'In any case, he certainly knows the market there. With his help, I think we have a real chance at getting into India.'

Marine handed me my cup and we both took a sip of coffee. I glanced into the open plan through the glass wall of the office. Claude was leaning back in his chair, smiling as he spoke, his phone clamped to one ear; Gilbert and Solange were standing by her desk, the two of them looking over some papers. Sophie, the keen young operations manager was gesticulating wildly as she explained something to a small group gathered round her desk. They all laughed and Sophie looked pleased.

I smiled. 'Yes,' I said, turning back to Marine, 'I've got a good feeling about this.'

'Did all the begging bother you? I've heard it's a real problem in India.'

I shook my head. 'To be honest, it wasn't that which shocked me most,' I replied. 'It was upsetting certainly, especially the children. But Paris has its share of homelessness, and I'm sure it's getting worse.' Marine nodded in agreement. 'I was more stunned by the rubbish.'

'The rubbish? More so than people sleeping rough?'

'The thing is, you have to see it to realise the extent of the problem,' I said. 'It's not just litter. In parts of the city there are great festering mounds of refuse. People routinely discard their rubbish, you see it all the time. And so much of it is plastic, so it just accumulates. It not only spoils the city; it's a serious environmental hazard.'

Marine took a sip of her coffee and raised her eyebrows. 'But Mumbai is supposed to be so modern?'

'Yes, and in many ways it is,' I answered. 'It's cosmopolitan, cultured, the old-banger taxis have been replaced, and there are high-rise buildings springing up everywhere. Obviously it's a major centre for Asian commerce—for international commerce as well...' I paused and shook my head. 'My hope is that as it develops, India will retain a sense of its own history and culture rather than repeating the mistakes that so much of the west has made.'

I glanced outside as a flock of pigeons swooped low past Des Invalides, flapping to rest on a rooftop. The irony didn't escape me that although my city hadn't gone down the route of filling itself with sky-scrapers, I was sitting in Paris's highest one.

'But yes, the rubbish,' I continued, turning back to Marine. 'Apparently there's a government initiative to clean up India. But Ard...' I checked myself. 'Someone told me that rather than wait for whatever the bureaucrats are planning, there's this sort of environmental vigilante who's already doing great things for the city.'

Marine put down her coffee cup and sat back in her seat.

A vigilante? What do you mean? Who told you?'

'Oh, someone I met at the conference told me about him. This vigilante—he goes by the name of Saucha—no one knows anything about him, except that he's a local who goes around clearing away rubbish from wasteland and making parks for children. I was taken to one of these 'Saucha parks'. It's impressive what he's doing with no official help, simply because he wants to address a problem and set a good example. Apparently it's working too; his parks are being copied and maintained by other local people, purely voluntarily.'

'That *is* impressive. And no one knows who this 'Saucha' is, you say?'

'That's right.'

'Then how do you know he's a man?'

'Good question!'

I smiled and stood up, taking my coffee over to the window, where I watched a single cloud in the otherwise clear sky, start to dissipate over La Défense.

'In any case,' I said still gazing out, 'he or she made a big impression on me.' I turned to face Marine. 'I've begun to think seriously about what more *we* could do. Our vision for the company talks a grand story about the environment and our local and international communities. But beyond recycling, and getting rid of plastic cups from the office, we've done precious little else.'

'Oh come on, don't beat yourself up,' Marine countered. She picked up her coffee and came to join me by the window, seating herself on the little ledge. 'Besides, you've been in post for less than three years. Our 'people, planet, profit' vision didn't exist before that. Okay, we haven't focused on the 'planet' leg of the three-legged stool, but look at what we've achieved in terms of our people; the personnel-restructuring, the overhaul of our employment policies, the equal pay initiative—all that has made a real difference to our staff and their families.' I followed her glance to her desk and a glass-framed photograph of her son, grinning widely and holding up a certificate. 'You only have to look at how absence rates have fallen, to see that it's working,' Marine continued, nodding towards the open-plan. 'And then there's the little matter of building and consolidating our client base—no mean feat with the economy on its knees. I'm sure we all appreciate the dividend payments that prove it! It's a cliché, I know, but Rome wasn't built in a day.'

As she spoke, I nodded slowly, my father's voice coming back to me; *don't just aim higher girl, aim deeper.*

'Yes, okay,' I replied. 'But now it's time for the next step. Our India expansion is a real opportunity, in more ways than one.'

We both looked round as Tristan appeared at the door of the office, and indicated through the glass that he was coming in.

'Afternoon ladies, sorry to interrupt your chat.' Immediately my hackles rose. *Ladies? Chat?* 'Could I borrow you Marine, there's something I'd like to discuss.'

'Tristan, this isn't a 'chat,' we're in a meeting,' I replied curtly.

'Oh?' His eyes flicked from me standing by the window, coffee in hand, to Marine perched on the ledge beside me. 'This is important,' he said. 'If you wouldn't mind giving me a moment of your time, Marine?'

'Tristan,' Marine snapped, '*this* meeting is important, so if *you* wouldn't mind, we'd like to continue!'

I looked impatiently at my watch. 'Look, we're due to finish in twenty minutes. I'm sure whatever it is can wait until then.'

Tristan looked as though he was going to say more, but I interjected. 'Close the door on your way out, would you please?'

'Can you fucking believe that man!' Marine exclaimed once the door had closed behind him. 'I'm convinced his obnoxiousness is deliberate. It's like he looks for every opportunity to undermine you.'

I looked at her guardedly.

'Let's get back to business,' I said.

We moved back to the meeting table and sat down.

'What all this is leading to,' I continued, 'is a set of ideas I have concerning our environmental responsibility. First, the India expansion.' Marine nodded. 'We can source local suppliers who are committed to green policies and practices. I want locally sourced and produced eco-merchandising. I want greener transport options; awareness of environmental issues built into our marketing. And above all, no plastics. None. No plastic bags for merchandise, no plastic pens, and definitely no plastic water bottles.'

Marine raised her eyebrows. 'That's quite some thinking you've been doing.'

'Yes, and it's not going to stop at India. There's no reason why we shouldn't take this strategy right across our organisation.'

'You know, all that'll take time,' Marine replied. 'We're tied into all sorts of supplier and partner contracts, we can't just change over-night.'

'I know. But we've got to start somewhere.'

'And switching to greener suppliers is likely to be more costly.'

'Not necessarily. Part of the planning will be to assess that properly. It won't be a short term project. But with the India initiative, we're in a great position to make a start.'

Marine nodded. 'You know, this could work,' she said. 'You're right, it's a long term project but we could aim at setting an industry standard—it could be really very exciting.' Suddenly Marine smiled broadly at me. 'I think I have the perfect name for it.'

'Oh?' It was my turn to raise my eyebrows.

'Project Saucha!'

Insomnia

14.47 Father... I remember... I must have been four, maybe five years old.... I was sitting on the floor in the salon, drawing with my big, fat crayons, the ones Aunt Constance had given me for my birthday. I liked the way if I dug them hard, they smudged into the paper.

'Be careful,' you said over the top of your big newspaper. 'Your aunt Constance will tell us off next time she visits if you mark the parquet.'

'What shall I draw, Papa?'

'Why don't you draw us?'

I took a crayon and began. Green, then dark blue. I took my time getting your glasses just right, the buttons on your jacket, your shiny brown shoes with their long laces.

'Are my feet really that big?' you asked, tickling me under the arm with a black-socked foot.

I giggled and pinched your toe. I drew myself by your side, my dress yellow with red polka-dots, like my favourite one, an orange hand reaching up to yours, fingers entwined. I scribbled in my big, bushy hair with the black crayon.

'Why don't you have hair, Papa?'

'My brain is so big, it pushed out all my hair,' my father said.

He winked at me. 'No it didn't!'

I held up the page to show him. He put down his newspaper and lowered his glasses.

'It's very good,' he said at last and I beamed. 'But why is this side blank?' He pointed to the right of the page where there was an empty space. I looked up at him.

'That's for when Mama comes back.'

Paris, Salon d'Art, Quartier Latin

'What the heck?' Theo-Paul boomed into the phone as I opened the door to my apartment. 'I need a night out and I'm sure you do too. I'll pick you up in an hour.'

It seemed a better prospect than another evening at home trying and failing to write my father's eulogy, so here I sit with him at the Salon d'Art, not far from République. It's the first time I've been and I look around the cosy little café with its long, dark-wood bar and deep red banquettes. Theo-Paul peers over the top of his glasses, holding the menu at arm's length. I detect a vulnerability about him, perhaps because he's unaware of my scrutiny. The word 'dependable' springs to mind, although I'm certain I can depend only on Theo-Paul's presence, not his understanding. I watch him turn a page and I think about my father imploring me to marry. Would Theo-Paul's kind of dependability be enough? *'I'm choosy about my lovers...'* Ardash had said. I shove away the thought and pick up my menu.

Theo-Paul puts his hand in the air and mouths at the waiter that he'd like the wine list. I glance around at the people seated at the tightly packed tables. The couple to our left is talking about a daughter who apparently has marriage problems. I watch them, eavesdropping as the woman lists her son-in-law's failings. 'He was never right for her,' she says. 'Didn't I say that right from the start?' She sounds triumphant and clearly the question is rhetorical. The man must realise this because he doesn't answer. He is looking around him as though planning an escape but the woman continues, regardless.

I turn to my right where a man is speaking at length about an article he has read in Le Figaro. 'He's got it absolutely spot on,' the man is saying, 'I don't know why the unions can't see it, they'll have this country on its knees before long!' The woman opposite him is biting her lip and playing with her cutlery. Neither is looking at the other and I have the impression the man would be equally happy airing his opinions to anyone.

I look at Theo-Paul as he squints at the wine list and try to think what we might be discussing if we'd been married for years. *I'm always honest...*' Ardash had said. I lean forward and speak quietly.

'Do you think these couples here are happy?'

'Maybe they are content,' he answers without looking up.

'What do you think about commitment?'

'Christ, what a question!' Theo-Paul peers at me over the top of his glasses.

'I mean...no, it's okay, forget it.' I go back to looking at the menu.

'Thank God,' Theo-Paul says. 'I thought for a moment you were going to get all deep and meaningful! What are you going to eat?' I sigh.

'People eat too much,' I say, snapping my menu shut. 'I'll just have a salad.'

'Who you are trying to torment?' Theo-Paul asks, 'me or yourself?' He hails a waiter and orders a blue fillet steak and a bottle of Pomerol. 'Make sure the steak is very blue,' he insists. 'And bring a side order of frites.'

He folds his glasses and places them on the table. As he is ordering, I stare past at a cloud of dust mites dancing in the light as a waitress shakes out a tablecloth, and I think it's one of the most beautiful sights I've ever seen. I consider sharing this, but think better of it.

'Theo-Paul,' I say after the waiter nods and leaves with our order. 'I'm having tremendous difficulty writing my father's eulogy.' I wonder if I'm setting him a test and I watch as Theo-Paul tears apart a piece of bread from the basket in front of us without looking up. 'I want to say something genuine, but I can't find the words.'

107

'Aren't these things fairly standard? His marriage, blah, blah blah, his job, blah, blah blah, what made him a good man, that sort of thing?' He picks up his glasses and starts to clean them with his napkin. 'I'm sure the right words will come in time,' he says.

I place my chin in my cupped hand and look at him. Someone else might feel offended at Theo-Paul's lack of sensitivity, but I knew before asking that this isn't the kind of territory where he feels at home. I wonder whether he's regretting asking me to dinner. The wine waiter arrives with our Pomerol and Theo-Paul looks relieved as he replaces his glasses and busies himself inspecting the label. I wonder whether I too am relieved.

Over our meal, Theo-Paul surprises me by asking a question.

'Listen,' he says, 'I've been thinking. How about sometime soon, you and I spoil ourselves and take off to Stockholm for a weekend?'

I look up at him over the top of my wine glass and frown suspiciously.

'Stockholm!' I exclaim. 'Why?'

'I don't know,' he retorts, 'the charm of the Baltic, the *Brännvin*? Do you need a reason to enjoy a weekend trip?' He hesitates. 'I'm sure you'll be glad of a break; especially after the...you know... after...' he looks down and pushes a piece of steak around his plate.

'The funeral, Theo-Paul,' I say, 'after the funeral. You don't have to avoid mention of it.' I smile at him. 'Is this you trying to do your bit for the bereaved friend?' Theo-Paul doesn't reply.

'How's your steak?' I ask.

'It's over-cooked. Don't change the subject. The point is, are you coming to Stockholm or not?'

The wine makes the quiet buzz of conversation in the restaurant sound soothing in spite of the boredom I suspect is beneath much of it. I look around and notice that many of the older women have desperately short hair. I imagine them in the solitude of their marital bedrooms cutting it off to punish their men. I look at Theo-Paul and find that he is looking at me as he chews his steak. '...*you and I are not so different...*' Ardash had said...

'Have you heard of Edmund Burke?' I ask. Theo-Paul raises his eyebrows.

'He defined the source of the sublime as anything that excites ideas of terror, pain or peril in the mind of a person who knows they're not in any danger.'

'Ah,' he answers, before taking a large sip of his Pomerol. 'You're coming to Stockholm then?'

Later, Theo-Paul kisses me on each cheek as he drops me off at my apartment and I watch as he climbs back into the taxi. 'Think about the trip,' he calls before disappearing into the night. I turn and press the code into the keypad by the lobby door and step into the semi-darkness inside.

'...*I never discuss my lovers with any others...*'

'Father,' I think as I climb the stairs, 'if I go to Stockholm, should I tell Ardash?'

In my apartment, I kick off my shoes, shrug off my jacket and sit down heavily on the couch. I feel suddenly and unaccountably angry, and tears prick the corners of my eyes, spilling over down my cheeks. I wipe them away brusquely with the back of my hand. I ought to go straight to bed I think, but I continue to sit there at the centre of a strange bitterness, the source of which I can't pinpoint except that it is has something to do with Ardash. '...*I'd like to get to know you more...*' I look around the room. The soft glow from the side lamp is casting long shadows from the palm plant onto the wall, and the books lining the shelves look regal and proud in the dark wood. I look at the Japanese vase and frown. I've inhabited this beautiful space so well I think, I've created it around me with such care and precision, and I've never shared it with anyone else nor wanted to. Why do I feel so alone here now?

The thought of lying against a warm, hard, male body is enormously comforting and I wonder if I regret not inviting Theo-Paul up. I glance at my watch. Almost eleven o clock. I rummage in my handbag for my phone and stare at it, wondering if this is a good idea. Eventually I press the button and listen to the droning purr for a moment... two... three... No answer. I call his landline number. Ardash isn't home. Or he is busy. I throw the phone onto the couch. I tell myself through my tears that it doesn't matter who Ardash is with, a lover, a potential lover. I tell myself it is good that he isn't here when I need him. I decide to go to Stockholm with Theo-Paul.

Achille de Quincy—before my death

The question of marriage. Never an easy one, I suspect, for a father, and certainly not a question one wants to contemplate on his deathbed. But avoiding it won't change the fact. She will probably never marry. Of course I wanted her to, what parent wouldn't? I still do. But over the years, I've become less and less certain it will happen for her. Even now I worry about that. Perhaps especially now. I think she'd make a wonderful wife, but of course I'm biased. She'd certainly make an interesting wife. And, like she does with any venture she undertakes, I don't doubt that she'd throw herself whole-heartedly into matrimony, she'd make it her mission to 'do marriage' in the best possible way. No, it isn't a question of whether I want her to marry, but to whom.

I remember the first chap she brought home, a tall, lean, dapper young man from The Rhône, who was studying business with her at HEC. Lawrence was his name. He came for afternoon tea one Sunday and I watched her with him, as she fetched the cups and the cakes, trying to see into her motivation. She looked young and fresh in her jeans and jumper, her feet bare and her hair tied in a lose chignon, curls falling prettily around her face. She was charming and accommodating but not flirty, and I caught a glimpse of her as Lawrence must see her, enigmatic, aloof, a challenge. She clearly hadn't lost her head over him and I was glad. There was nothing intrinsically wrong with the boy and I can't say I disliked him. But in him I saw a kind of underlying scurrying fervour, as though he felt life might not grant him the time to unfold naturally. I suppose his impatience was no different from that of any other young man his age, and he was polite and intelligent after a fashion. His father owned a string of dairies near Lyon, and if I remember rightly had insisted on the boy studying commerce before entering the family business. A worthy enough future.

'What did you think of him?' she asked after he'd gone.

'Good on paper,' I'd replied.

I wasn't surprised when she dropped him in her second year, saying he was getting too demanding and distracting her from her studies.

There were others of course. There were a few Jean-Lucs or Jean-Pauls or Jean-Yves over the years. Clean-cut young men with tidy haircuts, set for generic business careers. In the main, they depressed me. Don't misunderstand; by this time, my girl was set for a business career herself. I didn't have a problem with that. No, what I found questionable about them was all their posturing, their bluster, the unexamined aggrandisement of their lives and their plans. There's nothing wrong with ambition, it isn't that, and I'd have been disappointed if they didn't have a healthy dose of it. But it seemed to me that all those Jean-somethings had very little about them *but* ambition. You see their type daily in the city, dynamic, driven, clever. Types who seem to occupy their self-importance with a sense of entitlement and who have a collective blindness regarding anyone who doesn't fit their social goals.

There are egotistical men in medicine, of course there are, but I have an idea that had she gone into that, she'd have been likely to meet a more contingent type of chap, one who would rather examine a point of view than defend a position. It must be the scientist in me. Or the healer. But given the circle she moved in, it was aspiring business-men she met and I never saw one of them who had an idea of what it was beyond money and power they were striving for.

No. My girl is better than that. She was always deeper, more sensitive, more nuanced than those one dimensional young things. She is driven yes, but what drives her will never be satisfied by the size of her bank account or that of

112

her husband and I knew that all along. But what good does it do a father to know his child so well, when we must each choose our own path? Even now though, when soon I am to enter whatever lies beyond, and she is left to face her life alone, I would still say to her *girl, don't aim higher, but deeper.*

Paris, Le Poissonnier and an elegant apartment on the top floor of a building near Bastille

'I'm never afraid, I'm just preparing for pain.'

We're dining at Le Poissonnier and Ardash, eating quail's eggs, is taking his time peeling each one carefully. 'Maybe a part of me is always expecting pain,' he says, dipping a peeled egg into the little dish of celery salt in front of him. I look at my reflection in my wine glass and wonder whether I see myself reflected in Ardash's contradictory independence.

I hadn't called Ardash for some time after his revelation in Paris, but thought a lot about what he'd said. Eventually I'd emailed him, saying simply, *Come to Paris. Let's see what happens.*

'What do you think would happen if you found this pain?' I ask him now. I flick a glance to my right, but the couple there are engaged in conversation, their hands clasped together across the table.

'Pain is under-rated,' Ardash replies looking intently at me. He places another quail's egg slowly into his mouth without breaking eye-contact.

'I would imagine,' I say, 'that the kind of pain you're talking about is related to trust. Are you saying that you don't trust people?' He seems to consider this.

'Trust is an interesting concept,' he replies at last. 'It seems to me that trusting someone is to make unreasonable demands on them.'

'Surely trust is synonymous with risk? And you seem to be quite a risk taker.' I reach for my glass and think of him dirt-biking in Mumbai. After taking a long, slow, sip, I replace it in front of me and run my fingers up and down the stem. Ardash watches.

'There are different kinds of risk,' he answers, after a pause. 'The risk involved in trusting another person seems to me to be unworthy. I believe that rather than opening up possibilities trust closes them down. It serves only to limit us in our choices.' He sits back in his chair and glances around the candle-lit restaurant. 'Look around you,' he says quietly, indicating the other diners with a nod of his head. The place is full of couples having hushed and intimate conversations, and I think fleetingly of Theo-Paul. 'I'd imagine that each person here feels they can trust their partner,' Ardash continues. 'Or at least that they'd like to be able to.' I nod in agreement. 'What they actually mean, though, is that they expect their partner to behave in such a way that won't hurt them.' I nod at him again, as the man on our right leans forward to kiss the woman.

'Okay,' I say, looking back at Ardash. What he said doesn't sound unreasonable to me. 'And...?'

'Well, think about it,' he replies. 'When I say 'I trust you' what I really mean is 'don't do anything you know I won't like."' He pauses again. 'Trust is a much unexamined concept.'

I think about this as the waiter arrives and offers us more bread. I shake my head at him and watch Ardash take a piece. I suppose because he's honest about the possibilities within a relationship, trust isn't necessary. It's a novel notion I think, as Ardash tears his bread roll in two and starts to devour one of the halves.

'So what you're saying is that when we have full honesty, we don't need trust?' I ask.

Ardash swallows his bread. 'Exactly.' I hold his gaze.

'That sounds dangerous,' I say.

'As I say, pain is under-rated.' He picks up the bottle to pour us both more wine. 'Tell me about Theo-Paul.'

*

Earlier that day, Theo-Paul had called me at work. 'I've got the tickets,' he'd boomed. I moved the phone away from my ear. 'So there's no backing out now.'

'Stop shouting,' I said, walking around my desk and closing my office door. 'I'm not going to back out.'

'I never know what you're going to do.' I could sense Theo-Paul's wry smile.

'That's why you like me,' I answered, moving to the window. It was drizzling but still sunny and I watched as light rain fell in a pretty haze to the glistening roads below.

'What have you told Marine?' Theo-Paul asked.

'About what?'

'About going away with me of course.'

I frowned. 'I haven't told her anything. What does it have to do with her?'

'Oh come on. Won't she ask?'

'Look,' I said, 'you're not married to her anymore and what I choose to do with my weekends is no one's concern but mine.'

'Okay, okay, settle down.' He paused for a moment. 'Do you know what day it is?'

'Of course I do,' I said brusquely, 'it's Friday.' I glanced at my watch. My next meeting was in twenty minutes and I wanted to send a few emails first.

'Not only that,' Theo-Paul said, a hint of a tease in his voice. 'It's our anniversary.' I tutted.

'Theo-Paul, we're not an item, we don't have an anniversary,' I said.

'Nonsense! It's the anniversary of when I first met you. Which curiously is also the anniversary of my divorce. Obviously not in the same year.' He chuckled. 'How about meeting for dinner later?'

'Sorry, not possible tonight,' I said as I walked back to my desk. 'I have plans.'

*

116

'I've known him for a few years,' I tell Ardash, picking up the last of the quail's eggs and dipping it in the salt. 'He used to be married to a colleague of mine.'

'Interesting,' Ardash replies. 'Are you the reason they aren't married anymore?' I shake my head as I eat the egg. The waiter hovers nearby waiting to clear our plates.

'I have no idea,' I say, picking up my glass.

'I'm not sure I believe that.'

'Well,' I answer, 'he didn't leave her to be with me. Apparently their marriage was already failing when I met him.'

'But you see a lot of him?'

I'm always honest, he'd said… I don't like this questioning but I reply anyway. 'I suppose you'd say we're good friends.'

'Friends.' Ardash levels a steady gaze at me. 'So why aren't you together?'

'Together?' I say. 'What does that mean?'

Ardash smiles. 'Good question. Why aren't you married, living together?'

'Ah, I see,' I reply, before pausing. *Honesty? Risk?* 'To tell the truth,' I reply at last, 'I have thought about it. There are lots of reasons why it could work. We're the same age, we have similar backgrounds and jobs, I can talk with him, especially about work. He doesn't make many demands on me and I like that. I suppose we've become good friends over the last few years.' I think for a moment. 'I'd say we're a good match 'on paper''. As I speak, I watch the veins in Ardash's neck tense, un-tense and tense again. 'I think my father would have approved, had he met him. Look, do you want to hear all this?'

'I wouldn't have asked if not. So? Why aren't you married?'

I pause for a moment, searching for the right phrase. 'Like I say, we're good 'on paper'. But…he doesn't…he isn't…' I search for the right phrase. '…I'm not sure I'd be happier with him than on my own.'

117

My Andouillette arrives, quickly followed by Ardash's Tartiflette and a dish of Gratin Dauphinois, and I busy myself making space on the table and serving out the potatoes.

'Bon appétit,' I say, picking up my fork.

Ardash drains his glass. 'Are you having sex with him?'

I pause, my fork midway to my mouth. 'You're a strange contradiction,' I say, shaking my head. 'You're so guarding of your own freedom and yet you probe into mine as though you have the right to demand what you don't give.'

'You may be right,' Ardash says, cutting into his Tartiflette. 'Tell me how you and Theo-Paul met.'

Five years earlier, Marine and I were, unusually, having lunch together. I was regretting it. 'Listen, we're having a little soirée at our place,' Marine said over our salads. 'Nothing grand, just a few close friends for drinks and nibbles. Do please come.' I shoved a tomato around my plate and didn't reply.

'This place is great,' Marine said, looking around at the boats moored on either side of the canal St Martin. 'Perfect place for me eh? Marine? See?' I smiled thinly and sipped my water. 'Seriously, I'd love you to come.' She leaned forward and lowered her voice. 'Between you and me, things aren't great with Theo at the moment. He can be a bit... a bit unpredictable at times. Moody. He was never very sociable, but he's getting worse. Sometimes he's downright rude to our friends. I'm hoping this little soirée will bring him out of himself. It would mean so much to me to have your support.' I wondered why but didn't ask.

The soirée turned out to be a full scale party and I was pleased I'd arrived late.

'I'm so glad you made it,' Marine said over the sound of piano music. She took my coat and ushered me into the salon.

'Marine, I can't stay long,' I said, glancing around at the modern-art on the walls, the oranges and reds of the paintings reflecting the colours of the cushions on the black leather sofa. It was the first time I'd been at Marine's apartment and I was intrigued, in spite of myself. 'I want to be up early tomorrow to get some work done.'

'Nonsense, work on a Sunday?' she said a little too brightly. 'Come and meet Theo. He'll talk you out of your work-a-holism.'

Theo-Paul was alone on the balcony, gazing down at the dark street below, a glass of Cognac in one hand, a cigar in the other, which Marine promptly removed.

'He thinks he can get away with that on the balcony,' she tutted.

Theo-Paul drained his glass and took in my black Chanel dress, or more probably what was inside it.

'Am I allowed another one of these?' he said, shaking his empty glass at Marine.

'Oh for goodness sake,' Marine replied. 'I'll get you both a drink. Now please be nice.'

'I think she meant you,' Theo-Paul said, once Marine had bustled off to make the drinks. He'd gone back to staring over the balcony.

'I doubt it,' I replied. 'She knows that won't happen.'

'Ah.' Theo-Paul, turned to look at me. 'You must be the other woman on the board.'

'Indeed,' I said holding his gaze. 'I'm the other woman.' Neither of us spoke.

'Drinks!' Marine trilled tinkling the ice in two glasses of Cognac. 'Oh good, you're talking, that's nice.'

'Jesus Marine, ice? In Cognac?' In one swift movement Theo-Paul scooped the ice out of both glasses and threw it over the balcony.

'For fuck's sake Theo,' Marine muttered thrusting the glasses at him before turning and marching back into the apartment. I smiled. Theo-Paul noticed.

*

'We met at a party,' I tell Ardash. My Andouillette tastes too salty and I push it around the plate. Ardash sits back in his seat and looks at me. He hasn't touched much of his meal either.

'This place isn't what it used to be,' I say, pushing my plate away.

'Are you having sex with him?' Ardash asks again. The conversation is beginning to feel like an inquisition and I decide to put an end to it.

'Ardash, really,' I say, sitting back in my chair. 'This is getting tiresome.'

'I assume therefore that you are.'

'You can assume what you want. You made it perfectly clear that you have a whole other part of your life that doesn't involve me. Perhaps I'd like to retain the same degree of freedom myself.'

Ardash's lips curl into a slow smile. He moves his hand towards mine and starts to stroke the inside of my wrist with his thumb. I let him.

'Real freedom is being able to say anything to each other,' he says.

I laugh. 'Do you realise what a contradiction you are?'

He pulls me towards him, his hand tight around mine.

'How about we skip dessert and go back to your apartment?'

Paris, Père Lachaise

Rain has been falling lightly all day, and although not cold, I draw my wrap around myself more closely, as I shiver in the still afternoon air. My aunts stand in a row opposite, leaning on the arms of uncles or cousins I don't recognise, the rain misting their pill-box hats and the shoulders of their coats, too heavy for the season. One aunt is sniffing into a handkerchief and crying audibly, her face buried in the shoulder of her son who looks as ancient and gnarled as she does. I look down into the grave at my father's coffin as the priest speaks.

'Lord our God, you are the source of life. In you we live and move and have our being. Keep us in life and death in your love, and, by your grace, lead us to your kingdom, through your son, Jesus Christ, our Lord.'

I'm only half listening and I drift off amidst the priest's hypnotic cadences into a day much like this one—perhaps twenty years ago, could it have been so long?—where my father and I were packing up the remains of our picnic in the Jardin des Plantes before everything got wet, and hurrying off into a nearby café. It was my birthday and before the rain started, my father had given me a book, beautifully gift wrapped in red paper. I'd smiled at how pleased he looked as I turned it around in my hands, joking with him about what the gift could be.

'Socks?' I'd teased, and he cuffed me playfully. I unwrapped the parcel slowly and carefully, savouring its bright red paper and trim before sliding out the book. 'One Hundred Things to Do Before You Die,' I read aloud.

'You know girl, when I was young, I didn't experience as much as I might have,' my father said. 'Perhaps I was too busy working. Or maybe I didn't have the imagination.'

He turned to the first page where he'd written an inscription. *'Be sure to live before you die.'* I'd hugged him and kissed him warmly on each cheek. Now, as a chilly wind starts to get up, I think about that birthday book gathering dust on its shelf. It feels like a betrayal.

Some mumbled 'amens' bring me back to the graveside. The priest is leading another prayer.

'Lord Jesus Christ,' he intones, 'we thank you for all the benefits you have won for us, for all the pains and insults you have borne for us...'

I try to follow his words, but staring down into the grave, my mind latches itself onto the word 'coffin' and repeats it over and over again. In spite of this repetition, I can't formulate anything coherent out of the word. It's as though its meaning is disappearing into the earth along with my father and I feel sudden terror at losing an understanding of a word that I once knew how to use. I take a deep breath and will my heart to stop pounding in my chest. I stare at the coffin, wanting to yell 'no!' Instead I close my eyes and try to stay with the sound, if not the sense of the priest's words.

I know that soon it will be time for me to speak and I begin to ready myself, taking some deep breaths and pressing the palms of my sweating hands together in front of me. I take a sheet of paper out of my handbag and unfold it carefully, refold it, then unfold it again. I look at the sheet with its neatly typed paragraph and a wave of sorrow washes over me. Just one paragraph was all I had managed in the end and I wonder what grief is, if not the anguish of torment. I am willing myself not to cry. The priest nods at me and I clear my throat to speak, but my voice catches and I have to stop for a second or two before starting again. I don't look up at my aunts but take a deep breath and begin to read.

It seems incomprehensible to me that the immensity of a lived life can be laid down on paper using mere words. No amount of clever combinations of words and grammar formed into sentences and paragraphs can recreate the truth and the vitality of a human being who once lived and breathed here with us, and who is now gone. And yet words are among the only tools we have with which to ensure that a life is not lost, that it is given its due, that it is suitably recognised for the mystery and worth of what it was, and honoured accordingly. In relation to my father, that task has fallen to me and I have felt and still feel utterly unequal to it. All I have is my own truth, my own version of my father. Each one of you will have your own version of the man, as brother, uncle, friend. All these truths, all these ways to know and understand this man are equally valid but can be only fragments. Because of course ultimately, no one could know the inner core, the quiet reality, the ultimate truth of the man he was, but my father himself. I had hoped, here, to be able to do my father some degree of justice with my own version of a man that I loved so dearly and whose loss I bear so deeply. But I can't. I simply don't have the words with which to bear my father up, the words which will capture and illuminate his essence. I hope that my insufficiency here before you today speaks not of a lack of willingness nor a lack of care, but rather of the deepest sorrow that a daughter feels at having lost a father she loved and the simple fact that that loss took all meaningful words away from her. The best I can do here today is to ask you to take a moment or two to consider the man that you knew, the man who touched your life, the man who was as unique in relation to you as you were to him. If it moves you to do so, Father Maurice has pens and paper for you to write a few words of your own to my father, which we can leave here at his final resting place to go with him wherever his journey now takes him.'

'Thank you so much for coming,' I say over and again to the aunts, the uncles and the cousins after the service. I nod and smile wanly, as I kiss papery cheeks without being certain to which aunt or cousin they belong.

'Poor girl,' I hear an elderly female voice whisper not at all quietly, 'she and her father were so close.'

I have no idea how I feel. Resolute, I think, although that sounds more like a state of mind than a feeling. 'Is it possible to feel nothing at all, Father?' I ask, gazing at the coffin, the little sheets of folded paper lying on top looking as fragile and vulnerable as the words they contain. Each of their writers had kissed the carefully folded sheets before letting them flutter into the grave and shuffling back to their place. 'Lovely idea,' I'd heard one of the cousins murmur. My eulogy is lying folded on the coffin along with the other notes. 'Father,' I say staring at them, 'it was the most honest I could be.'

The priest's warm, if rather generic homily had caused an outpouring of grief from my eldest aunt in the form of hiccupping little sniffs and snuffles and I chided myself for wondering whether at least a part of her grief was for herself now that no elder sibling or parent stood between her and death. Her sisters are clucking around her now and as they begin to vie for the attention of the priest I feel glad that I haven't entirely bared my soul. Two large men standing to one side of the little group catch my eye, their gloved hands crossed over each other resting on their shovels in front of them. In spite of their respectfully bowed heads, their presence distresses me, and I quickly turn away.

'Marine!' I jolt at her sudden presence next to me, my hand swiftly shooting up to my face to wipe away any stray tears. 'I hadn't expected you here.' She lays a hand on my arm.

'I know,' she says gently. 'I won't stay and intrude. But I wanted to be here to show my support.'

'How kind of you,' I reply, surprised to notice that I really mean it. Even so, I feel glad she isn't staying. The sight of Marine feels confusing, like seeing your usual bank clerk in a café, familiar but out of place.

'Take what time you need,' she says. 'No one is expecting you at the office tomorrow. And I'm a good listener if you ever want to talk.' She squeezes my arm, kisses me on each cheek and turns to go.

'Marine...' I say. She turns back. 'Thank you.'

Paris, mostly the Montparnasse Tower

But the next day I did go to the office. I didn't precisely articulate the thought, but something seemed to be prompting me to keep busy, to keep up a 'normal' routine, not to give myself time to think too much. I pulled back my bedroom curtains, allowing the early morning light to soften my tiredness and although my eyes and head ached from the accumulation of broken nights, now that the funeral was over, I felt something akin to relief. *Life goes on*, I thought, turning away from the window and although I hated myself for sinking to such a trite cliché, it was clearly an undeniable truth.

In the shower I stood for a long time letting the warm water wash over me, not thinking about the day ahead, but simply savouring the comfort of the steamy heat. When eventually I emerged, glowing and damp, I stood in front of my wardrobe wrapped in my towel, my hair wrapped in a smaller one, staring at all the work dresses and jackets neatly arranged by colour. *Really, what difference does it make*, I thought pulling out a navy dress and jacket at random. I had a sudden and bizarre urge to throw them both out of the window and I barked a half laugh, half sob into the silence of my bedroom. Instead, I tossed the clothes onto the bed and turned to reach for the matching shoes.

After blasting hot air from the hairdryer over my damp hair and pulling it into a tight bun, I dressed quickly and perfunctorily. I stood looking at myself in the mirror. *Oh god*, I thought, *I can't go to the office looking like this*. Without make-up and with my hair scraped back I looked pale and worn-out. *Old*, I thought. I wanted to cry. If I ripped off these preposterous clothes, threw myself back into bed and yanked the duvet up over my head, would I stop feeling? I wanted nothing more than to sleep and sleep and sleep. But instead I grabbed my makeup bag from the dressing table and threw it savagely onto the bed.

'How is it, Father,' I asked, 'that men can look fully competent and in control without having to apply this ridiculous war-paint, whereas without it women just look tired?' *Well, it is what it is*, I grumbled as I squeezed foundation cream onto a ball of cotton wool.

Now, squeezed into a crowded carriage on the metro, I recall a conversation that Tristan and François had a long time ago about a bereaved colleague. It was in Troyes and the three of us were having a brief lunch before a meeting. I remember feeling shocked by their attitude.

'A day for the funeral is all she's entitled to,' Tristan had said. 'I think we've been very generous giving her two. She has no right to any more, and frankly, I'm surprised she's asked.' I looked at François, expecting him to show more empathy, but he'd agreed with Tristan.

'Indeed,' he said. 'It'd be different if she'd lost a child or a husband, but it was her mother. I mean, forgive me for stating the obvious but she was an old woman, she was already on borrowed time.' He took a large bite of his sandwich. 'You're absolutely right, Tristan,' he said through his mouthful. 'More than a day is self-indulgence.'

I'd looked from one to the other. 'Self-indulgence?' I said. They both turned to me in surprise. 'Surely as a responsible company we want our staff to feel cared for. And in any case, from a purely business point of view, do you really think anyone can give their best a day after the funeral of their mother?' Tristan and François looked at each other with what I thought was silent complicity.

'Much better to keep up a normal routine,' Tristan said.

'Indeed,' François had replied. 'Better all round.'

The irony of the fact that I'm choosing to deal with my own bereavement in exactly the way I'd objected to bothers me, and I wonder, somewhat ridiculously, whether I should have taken an extra day just to prove myself right. When I became CEO I'd insisted we revisit our time-off policy.

'Marine,' I'd said, 'I want you to work with the staff to develop a more compassionate and flexible way of dealing with personal issues.'

I sigh and I look around the carriage. The metro is full of tired-looking people, wearing the standard uniform of the business commuter, all reading newspapers, fiddling with their mobile phones or staring vacantly into space. *'What am I trying to prove, Father?'* I ask silently. I want to scream.

As I leave the metro and push my way up the steps to the concourse, the sheer size of the Montparnasse Tower depresses me, and I wonder whether the designers intended it to diminish us as humans. I shove the feeling away and nod at the security man as he stands aside to let me enter. There are four or five people standing in the lift lobby and two more enter while we are waiting. The woman to my left glances at me as the lift arrives and I straighten my dress. We all step in, shuffle to our places and stare straight ahead. Only as the lift stops and someone gets out do we nod or wish the person leaving a mumbled good day. I glance at my watch. It's 7.55.

Claude has arrived before me, which isn't unusual, we are generally the first two here. He looks up in surprise when I enter the open plan section of our offices. I feel annoyed that he appears not to have expected me. I nod at him and he goes to speak but I cut in.

'Bonjour, Claude,' I say, 'I'm glad you're early, are you able to have that report on the Madrid account on my desk a little earlier than planned?'

'Yes of course,' he answers quickly. 'I'm working on it now. Will twelve be okay? There are still a few things I need to chase. Coffee?'

I soften a little. 'Thank you Claude, twelve is fine,' I say. 'And yes, coffee would be lovely.'

In my office, I set my laptop on my desk, plug it in, flip up the lid and press a few keys. While I'm waiting for it to start up, I walk over to the plate glass window and stand there gazing out across Paris. In the softness of the early morning light, the creamy-white buildings look almost North African against the pale blue of the sky. I stare ahead, along my line of vision to the Eiffel Tower and to La Défense beyond. There are a few lights on in the knot of towers there, and usually when I see them I feel a degree of empathy with the people in those offices who, like me have decided to get a head start on the day. Today though, I catch myself wondering what it is that we're all doing here. What worries me, I realise, isn't that I don't know the answer to that question, but the fact that I'm asking it. The strangeness of this line of enquiry makes me feel agitated and I'm relieved when a knock on my door interrupts my reverie. I turn to find Claude with a cup of coffee poking his head round my door.

'That's lovely Claude, thank you. Put it on my desk will you?' We both move to the desk. 'Claude, I want to go through your report with you after lunch,' I say, in what I hope is a no-nonsense voice. 'Can you schedule some time this afternoon? At say, 1.30?'

'No problem,' Claude replies. 'The team meeting is at 2.00. Will half an hour will be enough?'

'Good, thank you Claude, yes half an hour will be fine. I'll let you get on.'

Claude smiles and leaves, closing the door carefully behind him. Picking up my coffee, I watch him through the glass walls of my office as he walks back to his desk. I wonder what his work means to him. It's clearly more than just the salary, and I feel something akin to pity for him until I realise that his motivation must be identical to my own. 'What is it that we all want, Father?' I say.

Solange arrives with Gilbert. I watch her hobble in, her broken foot having been in plaster for over a week. Claude remains standing to shake hands with her and Gilbert before sitting down in front of his computer. Solange hobbles off to make coffee, waving to me on the way and pointing towards the kitchen with a questioning look on her face. I raise my coffee-cup to show her that I already have one. Gilbert nods to me and I watch him as he settles himself at his desk. He says something to Claude and they both laugh good-naturedly. I feel a sudden wave of warmth towards them all, here at the office bright and early and cheerful, ready to begin the day's work. I look at my computer with a sigh and prepare to begin my own day.

Typically, my office days begin with a check of my on-line calendar to make sure I know my schedule. Today is no different, and clicking a button on my keyboard, I see that in addition to the meeting with Claude, I have a phone meeting scheduled with the CEO of our Luxembourg partners at 2.30, and a debriefing from the sales-team meeting at 4.00. I have a Skype call in my diary with Roshan Naik at 9.30 but it hasn't been confirmed. I feel irritated by this but remind myself that it's possible I have an email waiting for me which will confirm the call or not. *Right*, I think, *I'd better deal with that first.*

My in-box is very full since I wasn't in the office yesterday, and I scan down it looking for Roshan Naik's name. I sigh, wondering how long it will take to clear this backlog. Nothing from Mumbai. *Ridiculous*, I think, I emailed him more than a week ago, is it so difficult to send a reply? I run a quick search in case I've missed something but I haven't. *Surely* I think as I pick up my phone, *politeness dictates that even if he can't confirm the meeting, a brief holding email to say so would be easy enough to send.* I dial Solange's number.

'Solange, were there any phone messages for me yesterday?'

'Bonjour to you,' Solange answers in a sing song voice. 'Yes, I'm just compiling them for you now. You had one from that new supplier, the one near Saint Michel—he said he'll call back today at about mid-morning; one from Tristan—I think he forgot why you were off yesterday. He didn't leave a message; there was a call from Madrid confirming your meeting next month—I confirmed that for you and updated your diary, I hope you don't mind. There were a few others, I've got the details for you here.'

'Ok, thank you Solange. Nothing from Mumbai? From Mr Naik or his office?'

'Sorry, nothing from there,' Solange replies. 'Are you sure you wouldn't like a fresh coffee?'

'I'm fine, thanks Solange,' I say, and replace the receiver.

Damn, I think, staring at my screen. I retrieve a business card from the little box on my desk, pick up the phone once again and dial a number. An automated voice talks to me in Hindi before telling me in English with a strong Indian accent that Mr Naik is currently unavailable. I replace the phone decisively. I will have to assume that the 9.30 meeting is not happening. Solange appears at my door and I wave her in.

'Your messages,' she says and brings a sheaf of papers to my desk. 'I forgot, there was one from that chap in Poitiers. He wants you to call him back before 11.00 today if you can. He says he may have some interesting news for you and that he'd like to set up a meeting.'

'Thank you,' I say. 'Just leave the messages there will you?' Solange places the papers on my desk and hovers for a moment. I sigh inwardly.

'How are you doing?' she asks. 'Did the funeral go well?'

'I'm fine, thank you,' I say curtly. 'I won't keep you any longer.' Solange nods and scurries out of my office and I carry on scanning through my emails. I see her say something to Claude and I suppress a wave of irritation as they look round at me. My phone rings. It's Gilbert.

'Good morning Gilbert,' I say. 'What can I do for you?'

'Just checking we're still good for our 11.00 catch up,' he says in his characteristically cheerful voice.

'Yes, no problem,' I reply.

'I finished my report on the Luxembourg project,' he continues. 'Can I pop in to you now? There are a couple of things I wouldn't mind running past you before I give it to Monsieur Ploum.'

Why is 'Monsieur Ploum' *not writing his own report*, I wonder, remembering Tristan telling me it would be late.

'Yes okay, bring it in.' I rub my temples with my hands and open a drawer in my desk, fishing around for a packet of pain-killers. As I swallow two tablets with a swig of coffee, the light on my phone begins to flash. *It's going to be a long day*, I think as I press a button. As I do so, I watch Gilbert get up from his desk and walk over to my office, clutching the report. I glance at the time. It isn't yet 9.00.

Achille De Quincy—Before my death

...I must think while I still can, force my mind to make sense of it all, of what this life has been... What I've considered so far is incongruous; it's partial, not the full truth of her and as such fails both of us. Courage, man. If I can't look truth in the eyes on my deathbed, there's no facing it at all, and what use could there be in denials now? *Deathbed.* What a ridiculous word. I try to forge comprehension out of the cliché but the full import of it eludes me and when I try to understand, I find myself hovering on the edges of dreaming, not knowing if I'm awake or asleep. ... I must not fade yet...

Sometimes there is a flash of understanding and for a moment I know what I need to say to her. But it slips away like a receding dream and I am left grasping after mist. When she is here, I have the sense that what I took for reality has fooled me, and all I find to say to her are truisms. I must concentrate. I must work harder, fix my mind to finding the right words, the words which will bring my fragmented thoughts into perspective, for me and for her. But I am so tired...

...and so, the truth of her. Yes, she was fey and quiet and she preferred her own company. I won't deny it; as a child she had a strange way about her. But she was only like that *after.* Before, she was as friendly and playful as any of her cousins, always laughing, always up to some kind of mischief. 'You've got your hands full with that one alright,' her aunts would say, 'there's just no silencing her.' We used to joke that a career as a barrister awaited her, the way she would talk nine to the dozen and always end up getting her own way. I don't think she remembers Pauline. If she does she's never told me and I've never asked. Where would be the sense in it? It wouldn't get us anywhere...

132

Insomnia

1.48 'Sell up, take the money and run...' I stare at the ceiling. The fact that I know every crack and mark by heart annoys me. I've read the same paragraph of my novel three times, but my mind keeps returning to Theo-Paul's words. I throw down the book and grab my pain killers, hoping these and the half a litre of water I drink will stave off the worst of the inevitable hangover. *What was I thinking, why did I drink so much?* I briefly entertain the idea of cancelling tomorrow's meeting, but know that's the wine talking. I know it shouldn't surprise me, but I can barely believe it. *François wants to sell the business!*

2.09. Bastard! Narcissism, that's what it is. His mission complete, his fortune made. 'When you're at the top of the tree,' he once told me, 'there's no one to give you a pat on the back. Your only validation is the money you make.'

2.29 Back from the bathroom and I flop onto the bed. *For Christ's sake! What about my plans for the business?* I punch a pillow, yank the duvet more tightly around myself.

3.00 Ardash. Where are you, who are you with? Are you kissing her, fucking her? Are you sleeping in each other's arms? *I HATE YOU! I WANT YOU!* Hot tears. I sob, deeply, I bury my face in the pillow, *Father*, I whimper, *Father...* and I cry and I cry and I cry.

3.50 ...meetings, money, men...

6.45 The alarm! I must have slept. Fuddled, blinking, struggling to the edge of the bed, I rub my eyes and *Damn!* Getting up, stub my toe. My meeting... My head sinks to my hands.

Paris, Ile Saint Louis
and the train to Poitiers

Merde. Have there ever been more people here? A man tries to jostle past me and I nudge him back irritably, swearing under my breath as coffee splashes from my paper cup onto my shoes. My head is throbbing as I elbow my way along the platform toward the carriage door, bumping legs and bags with my laptop case. Inside, suited men and women wrestle briefcases and hold-alls into luggage racks and under tables and I join them in staking out the little space that will become my territory for the next few hours.

As I set out my laptop and phone on the table in front of me, a commotion begins outside and I look out of the window to see a young woman struggling with a pushchair in one of the train's doorways. She's yelling at her child to keep still as she fights with the pram and a large suitcase. The child starts crying which sets the suit-wearers tutting and muttering as a train guards rushes over to manhandle the pushchair onto the train. This child is still wailing as she and her mother take the seat behind mine. *For God's sake.* I close my eyes and rub my temples.

'I'm not at all happy about the meeting I have tomorrow.' I'd noticed that since my father died I'd been phoning Theo-Paul more often. He seemed to like it. 'It's with a contact who may have a potential buyer for the business.' I frowned, swung my feet up onto the sofa and pressed the remote button of my sound system to start some music.

'Why aren't you happy?' Theo-Paul answered. 'That's good news isn't it? What the heck is that you're listening to?'

'Tosca,' I replied. 'It's about lust and murder. The heroine throws herself over a cliff in the end.'

'Christ, great taste in music you have!'

'I'm so disappointed. I mean, it's clearly the logical next step for François, but there's so much I want still to do in the business.' I took a sip of my wine. 'And besides that, I don't think it's the right thing to do.'

'Mad. The right thing for who? I don't know why you don't sell up, take the money and run.' I could hear Theo-Paul sipping his wine.

'I'm not going to pretend I'm being totally altruistic,' I said. 'Selling isn't what I want to do just now. I'm more motivated to see if I can achieve something *within* the business rather than simply building it up to sell it. And I actually do think that would be in the best interests of the company as well. You know what would happen if we sold. The acquiring company would have no interest in continuing with my corporate vision. It would be run purely for profit.'

'Well, you're the CEO,' Theo-Paul said. 'Why are you going ahead with it?'

'It's what François wants,' I said. 'And he's still the majority shareholder, even if he has retired.'

'Okay, this is a two glass conversation,' Theo-Paul said. 'Hold on while I get a re-fill'.

Whilst he was away I walked through to the kitchen to re-fill my own glass, wondering whether it was a sensible thing to do the night before an important meeting. *Oh stuff it*, I thought, taking the open bottle of Chablis from the fridge. *Besides, it might help me sleep.*

'If you did sell the business,' Theo-Paul said when we were both back, 'what would happen to your job?'

'Well, François and I have discussed that,' I replied. 'Clearly the acquiring company would have its own strategic vision for us, their own plans for the future of the business. Having said that, in all likelihood they'd want to maintain the existing leadership team, at least for a while. And I'd negotiate an earn-out and possibly even a re-allocation of shares in addition to my percentage of the sale price. It could be a very nice package, but...'

'But?' Theo-Paul retorted with a snort. 'I can't see any 'but' in that little scenario!'

Ardash's words came back to me. 'In the right hands business can be a powerful force for good.'

'Theo-Paul, I have ideas I want to implement. There's no guarantee the acquiring company will share my vision, and I want the company to do something worthwhile as well as making money.'

'Very noble,' Theo-Paul said. 'But stupid. You're not going to 'make a difference' or whatever it is you think you can do by running a company. No one ever does. No, what you need to do is make your money. After that, you'll be able to... I don't know, set up a charity, whatever you want. And you know as well as I do that the real money is in selling businesses, not running them.'

After the call I lay back on my sofa listening to the music and sipping my wine, thinking about what Theo-Paul had said. Was he right, is it not possible for business to 'make a difference,' as he'd put it? If so, why not just sell up? But, surely, business can make a positive contribution beyond merely providing jobs? Haven't we made a good start? Ardash certainly thought so. '... *business has a moral obligation to use its power to make life better for people,*' he'd said. Saucha flashed into my mind, and his mission to make little green spaces in the heart of Mumbai. *'I'm guessing you appreciate acorns,'*

I closed my eyes and wondered whether it was a good idea to call him. Probably not, I thought, trying not to imagine him in bed with some beautiful English Rose. I drained my glass, noticing that most of the bottle was gone. *I may as well finish it now.* I poured another glass.

After a few moments, I stood, turned up the music and wandered, with my wine out onto the balcony. I shivered and pulled my wrap closer around me, as Tosca followed me into the chilly night. Little clouds were scudding across the sky, back-lighted by a hazy half-moon. Looking across at the apartment opposite, I saw that the curtains were drawn, the light from inside silhouetting the geraniums on the balcony. I thought I could see the shadow of the woman moving around inside. I nodded to myself, turned and went to get my phone.

Back outside, my glass in one hand and my phone to my ear I leant on the railing and listened to the purr of Ardash's mobile. *If he doesn't answer, I'll throw my phone into the Seine!*

'Hello?' he said, making me jump.

'Are you alone?' I asked.

'Do you really want to know?' I was silent. 'Is that Tosca you're listening to?'

'Yes it is,' I replied.

'She paid the ultimate price for acting on her passion.'

Neither of us spoke. After some moments I said, 'I have a question for you.'

'Go on.'

'Do you think your lifestyle is a way for you to manage your conflicting needs for connection and freedom?' *Where did that come from?!* I took a large gulp of wine.

Ardash was silent for some moments before replying. 'Are you asking for us to be exclusive?'

Across from my balcony the light from the geranium-apartment suddenly went out and I found myself staring into darkness.

'No,' I answered.

I think about Ardash as the train pulls into Orleans, and as people leave and board the train, I stare absently out of the window at a woman with an expensive looking haircut. She's wearing a stylish green jacket and is leading two little designer dogs along the platform. *I don't want to be a keeper of slaves*, I think as she steers the dogs through the exit. My mood, I notice as we pull out of the station, is in danger of slipping from tiredness into melancholy. *For God's sake, how am I meant to function without a normal night's sleep?* I decide to go to the buffet car for some coffee before the full force of self-pity rolls in. 'I must be careful, Father,' I tell myself. I imagine his voice: *'Too much wine and not enough sleep are not happy bed-fellows!'*

As I sway along the carriage, I notice a man who also has a dog, bigger than the two on the platform, and clearly ill-at-ease on the pitching train. As I lurch past, he says to it, 'Do as you're told or you'll get off.' This makes me smile and I feel a little prick of gratitude. 'Nice dog,' I say. Back at my seat, I fish around in my case for a packet of pain-killers, wondering whether I'm becoming addicted to them. Not caring, I pop two into my mouth before taking a sip of coffee, annoyed that the cup is plastic.

Tristan will get on at Saint Pierre-des-Corps, where he has spent the weekend. As we pull into the station, I watch for him among the other business suits, and soon spot his balding head bobbing in the crowd. I steel myself. Tristan will no doubt practise his best invective and I will have to talk as though this meeting matters to me.

My thoughts flash to Ardash. *Real freedom is being able to say anything to each other.* I'm trapped. *Here we go*, I think, steeling myself against his inevitable unpleasantness as Tristan lurches along the carriage. He flops, panting and sweating into the seat next to me.

'Late!' he says, as though I have the power to influence the speed of the train. He mops his brow with a handkerchief. 'I assume you're fully prepared?'

'Good morning to you, Tristan,' I say coldly, 'Yes, I'm fully prepared, thank you for asking. Are you?'

Poitiers

In spite of the lateness of the train we arrive at Poitiers with time to spare and decide to go for coffee.

'So why this guy in particular?' Tristan says as he settles himself into the window seat of the busy little café. 'Damn it!' He twists round in his seat, hand in the air and snaps his fingers at a harassed looking waitress.

'I've already told you, he's one of the leading industry analysts. I met him years ago at a symposium. He's extremely well connected. Knows who to watch, who the rising stars are, who to avoid. He knows who's in the market for acquisitions and who has money to invest.'

'Yeah? Plenty like that.' Tristan stirs his coffee savagely.

'The point is, Tristan, I Trust him. And I'm confident he can provide a useful introduction for us.' Tristan makes a dismissive noise.

'We'll see.'

My contact is already at the table when we arrive at the restaurant of the Hotel Grand Opéra, and he stands to greet us, kissing me warmly on each cheek as Tristan takes in the beautifully laid tables and the glass roof above us.

'Bonjour, good to see you, good to see you,' Michel says, clasping my shoulders.

'You too, Michel,' I say. 'It's been a while.'

'Too long, too long.' Michel looks expectantly at Tristan.

'Michel, this is Tristan Ploum,' I say. 'Tristan is our Sales Director.'

Michel smiles broadly and thrusts out his hand at Tristan. 'Pleased to meet you.'

'Not at all, the pleasure is mine,' says Tristan, with a smile on his face that doesn't reach his eyes. He pumps Michel's hand hard with his own. 'I've heard a lot about you, all of it good,' he says. I smile at him thinly as we all take our seats.

As we get comfortable at the table and pick up our menus, there is the usual, ritual exchange of the fortunes of various individuals and companies we all know. I watch in veiled amusement as Tristan prowls around Michel, working hard to demonstrate how well connected he is by reeling off names of people and companies in fast succession. Michel is charming and smiling and I appreciate his easy, open manner. A waitress arrives and we take it in turns to give our orders.

'How is François? And how is your re-structure going?' Michel asks as we hand back the menus. 'Last time we met, you were in the planning stages if I remember rightly.'

'François is well, thank you. Enjoying retirement. And the restructure is complete.' I glance at Tristan, who is focusing intently on his sparking mineral water. 'We have the right people in the right roles and a strong senior management team supporting our aims.'

'Excellent, excellent,' says Michel. 'I hear that your equal-pay initiative has sparked some talk in the industry. All to the good in my opinion. Tristan, perhaps you might like to bring me up to date on your medium to long-term plans. I gather you have some exciting projects on the go? One of them in Mumbai, if I'm not mistaken? I'm keen to hear about that.'

Tristan waxes lyrical about the opportunities in India he was previously so quick to dismiss. He doesn't mention what we hope to achieve in terms of environmental policies. 'Project Saucha?' he'd sneered when Marine and I briefed him on our plans. 'Sounds like a dodgy Thai night-club!'

I begin to speak but Tristan cuts across me.

'I think you'll agree Michel,' he says holding up a hand, 'that what we have planned is ambitious but spot-on in today's market.' *Damn you*, I say silently. It's imperative that Michel retains the impression that Tristan and I are of one mind, so I let him continue, nodding and smiling to ensure that my annoyance doesn't show. Thankfully, Michel seems not to notice anything amiss, and he nods and smiles too, and asks a number of questions.

'When are you expecting the India expansion to begin realising revenue?' he asks.

I start to answer but again, Tristan cuts across me, giving a wildly optimistic answer. I don't contradict him but notice that my fingernails are digging into the palm of my hand.

'We have ambitious stretch-targets,' I say decisively, casting a look at Tristan. 'Of course a lot depends on the success of our new projects, not just in India. For example, Tristan has been working on a Luxembourg-based partnership. But our core business is solid and we're in the right place to exploit the opportunities.' Tristan makes a strange noise and Michel and I look at him. He coughs.

'Sorry' he says. 'Piece of beef stuck.' I hand him his glass of water.

'Yes indeed, you seem to be robust in spite of the economic down-turn,' Michel says.

'We're optimistic,' I reply before Tristan can answer. 'We've worked hard to retain and expand our client base, and our continual focus on being ahead of the innovation curve has kept us competitive and agile. Plus we have a very loyal and committed workforce who share our vision and our values.' I think about our pathetic contingency fund and hope what I've said remains true.

The waiter arrives to suggest dessert but after I decline, the others do too.

'Women!' Tristan quips. 'Always thinking of their figures.' He winks at Michel. I smile thinly and glance at his ample paunch, feeling gratified that Michel doesn't laugh.

'Well,' he says, 'if I'm reading things correctly, I think you may well be interested in TKG Associates. Do you know of them?' Tristan and I both sit forward.

'No, I don't.'

'Yes I think so.'

Tristan and I reply at the same time. I can tell that Tristan doesn't know them.

'Where are they based?' I ask.

'They're based in Troyes.' Tristan starts and we look at each other for the briefest of moments.

'I think they could be very interesting for you,' Michel repeats, thankfully unaware of our discomfiture.

'Oh, in what way?' Tristan asks cautiously.

'They're in the market for acquisitions—particularly companies with an interest in the Asian market.'

Michel has said the magic word. I watch Tristan's lips twitch and sit back in my chair, relieved in spite of my complicity in bringing about a chain of events I don't want. I turn to order coffee.

On the train back to Paris, I gaze out of the window into the fading twilight, the Loire snaking alongside us, and I think absently that it's easier to see the true shape of things in the near-darkness. My head is pounding and I've run out of pain-killers. Tristan has been chattering excitedly about how he thinks we ought to proceed with TKG Associates since we boarded the train. Neither of us mentions the fact that they are based in Troyes. *Hopefully, they'll meet us in Paris*, I think. I wonder whether to confront Tristan about his behaviour in the meeting but decide I just want to get this train journey over with, get home and sleep.

'You do realise how big this could be?' Tristan says when he finally notices that my responses are minimal.

'Slow down Tristan,' I reply. 'This could well be big but I want to do some research before I take it to the board. I certainly don't want to approach TKG yet.'

'Why are you being so cautious?' he says. 'Can't you see an opportunity when it's presented? When was the last time something like this landed in our lap? I can't wait to tell François.' I rest my hands on my temples for a moment.

'Look Tristan,' I say, turning to face him. 'This hasn't just 'landed in our lap'. And we need to get it right. We're not moving ahead with TKG until I'm convinced it's right for the company. And then, not without the full backing of the board. And *I* will discuss this with François and not you.'

'Oh, so this is your baby, is it?' Tristan's lips curl into that ugly sneer I've come to know so well.

'For now Tristan,' I say, 'yes it is.'

Paris, Café La Tour

Ardash is in London. He may be in London. We didn't talk about his plans the last time he was in Paris. But I know that when I don't hear from him, it is usually because he is with his other lover. Lovers perhaps. I'm pretty certain she is based in London too, and this depresses me. *I don't like being number two,* I think as I wait for Marine at the Café La Tour before our afternoon conference call with Roshan Naik. I wonder, as I hand the menu back to the waiter, whether the distance Ardash and I create with our alternating intensity and silence is making what we have more or less powerful? *It's a bi-polar relationship,* I think as a man arrives at the café and greets a woman who is sitting at a table by the door. I watch as she stands and they kiss each other deeply, enjoying the fact that the man is running his hand up and down the woman's back. *What do Ardash and I have?* I wonder. *Do we have anything at all when we're not together?* I wonder about the woman he is with now. I imagine Ardash's appreciative gaze moving over her body, lingering at her curves. I see him running his hand up and down her back, stroking her wrist with his thumb. I imagine him leaning forward to kiss her, their lips parting slowly as they move to receive each other...

'Sorry, I didn't mean to startle you.' Marine pulls out a chair and sits down. 'You were deep in thought. Penny for them?' I don't answer her but smile instead, making a conscious effort to put thoughts of Ardash out of my mind.

'I hope you don't mind, I ordered for us,' I say. 'I thought it would save time.'

'Lovely, thank you,' Marine replies, eyeing our coffee and the brie and tomato sandwiches which are ready on the table. She takes off her jacket and sits down, placing her handbag beside her. 'There was a huge queue at the bank,' she says. 'We've got about forty minutes before the meeting though, so we should be okay.' She picks up a sandwich from the plate and takes a delicate bite.

'Actually, we've got longer,' I reply. 'I contacted Roshan and he's happy to meet at half past instead. I wanted time to go properly through our meeting strategy.'

'Excellent,' Marine says, dabbing her lips with a napkin. 'I've got my proposal here and I've read your briefing paper. I'm looking forward to hearing what Roshan has to say.'

I sip my coffee. 'Good,' I say, nodding. 'Now that the set up phase of Tristan's project is complete Gilbert can be freed up to work with you. And of course you'll want to work closely with Jean on the figures. Tristan may well want an input and that's fine, but Project Saucha will essentially be yours.'

I reach forward with my free hand to take a sandwich from the plate. Marine watches, and frowns but doesn't reply. She seems suddenly distracted.

'Something wrong?' I ask. She's silent for a moment longer and is looking at me strangely. I choose to ignore it.

Marine reaches into her briefcase and retrieves two neatly bound bundles.

'You've seen the draft,' she says, 'but I worked on this last night.'

I nod as she takes me through the detail of her proposal.

'Excellent,' I murmur, turning a page. I wonder, given Roshan's obvious bias, whether putting a woman in charge of this project is the best way forward, but tell myself that what's important is skill, not gender.

'Of course, these are just ideas,' she says once I've finished reading. 'If we're all agreed by the end of our meeting, we can go ahead and start the detailed planning.'

I take the final sandwich and glance at my watch. 'We'd better get going,' I say. 'I don't want to keep Roshan waiting.' Marine nods, but frowns again.

'Marine, what? You look as though you want to say something.'

'Look...' she says. 'Please tell me to mind my own business...' she points to my wrist. 'But are those bruises?'

I look down and curse the fact that I've taken off my jacket, revealing an angry blue-black weal beneath the pale silk of my blouse. It's obvious from the way the long, thin shapes of the bruises curl around that it has been made by someone's hand. I look Marine in the eyes.

'I did that at the gym,' I say. 'Shall we get to our meeting?' I continue to hold her gaze as I slip on my jacket. She gives me a complex look but doesn't pursue the subject.

Paris, Ile Saint Louis

'You're going to Stockholm with him?' Ardash's voice was quiet and even, through the strains of Bach's St Matthew Passion, as candlelight glinted in the bottle of 2003 Château La Fleur de Bouard. 'That is certainly interesting.'

We were at my apartment, and had just finished eating the Mushrooms Bordelaise I'd served with a warm, crusty baguette, and in spite of my misgivings about the conversation to come, it gave me a great sense of satisfaction to watch Ardash mopping up the last of his sauce with a hunk of the bread. The curtains fluttered lightly in the warm breeze wafting through the open balcony doors. Ardash levelled a steady gaze at me across the table.

'Yes,' I said, trying to keep my voice light. 'It's just a weekend trip.' *And I doubt you'll be alone,* I thought. Ardash was silent for a moment before answering.

'And why are you telling me this?' I looked at him, but couldn't read his expression.

'Well, for the sake of honesty. I didn't want to keep it a secret from you.' Ardash didn't reply and I watched the veins in his neck bulge. It had taken me some time to decide to tell him about my weekend away with Theo-Paul. Although I felt fairly certain that Ardash wouldn't ask if I didn't volunteer the information, the idea of having something that felt like a secret seemed contrary to the spirit of honesty that rested between us.

'Would you prefer I didn't go?' I asked, surprising myself with the question.

'That is your choice entirely,' Ardash replied. His voice was still quiet, and it was clear from the tightening of his jaw that he was displeased. A pang of annoyance made me snappy, and I made an effort to keep my voice even.

'Yes I know that,' I answered. 'I'm not asking for your permission, just your opinion.' I watched the light from the candle flickering in the dark bottle.

'Don't play with me,' Ardash replied.

I looked at him through the candlelight.

'Play with you?' I said. 'What makes you think I'm playing with you?' Ardash didn't answer but maintained his steady stare.

'You know, I feel a bit confused,' I said at last. 'You prefer being non-exclusive. Fair enough, I can live with that. You were honest with me from the beginning and I respected that. I still do. And in fact it turns out that not only can I live with you having other lovers, but I also prefer not to be restricted.' I looked at him carefully trying to gauge what his response would be. 'But Ardash,' I continued. 'Since this is the case, you must accept that I too may have other lovers. Or do you prefer that I don't tell you the truth?'

Ardash was looking at me carefully.

'Truth,' he said, 'ought not to be used as a weapon.'

I shook my head. 'I'm not sure why you think I'm doing that,' I answered. 'That isn't my intention at all.'

'I told you right from the start, *I* don't inflict hurt by talking about my lovers.' Ardash spoke slowly and quietly and I watched his Adam's apple rise and fall with his words. 'They simply know that the possibility is there, that's all. Not the details. I would ask you to extend the same courtesy to me.'

'You know that I'm going to Stockholm with Theo-Paul, that's all,' I said, growing anger sharpening my voice. 'I won't tell you the details, but neither do I want to censor myself. And besides,' I drained my glass and put it on the table a little too hard, 'have you forgotten that you've asked me several times whether or not I'm having sex with him? Do you not see just a little hypocrisy there?' I stood up and began to clear the plates. Ardash sat drinking his wine in silence.

In the kitchen I stood for a moment, my arms outstretched, leaning on the sink. I glanced through the door to the salon where the music and the candlelight created a deceptive softness that engulfed Ardash as he stared out of the window. I watched as he picked up the bottle and poured himself another glass of wine, swilling it around in front of him before taking a large sip. A sudden rush of anger ignited my resolve.

'Look Ardash,' I said, returning to the salon and trying hard not to raise my voice. 'I don't create your rules and you don't create mine. You are here because we both choose it. If you are unhappy,' I turned and gestured towards the door... 'Then you are free to go.'

Ardash's voice was quieter still. 'Thank you,' he said, 'for that reminder of what I am free to do.' He put his wine glass down carefully. 'And for alluding to my *'rules'.*' He twisted the word into something ugly, and paused, staring right into me. 'But I can assure you, I have no *rules.*'

I took a long, slow breath. Without breaking eye contact, I reached forward across the table for the wine bottle.

Suddenly, Ardash's hand shot out and grabbed my wrist, his fingers savagely tight. He said nothing. Neither of us moved. The candle guttered and threw wild shadows against the wall as the final chorus of the St Matthew Passion crashed between us. I held my breath and, ignoring the pain, kept my eyes firmly locked on his.

When he released his grip I picked up the wine bottle and poured myself a glass. A set of livid red weals was already beginning to swell on my wrist. As we raised our glasses to our lips, I looked out to the apartment opposite just in time to see the door of the geranium balcony slam shut.

Paris, Montparnasse Tower

'How did that happen?' I demand. 'We put back the meeting to half past.'

Marine and I have arrived at the office, where Jean tells us as he throws on his jacket, that Tristan is already in the conference call with Roshan Naik.

'They've been talking for the last half an hour,' Jean answers. 'Said since he had the opportunity, he wanted to get the measure of our friend Naik for himself.'

'Did he now?' I reply, frowning.

'I thought that wouldn't go down too well,' Jean says, 'so I dialled you in so that you could join as soon as you arrive. I'd have gone in myself but I needed to finalise these figures for Luc. I'm off to meet him now- -I'm late actually. I'm on my mobile if you need me.' Jean grabs his laptop case and rushes out of the door glancing at his watch as he goes.

I hear Tristan and Roshan laughing together as Marine opens the door to the conference room. As we enter, we see Naik's face filling half the screen and Tristan's the other half.

'Ah, here they are at last,' Tristan says, making a show of looking at his watch. 'Good lunch?'

'Mr Naik,' I say, ignoring Tristan. 'Very good to see you again. I trust you are well? You've started early I see.'

'Indeed,' says Roshan, the digitised version of his clipped accent juddering slightly on the screen. 'Do forgive us for making an early start. Your man here is so keen and full of ideas. It is most refreshing to talk with a man of such drive and energy.'

'Not at all,' I answer, flicking a glance at Tristan. 'Let me introduce you to Marine Roussel, our Business Development Director.'

'Good to meet you, Mr Naik,' Marine says.

Roshan nods at Marine, his exaggerated bow suggesting that he is used to the over-stated gestures that video-conferencing requires.

'I was very keen to meet Mr Naik,' Tristan says, as Marine and I settle in front of the screen.

'Oh please Tristan, as I told you before, do call me Roshan.'

'Thank you Roshan.' Tristan's voice is oily. 'It sounds to me as though we have an excellent opportunity here which can only be extremely mutually beneficial.' Marine and I exchange a glance and I stop myself from rolling my eyes at his hypocrisy.

'Indeed,' I say. 'Which is precisely why we are all here. Has everyone read the briefing notes?' I flip up the screen of my laptop and click a few buttons.

'Yes, yes,' Tristan says. 'But I'm far more interested in what Roshan has to say. He has some excellent ideas about how this could work. Roshan, now that we are all here at last, perhaps you'd like to update the others on what you and I have been discussing.'

Tristan and Roshan spend the next twenty minutes presenting to us an outline plan that so closely resembles my briefing notes, it's hard to see what Tristan thinks is novel about it.

'So what we are suggesting,' he says, 'is that we share office space with Roshan out in Mumbai for a six month period, get a man out there to work closely with him and his team and start the project from the ground up.' Roshan is nodding energetically.

Roshan's half of the screen suddenly goes blank and we are left staring at an empty blue space.

'Dammit!' says Tristan. 'I'll dial him back up.'

'Give it a few seconds,' Marine says, 'he'll probably be doing that himself.'

Marine is proved right as Roshan's image appears on the screen once more.

'So sorry,' he says. 'Video-conferencing is always somewhat glitchy.'

'Not to worry,' I reply. 'I was about to say that if we sign this project off, Marine will handle the set up phase. She will produce a scoping document and project plan, along with full set-up and running costs, an operational plan, plus of course, a realistic revenue projection. Roshan, I'm sure these considerations are as important to you. We'll all feel more confident moving forward with a proper strategy in place.'

Tristan makes a show of winking at Roshan. 'What did I tell you, a details woman through and through.'

'Indeed,' says Roshan. 'But whilst you and I are warriors Tristan, there is some merit in planning.' I feel like pulling the plug on the conference call. Instead I say:

'Marine has some ideas about how we might proceed. Would you like to outline those now?'

'Certainly,' Marine says. 'I've done some initial work.' She clicks a few buttons on her laptop. 'I haven't circulated this yet, so I'll talk us through.'

Tristan is shaking his head.

'Sorry to cut across, Marine,' he says. But I'd like to put myself forward for this project. First, I have prior experience of working with Asian companies—an important consideration given the potential market. Second —and no offence meant here—but as a male, I think the cultural morés of the region will be somewhat easier for me to navigate. Right Roshan?'

'Well,' Roshan answers. 'Mumbai is a very progressive and modern place, we are certainly not backward in this respect. But there are those with a more... traditional outlook...' His voice breaks up as he speaks, but it's obvious he agrees with Tristan. Tristan looks triumphant.

'And I think Roshan and I have begun a very good working relationship already. Roshan, what do you think?' Roshan nods vigorously.

'I would be most honoured to work with a man of your calibre, Tristan,' he says.

I feel myself reddening with anger and take a long breath. I look at Marine. It's obvious that we need Roshan, but it's obvious too that he wants to work with Tristan. and I want this project to succeed.

I start to speak, but Marine cuts across me.

'Look, it's not a problem,' she says, fixing me with a meaningful look. 'It sounds as though, all things considered, it makes sense for Tristan to take this forward. I'm happy to share the work I've already done,' she says with finality.

Tristan grins widely and Roshan wobbles his head.

'Yes, yes of course,' he says. 'Tristan and I were saying before you joined us, that a joint approach is the best.'

Tristan curls his lips and I flick a glance at my briefing notes staring up at me from my lap top.

'And Luxembourg?' I say to him. 'I wouldn't want you to be distracted from that project.'

Tristan answers me quickly. 'No need to concern yourself about that,' he says. 'No, as Sales Director, this falls squarely into my lap.'

Does it? How?! I remain silent though, and Tristan continues.

'Roshan, what about if you and I schedule some time this week and we can get our outline plan knocked into shape.' Tristan bends to pick up his tablet and as he swipes it a few times, I watch the light glinting off his bald patch. I'm glad he isn't in the room with us.

'I think Roshan and I can get your scoping document and project plan done by the fifteenth,' he says, tapping the tablet. 'What do you think, is that realistic?' Roshan nods eagerly.

'Indeed, indeed,' he says. 'It will be a pleasure working with you Tristan.'

'No need for your notes, Marine,' Tristan says. 'I'll get stuck in myself, once Roshan and I have looked seriously at the project.'

Marine narrows her eyes but doesn't respond.

'Well, I think we're all done here,' Tristan continues. 'Roshan, do you mind if I Skype you one-to-one in about an hour? There are one or two things I want to follow up with you.'

I want nothing more than to put Tristan in his place, but tell myself that Roshan mustn't sense divisiveness. Instead I say, 'Thank you very much indeed for your time, Roshan. Tristan, I look forward to seeing the initial report on the fifteenth.'

Once the screen goes blank, I brace myself for Marine's tirade of anger, which although I feel, I don't want to share. Her jaw is tense and her face white, but she simply looks at me.

'That,' she says, her voice even, 'is what's called a *fait accompli*.' I want to shake her but, clenching my teeth, force myself to remember who the real source of my anger is.

'Does it hurt?' Marine asks. I'm momentarily confused until I see that she's looking at my wrist, which I'm clasping in my free hand. I realise I've been rubbing my bruise.

Achille De Quincy—Before my death

Sleeping more, now ...more sleeping than waking... I don't know for sure, it's hard to tell which are dreams and which aren't... I think I'm awake...

...everything...what was there, the things she did, words she spoke, the things that were between ...the scent of lemons... music ... *'Ne me quitte pas'* ...sunlight through dark hair...untying her apron, folding it once, twice, placing it neatly in the drawer...everything exists still...as though suspended in amber...

...she turned... that last titanic, innocently bare instant when her eyes found mine, and, locked within that singular intimacy, smiled...

...a smile which, had another future been our fate, would have been no more than a mere moment of domestic cordiality...

... red hands on yellow cotton, she smoothed the front of her dress...

'...Achille, watch the girl, I'm going to the baker's...'

Paris, Montparnasse Tower and Les Halles.

'I'm fucking furious! Does he not understand his own role in this business?' The sudden appearance of Marine at my desk makes my office feel claustrophobic in spite of Paris spread below us, and I have to resist gazing past her to the panorama outside. The early morning sky is what my father used to call a 'painter's sky', filled with a mass of dramatic white-grey clouds scudding along the horizon. I rub my temples as I look up at Marine. *What now*, I think?

'Are you okay?' she asks.

'Yes, yes, I'm fine,' I reply, clicking a couple of keys on my laptop and snapping the lid shut. 'Sit down and tell me what's happened.'

'I can tell you now, you're not going to like this.' Marine sits down heavily in a chair at my meeting table. I get up and join her, pulling up the chair opposite.

'This isn't like you Marine,' I say calmly. 'Come on, what's happened?'

'Okay.' She modulates her voice a little. 'Tristan came into my office late yesterday in response to my email about next month's P and L, which I wanted to go through with Jean. He told me—wait until you hear this—the Luxembourg partnership is unlikely to realise anything like the revenue he predicted for this quarter. Probably not much more than 15 per cent. And he intends to focus on India instead!' Marine's voice is rising and I glance past her at the open plan section beyond the glass walls. Everyone is getting on with their work and paying no attention to us.

'Just like that, he tells me, completely out of the blue.' Marine glares at me. 'I mean, how is that possible? Were you aware of this epic failure?'

I'm not, and I'm not sure I believe it. I think back to my meeting in Luxembourg and the confident optimism of our partners. *'Why not aim to be five times the size we are now in three years?'* I think of the upbeat picture Tristan painted at our last board meeting.

'That isn't what any of his reports have said,' I say carefully. 'He's been consistently projecting a healthy revenue from the new service.'

'Exactly!' Marine snaps. I shush her gently, glancing again at the desks outside. Marine lowers her voice.

'At the last board meeting, we all sat there and listened to him assuring us that based on his own business plan and the way the set-up phase was progressing, new business revenue would be right on target this quarter. It was going to hit the market with a huge flourish and knock the competition out of the water if I remember rightly! At the very least it was soon to be a major part of our overall revenue stream. It's in black and white in the minutes for God's sake.' Marine's eyebrows shoot to the top of her forehead. 'Ha! If you remember, he even joked that we'd have his resignation if he didn't hit his target.'

Tristan, resign! For a fraction of a moment, I saw a glimmer of light, but then frowned.

'I'm certain that's not going to happen,' I say. 'This is crazy, I can't believe he isn't going to come close, he was so confident. He must have said what has gone wrong? Or is he just being overly cautious?'

'Tristan, cautious?' Marine snorts. 'No, this is beyond caution. He says he needs more time. More time, I ask you! I mean, he's the Sales Director for God's sake! But the growth we've achieved under your stewardship certainly isn't thanks to him. What the heck has he been doing all that time?'

'The Luxembourg project is what he's been working on,' I say. 'Marine, this could be serious, revenue from the new service is integral to our budget. Tristan knows that. If he's right, we need a serious re-think about our strategy.' *Particularly* I think, *because we don't have the contingency fund I wanted.*

'I know,' Marine nods. 'I'm not afraid to say it, that man is riding on a reputation he built years ago and I for one am beginning to question what he brings to the table.'

'Steady on Marine,' I say, 'let's not get ahead of ourselves. I can think of no possible reason why the new service shouldn't start generating income soon. I'll call a meeting and we can discuss what has happened. In the meantime, get Jean to do some number crunching and assess the worst-case scenario impact. I'll get Luxembourg on the phone.'

After Marine leaves my office, I get up and walk to the window. I watch as a flock of birds glides across the painter's sky towards the Eiffel Tower. I'm adding up figures in my head. As long as our core business remains stable, we can weather this setback without having to take drastic steps. What I want to know is, why Tristan has been so insistently bullish in his projections. He must have had an inkling of this long before now. I also want to know why he went to Marine and not me to give the bad news, although the answer to this seems clear. I turn and look through the glass walls of my office to the open plan section beyond. People are sitting at desks, talking on phones, clicking their keyboards. I watch Claude point to Solange's plastered foot and say something to her as she passes. Solange gives him a playful swipe on the arm. They both laugh and Claude turns back to his screen, smiling. I think about all the families this company is supporting, all the mortgages, the university fees. I hear my father's voice; '*I'm proud of you, you know that don't you?*' I close my eyes and look away.

Paris, Montparnasse Tower

'Classic power tactic,' exclaims Marine, replacing the phone in its receiver. Tristan is working from home but is supposed to be attending the meeting I've called via conference-call. He's phoned to say he'll be late.

I sigh. 'I'll make us some coffee before we start.'

In the staff kitchen, I start to fill the kettle when Solange comes in.

'Oh can't complain, slow to heal but getting there,' she says in answer to my enquiry about her broken foot. She hobbles to the cupboard and bends with some difficulty to get some cups.

'Let me do that for you, Solange,' I say.

'Wouldn't hear of it,' she says, straightening up. 'It is funny enough seeing you directors making your own coffee.' I smile at her.

'No reason why we shouldn't,' I say.

She straightens herself and places four plastic cups on the counter. I frown.

'Why aren't you using proper cups?' I ask.

'Oh, they're all in the dishwasher.' Solange points to the silent machine in the corner.

I open its door and am faced with two rows of used mugs and a couple of plates.

'Solange!' I exclaim, 'I've made it clear that we don't use plastic cups anymore. It's why the coffee machine was sent back! There's no reason people can't rinse their own used cups.'

Solange mutters something as she begins taking cups from the dishwasher.

'I'd like a sign put up in here please,' I say, collecting the plastic cups together. '*No plastics*. And it's your job to enforce it, okay?'

Ten minutes later, back in the meeting room, I phone Tristan.

'Why aren't you ready to conference?' I ask.

'Doing it right now,' Tristan says. 'Just came off the phone with a potential client.'

'The meeting is starting now,' I say. I click a few buttons on my computer and before long Tristan's face fills the screen. His desk-lamp is highlighting his bald patch which shines at us resolutely.

'Right then,' he says. 'I don't have long. And I didn't get an agenda, so I don't know what this is about. Perhaps someone might care to enlighten me.'

'There isn't an agenda,' I say. 'And this is important, so we'll be staying for as long as required. In fact Tristan, this is about the discussion you had with Marine about your revenue stream projection for the Luxembourg partnership. I'd like to know, please, why you are suddenly projecting practically nothing for the next quarter when your reports consistently told a different story.'

'More time needed,' Tristan replies curtly.

'Would you care to tell me why?'

'The service wasn't well received by the test-market. I need to go back to the guys in Luxembourg and discuss how we refine the offering before we start the main marketing campaign.'

'But why is this the first we've heard of it?' Marine explodes.

I raise my hand to calm her down. 'Surely you had an idea of this at our last Board meeting?'

'No I didn't,' Tristan says evenly. 'I've only just had the report in about the test campaign.'

'But you were so confident,' says Marine. 'You even joked about resigning if you didn't make your target!'

'I certainly did not!' Tristan retorts. 'Where is that minuted?'

'Look,' I say as Marine starts to raise her voice again. 'This isn't helping. The CEO of the Luxembourg end is fuming. He expects us to be full steam ahead by next quarter. '

'You spoke to him?' Tristan blurts, his face contorted with anger.

'Of course I did!' I exclaim. 'Tristan, seriously, what can we expect?

A heated discussion ensues about the figures, after which Tristan says, 'Look, I think we all know that this is an over-reaction. Christ, I thought your new tree-hugging strategy meant we're all in it together and looking to the long term. I simply need more time, that's all. Now, I'd like to bring this meeting to a close, I have a lot to do.' Tristan leans forward ready to log out of the call.

I can feel myself going red with fury but force my voice into a semblance of composure. 'This meeting is not yet finished,' I say. 'I want a report on my desk by Friday detailing exactly what has happened and more to the point, how and when this is going to start making money. And Tristan?' He sits there glumly. 'I'm interested to know why you were so insistent about the amount of dividend paid if there was any possibility at all that this would happen.'

'The dividend is in relation to last year's profits not this...' Tristan starts, but I raise my hand.

'By Friday, please.'

After the meeting I walk quickly back to my office. I'm still fuming but I don't want the rest of the staff to see, and I curse the glass walls as I walk in and close the door behind me. I don't know whether I'm angrier with Tristan or with myself for not fighting harder for the contingency pot. '*Am I over-reacting, Father?*' I ask. I frown as Marine appears and makes a pretend knocking motion.

'Five minutes?' she says, opening the door. I want to yell at her to get out and leave me in peace but instead I say, 'Yes of course, come in.'

'Christ!' she says, walking across the office and sitting down at the meeting table. 'What the hell is he playing at?'

I don't respond.

'And what about 'Project Saucha'? Can he be trusted not to fuck that up too?'

I know, I know! A wave of fatigue rolls up from behind my eyes, and I put my finger-tips to my temples. Marine frowns.

'You look exhausted,' she says. 'This is the last thing you need, so soon after your father.'

What the hell does that have to do with it?

'I'm fine,' I say. 'Nothing worthwhile is ever easy.' *Is this worthwhile?*

Marine continues to sit there. *Please will you just leave!* I shout at her silently.

'Look Marine, I have a lot to do…' I begin, but she interrupts me.

'Listen, why don't we go out for a drink later? Let's finish before seven and grab a glass of wine. It'll do us both good.'

I try not to sigh audibly.

'That's very kind of you,' I say. 'But I have plans. Another time perhaps.'

Marine looks at me for a long moment. 'Another time then,' she says, and she gets up to leave.

Versailles

'Bonjour, François, it's good to see you, I'm glad you were free.' I kiss him on each cheek and he pats me warmly on the arm.

'Come on in,' he says, ushering me through the door. I breathe deeply the aroma of freshly baked cakes wafting through the hallway. 'Blondine has made *Financiers* for the occasion,' François says with a smile.

'Lovely,' I reply, taking off my jacket and glancing around at the blue toile walls and the creamy paintwork. 'The place is looking beautiful. Have you redecorated?'

'Oh, you know Blondine,' François chuckles. 'As soon as one room is finished she starts on the next. We had the hallway re-vamped last winter. They haven't done a bad job have they? Here, let me take that.'

François takes my jacket and I gaze up at the grand sweep of the curved stairway, the chandelier scattering diamonds of light across the ceiling.

'Beautiful,' I repeat.

'Apparently it's the turn of the kitchen next.' François shakes his head indulgently. 'What's wrong with the one we have, I couldn't say, but there we are, what do I know about such things? Come through, we're in the garden room.'

I follow François into the conservatory where we're greeted by a burst of colour from the garden beyond.

'Old age is catching up with me,' François says, the rattan chair creaking as he lowers himself stiffly into it. 'Old bones not what they used to be.'

'It happens to us all,' I say, taking the chair next to him.

'Not for a few years yet, for you,' he chuckles. 'But tell me, how are you doing? I haven't had a proper chance to say how sorry I am about your father.'

'Thank you François, I'm holding up,' I say. 'And do thank Blondine for the beautiful wreath. I'll be sending cards soon.' François nods and pats me on the hand.

'Here,' he says, 'Blondine has set it all out for us. You can be mother.'

'Isn't she joining us?' I reach forward to pour tea from the pot into two dainty little china tea-cups.

'Oh no, no, she'd rather let us natter away, bores her stiff, business-talk. I'm guessing this isn't a social call?'

I was still thinking, as I took the thirty minute train ride from Montparnasse to Versailles, about what I'd say to François. It seemed wrong simply to say, 'I don't trust Tristan.' I'd discussed it with Theo-Paul on the phone the night before.

'He just won't support me,' I'd said. 'And what makes it worse is that I'm beginning to feel as though Tristan is deliberately obstructing my efforts.'

'Is it that hard to work out?' Theo-Paul replied. 'He's probably still sore after—'

'That's hardly the point, we're grown-ups, not grudge-bearing teenagers. No. The point is, Tristan has openly opposed almost all of what I wanted from the start. The re-structuring, the flexible working, the lot. The last three years have been a constant fight with him.' I yanked the cashmere throw from the back of the sofa and pulled it round my shoulders. 'And now this. We're really counting on the Luxembourg revenue.'

'Look, I'll be frank.' Theo-Paul's voice was matter-of-fact. 'This 'broader vision' you're so keen to achieve... it seems so...I don't know, abstract. I'm not surprised the board aren't behind it. Do they really know what it's all about?'

'Abstract? How is rewarding our staff fairly abstract? How is it abstract to use only suppliers with sound environmental policies? And what does all that have to do with the fact that Tristan has fucked up Luxembourg? No, the problem is not our vision, it's him!'

'Hey come on, settle down.' Theo-Paul sounded as though he was calming a fractious child. 'I'm sure you're exaggerating. Besides, business is like that. Being CEO is a tough job, and you have to be tough to do it.'

'If you ask me, that's a pretty old fashioned view of business. Yes, a CEO needs strength, but that shouldn't have to mean aggression and constant fighting. Why not work together creatively to move the business forward? That's not unrealistic at all. Or abstract! But no, I'm certain Tristan goes to François with his tales of woe.'

'Well,' Theo-Paul said with finality, 'I doubt François will be concerned as long as you keep making money.'

'You're right François,' I say, helping myself to a *Financier*. 'I do have some concerns.' A fly is buzzing busily around the room and I swat it away from the cakes.

'Funny, Tristan came to me just last week and said the same thing.' François takes a sip of his tea. 'Do you two not communicate?'

I bite back my annoyance.

'My concerns are rather more to do with Tristan and his effect on the business,' I reply.

'Yes, he said something similar about you.' François reaches forward for a cake and takes two. 'These are delicious, Blondine has outdone herself.'

'So what are Tristan's concerns?' I ask, working hard to keep the anger out of my voice.

François leans back in his chair, bites into a cake and starts to chew it slowly. He takes another sip of his tea and the cup rattles in its saucer as he replaces it. He brushes some crumbs from his trousers. *Can you please just answer me!* I take a sip of my own tea. A clock in another room chimes prettily.

'Look,' François says at last. 'I'm an old man and I don't have time for beating about the bush.' He leans forward to put his teacup down before sitting back again in his seat. 'I don't pay much heed to Tristan's concerns. That's why I didn't bother calling you after I met with him. Yes, I listened to him and yes he made a number of salient points which I am sure he will continue to make at board meetings. He has an excellent commercial mind and I'm glad to have him on the team, especially now you've got TKG interested. But—and this is the point—in spite of the little hiccup about the dividends, I know the business is in good hands with you.'

'Hiccup?' I say, raising my eyebrows. François holds up his hand and his chair squeaks again.

'You made a mistake there. Don't worry, it came right in the end, but what you were suggesting wasn't the right thing. I didn't go into full detail at the time, but the point is, if the company is going to be acquired, we need to show healthy dividend payments. It isn't about rewarding ourselves with pay-outs. It's about showing optimism for the future and a firm belief in our strategy.'

I shake my head.

'I understand that,' I say, 'but I thought I made it clear at the meeting, how not paying full dividend payments *supports* our strategy.' My cake suddenly feels dry in my mouth and I reach forward to pour some more tea. 'Is that what Tristan wanted to discuss?' François sighs.

'Look,' he says. 'I trust you. I made that perfectly clear to Tristan. And I'm willing to overlook the issue of the dividend payments. You don't often make a mistake and as I've said it came right in the end. That's the purpose of a good board, to make sound *joint* decisions.'

It's clear that François isn't going to budge on this, and I decide to ignore it and get to the point of the meeting.

'Did Tristan tell you about the delay in the Luxembourg partnership?' I say.

'That's a detail,' François replies.

A detail?! I feel my face reddening and I go to speak but François holds up his hand.

'Business is like that,' he says. 'You have to be prepared for the unexpected. I have every confidence that Tristan will get Luxembourg under control. You'll just have to hold your nerve.'

Hold my nerve? Why are you lecturing me about business? Why aren't you questioning Tristan? My fury is threatening to make me say something I'll regret, and instead, I clench my jaw and focus on the fly, which is now butting itself against the glass of a window. François looks at me for a long moment.

'I'm surprised you're ignoring what's staring you in the face,' he says. 'A bright woman like you.'

I frown, and François shakes his head.

'Look. You and Tristan...you're both intelligent people. You both know what you're doing as far as the company goes. Both of you are perfectly capable of running this business. But you can't both keep running to me every time you have a spat. You're going to have to work your differences out yourselves.' François fixes me with a meaningful stare. 'After all, it's not as though you don't know what the root of his problem is.'

I nod slowly.

'I really believed we could develop a good working relationship,' I say with a sigh.

'I hoped so too, my dear, indeed I still do.' François takes a long sip of his tea before setting the cup rattling back in its saucer. 'Try to understand him. Tristan is older than you. He's a man. He's strongly motivated. And you have the job he thought was meant for him.'

François is right, of course.

'He's only too aware of all those energetic young things coming up behind him,' François continues. 'If Tristan is going to reach the top of his career, he needs to do it soon.

Do you understand me?' I nod once more. 'And it's not just the fact that you're younger and a woman.' François pauses.

'There's the little matter of…' he pauses and looks me in the eye. '…the matter of what happened in Troyes.'

I look at François for a long moment before going to speak, but he holds up a hand.

'The fact is, you're going to have to find a way of resolving this. A man is a man, when all's said and done. And a man whose pride has been hurt, won't take kindly to being subordinate to the woman who inflicted the wound.'

The road to Troyes

'You're renting a car? Why? It's an hour and a half on the train, direct link.'

'I'm not coming directly home after the meeting, I'm visiting someone.' I can tell by his face that Tristan doesn't believe my lie, and I can tell that he thinks he's scored some kind of victory when I don't offer him a lift.

'Suit yourself,' he says.

'The truth is,' I'd told Theo-Paul on the phone, 'I wish I didn't have to go to Troyes with him. We've never talked about what happened there. It's obvious that all his nastiness is about revenge. I can't see that the journey would be anything other than awful.'

'I told you he's still bearing a grudge,' Theo-Paul said.

'He's bearing a grudge's big brother!' I retorted. 'What happened in Troyes had bigger consequences than you know about. And I don't just mean for his marriage.'

In spite of my misgivings about the meeting, the car journey is surprisingly pleasant once I eventually crawl out of the environs of Paris. I can't remember the last time I drove, and the feeling of being in control of something fast and powerful is gratifying. I change to a lower gear and speed up to overtake a line of cars in the slow lane, enjoying the pull of the torque and the low, growling sound of the engine.

I had no choice but to meet with TKG Associates. It was highly unlikely that François would be persuaded against selling the business and if that remained the case, I was at least intent on finding a buyer who would support our aims.

'The meeting is purely exploratory,' I'd told the board. 'I've done some research, and I'm not convinced TKG are right for us. They have a very aggressive growth strategy, and I'm not at all sure they'd continue with our ethical vision.'

The meeting will be doubly difficult, not just assessing the kind of leadership TKG would impose, but at the same time reining Tristan in. He's been talking non-stop about the meeting all week, and last night I'd had a sudden thought. *He's planning to convince the acquiring company to promote him over me!* I'd thought back to what François had said: 'If Tristan is going to reach the top of his career, he needs to do it soon.'

That's the root of Tristan's sudden interest in India and in TKG - to fulfil his need to get to the top, and at the same time get his revenge on me. I speed up to overtake a lorry. Ambition is all well and good, but I can imagine what I'd be called if I behaved like him! I spot a speed-radar and, biting back my anger, drop back into the slow lane.

I see a sign for a service station and, pulling into the slip-lane, decide to take a break. Why, I think as I slow down, does François insist on having Tristan on the board? It makes no sense, especially as it's obvious he'll never accept me as his superior. God, I wish I could get rid of him. A nagging doubt suggests that in spite of his reassurances, François doesn't fully trust me. I think back to when he told me I'd made a mistake about the dividend payments. *A mistake,* I mutter, coming to a halt by the shop. Why is my difference of opinion considered a mistake? 'Male privilege,' Ardash had said. 'It would be different if you had a penis!' I slam the car door and march inside.

I'm still brooding as back in the car I speed into the fast lane. I notice that my knuckles have gone white as I clutch the steering wheel and I take a long, deep breath and loosen my hands. Damned Tristan, and damned TKG! *I need to stop thinking about it, Father,* I say. I pass a sign telling me that Troyes is 50 kilometres away, and in spite of myself, my mind springs back to the last time I was there. Well, Tristan got what he deserved, I think, without pleasure.

Making a conscious effort to drop it, my thoughts move to Ardash and an odd little conversation we had a while ago pops into my mind. Ardash had been in Paris on business and we were finishing lunch on the terrace of a café not far from my office, drinking cappuccino and enjoying the afternoon sun.

'Look at this building,' I'd said as we sipped our coffee.

I held out my hand to the Montparnasse Tower, soaring high above the other buildings, its neon corner lights competing with the blue of the sky for drama-value. Ardash's gaze followed my arm up to my office and beyond to the top.

'It's certainly impressive,' he said. 'I imagine it's a great place to work, the views must be stupendous. Isn't there a restaurant at the top? Let's go one evening.'

'The restaurant is on the 56th floor,' I said. 'Not quite the top. But yes, the views are stunning, especially at sunset, although of course, I see them practically every day.' I put my cup down and continued to look up at the tower. Ardash remained silent. 'You know,' I continued after a while, 'this building is 210 metres high and it was the tallest skyscraper in France until recently.' I smiled, thinking back to the day, years ago, when my father had pulled 'The Montparnasse Tower' out of our research box. 'It's still the 14th tallest building in Europe apparently. Did you know that?'

Ardash raised his eyebrows and shook his head.

'I admit, I did not know any of that,' he said, smiling. His chin was resting in his left hand, elbow on the table, his lips curled into a sexy little half smile. I uncrossed my legs.

'Know who designed it?' I asked. He shook his head again, still smiling.

'I'm afraid I don't,' he answered. 'My knowledge of French architecture is somewhat lacking.' He seemed amused and I could tell he was wondering where this was going. I wasn't sure myself.

'It was designed by Eugène Beaudouin, Urbain Cassan and Louis Hoym de Marien,' I said.

'I see,' Ardash replied slowly. I stared up at the tower. For some reason, its scale, its stature, its sheer *audacity* suddenly annoyed me. I folded my arms.

'I can well imagine,' I said, 'that those three men probably saw this as the culmination of their life's work, a towering monument to all that it represents. What does it symbolise to you?'

'The tower?'

'Yes the tower. What is it that it represents?' Ardash lifted an eyebrow.

'A nice place to have an office?' I could tell he was humouring me.

'Yes of course,' I answered. 'But what does it *represent*?'

'Okay,' he replied a little more seriously. He turned and lifted his head to look back at the tower. 'Let's go for the obvious. Strength. Ambition. Achievement.'

'Right. But what is at the root of all those things? What drove those three men to build such a humungous building?' I was beginning to think I was getting somewhere with this line of thought. Ardash looked back at me.

'A desire to succeed?' he answered. I looked at him for some long moments before answering.

'I'll tell you what I think it represents,' I said, lowering my voice. 'What that tower represents is the need to prove how big your erect penis is!'

Two men at the next table flicked glances at us and Ardash smiled without a hint of surprise in his face.

I'm still chuckling about this conversation when, in my car, my mobile phone startles me.

'Tristan, I was just thinking about you,' I say, smiling.

'Why?' Tristan demands, with suspicion.

172

'Oh nothing,' I say. 'Listen, I'll call you back, the traffic is slowing down, I think something has happened up ahead.'

Cars are flashing their hazard lights and are slowing to a stop. *Damn!* I ease on the brake and slow to a halt. I crane my neck to see what has caused the delay but all I can see are stationary cars in each lane. I glance at the clock on the dashboard. I have plenty of time, I think, and I switch on the radio and fiddle with the frequency until I hear a 1980's band singing a song I vaguely remember, which distracts me for a while.

But ten minutes later we're still stationary and people are beginning to get out of their cars to see what has happened. I try to tune in to some travel advice on the radio but can't find anything, so I open my door to join the people milling about in the road.

'No idea what's going on,' the man in front of me says to no one in particular. 'Bloody ridiculous this is!' I lock my door and wander towards him. Another man walks towards us from ahead.

'Pile up,' he says. 'Lorry apparently, and three or four cars. Right mess by all accounts. Police and ambulances are on their way.'

'Bloody hell,' the first man says. 'I've got to be in Sens by eleven.'

'No way we're going anywhere any time soon, mate,' replies the second man sounding somewhat triumphant. The sound of sirens proves him right.

'I told you, you should've got the train. I'm nearly there.' Tristan sounds so pleased that I can't help snapping my reply at him.

'Yes thank you for that, but even you can't predict road accidents.' I flop into the driver's seat and slam the car door too hard.

'Well, I'm going to have to meet TKG by myself aren't I?' *I hate you*, I say silently. 'There's no way we can cancel. It was hard enough getting a date everyone could make.'

I sigh. 'You'll have to start without me. I'll get there when I can. *If* I can by the look of things here.'

I glance around outside. In the rear-view mirror, three lanes of cars are backed up as far as I can see. In front, people are still standing around outside. The couple in the car next to me are arguing loudly. 'I told you, it's always like this!' I hear the man say.

'Tristan, listen to me,' I continue into my phone. 'Stick to the script, okay? You know this is a tentative meeting. Do not charge in and lay all our cards on the table.'

'I think,' Tristan sneers, 'I'm capable of that.'

In my mind I see his lips curl upwards in that way that I find so repulsive. I start to reply but Tristan cuts across me.

'Look, I'm going into a tunnel, I'll have to call you later.'

'Tristan, I want an update as soon as the meeting finishes,' I say, raising my voice.

'What was that? I can't hear you!' he shouts. The line goes dead.

Insomnia

4.37 *I must sleep.* A cat yowls outside, making me jump. I've been wondering whether I really made my father proud. Surely, that's the kind of thing all fathers say? Did he have a happy life, I wonder? Without my mother? Beneath the shifting questions lurks the real source of the pain. I know that regardless of whatever the answers might be, *I just want him back.* I still can't accept that I will never see him again. That we will never sit in companionable silence sipping coffee and reading the papers. His voice never again at the other end of the phone asking how my day went. No more will we share another meal, a walk, an opera. Never will I feel his reassuring hand on my shoulder. Or see his smile. *I will never see him again.* I thrash my feet against the duvet, kick it to the floor. I lie there sweating and sobbing into my pillow. *Why can I not sleep?*

5.22 My father, Tristan, TKG, Luxembourg…questions upon questions scratch away, as the dead hours pile up behind me. But they've become anaesthetised. They are nothing but sets of words. Sounds in my head which don't make any sense. Except that they carry with them a gnawing, underlying wretchedness. The place behind my eyes throbs with a dull ache, and I no longer feel anything but a sense of dread for the day which is dragging me into it. Light is teasing the edges of the curtains.

5.50 I reach for the pain-killers. I may as well get up.

Paris and Nice but mainly Madrid

Drinking coffee at the departure lounge of Charles De Gaulle airport, I swipe the screen of my smart phone and re-read Ardash's email. *You are fascinating and dangerous* he wrote. *You live deeply and passionately. So do I. Are you going to Madrid with him?* I stop reading and close the email.

I look down at my wrist. The bruises took days to fade, and although it had been annoying to have to consider the clothes I wore and whether the marks could be seen, I feel a strange sense of regret at not having them anymore. They'd seemed intimate and honest, as though with this secret, physical reminder, Ardash had shared a hidden part of himself with me.

That night, we'd made love with more heat, with more intensity than ever we had before. We'd drunk the last of the wine slowly, our eyes fixed on one another's and as if on cue, we put our empty glasses down and stood up. We faced each other in the candlelight for a long moment, neither of us breaking the silence. And then as one, we began to pull one another down onto the rug, tearing off clothes, grasping and sweating, our movements suffused with a powerful sense of urgency, freeing each other with our teeth, our nails, our skin…

Now, at the airport, I rub my wrist absently, sip my coffee and glance out of the window. It's a beautiful sunny day. I open Ardash's email again. *Can we love and hate in such a way that we forge a single naked meaning out of the dangerous possibilities of a life lived?* How damned poetic, I sigh and open the report I need to read. I wonder, as I lift my fingers to my temples, whether we who write reports hope one day to combine all those words in such a way that they say something worth saying. This makes me think of the difficulty I had in writing my father's eulogy and I suppress a wave of sorrow by taking a deep breath and trying once more to concentrate. But after reading the same sentence three times, I snap the lid of my laptop shut. I look out of the window again and focus on some baggage handlers in yellow overalls and huge leather gloves, haul suitcases onto a cart. They're not very careful and I'm pleased I've only brought a carry-on case.

Is it true that happiness is only real when shared?

Ardash had asked the question that night, in bed, and thinking about it now takes me back to a time a few years ago in Nice. I was there for a meeting but since I'd never been before, I'd planned to stay on for the weekend and explore the town. On the Saturday afternoon, following a morning of wandering through pretty streets, I'd sat at a café terrace overlooking the bay, drinking first a coffee and then a glass of Chablis. I'd stayed there for a long time, reading, watching the little white sailing boats bobbing in the sparkling blue water, enjoying the light, warm breeze and late afternoon sun. I remember feeling totally at peace sitting there alone, complete and completely happy. *Of course, my father was alive then*, I think, remembering how I used to call him each time I arrived at a hotel to let him know I'd arrived safely. I sigh and I wonder whether, for many people, the pursuit of happiness is the same thing as the pursuit of a relationship.

In the airport, I re-open Ardash's email and wonder whether this is true for me. *Are you going to Madrid with him?* Do I want an exclusive relationship with Ardash? But maybe he is right; eventually, one or both of us would inevitably deceive the other. I think about how many people I know who are divorced. I think about Theo-Paul. At least Ardash and I are honest, I tell myself. His email describes me as fascinating and dangerous. He is fascinating and exasperating! *Don't tell me the details*, he says in one breath. *Are you having sex with him?* he asks in the next. I wish I hadn't told him Theo-Paul's name. I don't know the name

177

of Ardash's other lover. I don't know anything about her. I feel disadvantaged, as though I've given away some of my power. '...Theo-Paul...' Ardash had repeated the first time I'd referred to him by name. I hadn't liked the way he'd said it.

My flight is on time, and as I journey by taxi into Madrid and through its congested roads, Mumbai springs to my mind. My phone rings, making me jump, and I immediately think it's Ardash.

'Just checking in,' Marine says. 'All is fine here. How was your journey?'

I rinse the disappointment from my voice. 'Hi, Marine,' I reply, with a glance at my watch. 'Fine. I'm on my way to the meeting now.'

'Great. Big one, this. Best of luck with it. Not that you need it.'

'Thanks, it'll be fine.'

I arrive at a smart, city-centre restaurant, bustling with discreetly hushed, lunch-time trade. Inside is all black and gold and glass, and mostly full of business people. My client chose it, and I can see why. The tables are arranged in semi-alcoves with L shaped banquettes creating a feeling of privacy. I look around as I take off my jacket, and note with amusement the trilby hats hanging on the walls. A waitress arrives and ushers me to a table.

'*Agua gaseosa, por favour*,' I say. It's pretty much the extent of my Spanish. When she leaves, I glance at my emails but decide that I don't have time to do any work before the client arrives. I look at the menu instead. The waitress returns with my sparkling water. I see that she's now wearing one of the trilby hats and I smile.

'¿Te gustaría hacer un pedido?' she asks.

I indicate as best I can that I am waiting for someone and she nods and leaves. As I sip my water, I realise that in spite of the feeling of privacy, I can hear the people at the next table and that they are speaking French. A prickle of illicit pleasure makes me listen.

'It's moored on the Canal du Midi,' a young man's voice is saying. 'It's an attractive houseboat, but it doesn't have an engine. I'd like to turn it into a gay cinema.' I'm intrigued. I listen as he continues to tell another man and a woman about his boat. I think he's a dreamer, and I like him for it. It occurs to me that in their conversations, some describe people and events. Others tell of their dreams. I wonder which kind I am.

'And you think this is a worthwhile project?' I detect a touch of derision in the woman's voice.

'There's more to life than making money,' the dreamer replies. *Well said*, I think.

I glance at my watch and then at the door of the restaurant. My client is late, and I feel a pang of annoyance. I check my phone but there's nothing from him. I sip my water and go back to listening. From what I manage to gather, the second man is a banker but it's clear that this isn't a business meeting, and that pleases me. The woman appears be the banker's wife.

'We must be heading back,' she says, and she scrapes her chair back loudly and gets up. She's gone for some minutes and after a brief silence I'm intrigued to hear the banker ask in a hushed and heavily accented voice: 'Do you think promiscuity always leads to jealousy?'

Interesting, I think, sitting very still in anticipation of the answer. I wonder, perhaps because of the dreamer's talk of a gay cinema, whether they're having an affair.

'It's a good question,' the dreamer says. 'I think it depends on how secure each person is about themselves. Whether or not they're living according to their own values.'

Excellent answer, I think.

'Do you think of me as promiscuous?' the banker asks.

'No,' the dreamer replies. 'I think you simply know what you want.' The banker starts to reply but the woman arrives and they stop abruptly and get up to leave. I crane my neck to see them and I think, as I watch them go, the banker and the woman elegantly dressed, the dreamer casual in jeans and a sweatshirt, that our inner life is a constant flow between observation, introspection and dreaming. I wonder as I spot my client heaving his bulky mass through the door, whether we do very much else with our thoughts. I put this to one side as Señor Pons waves at me and hurries over. He doesn't have good news.

Madrid

It's sunny and the heat rains down through the glass roof of the station. I'm walking around, trying to drink scalding-hot coffee from a paper cup. *At least the damn thing isn't plastic,* I mutter. I try to un-tense my shoulders and jaw as I think of the business we've lost; I wonder, as I pass hordes of chattering tourists, why people bother to talk to each other. It seems rare that people ever share and explore ideas or find creative solutions. Valentino Pons's face flashes into my mind and then Tristan's and I imagine slapping them both.

I come to a halt by the station entrance and, looking up, notice the birds' nests in some trees, the birds flapping and squawking around them. *A murder of crows.* My phone rings, making me jump and I glance down at the display. It's Marine. I don't answer. I can't face a discussion now. Opposite the station I notice a yard full of gas canisters. The phrase 'the brighter the light, the darker the shadow' springs to mind as I imagine them all exploding in a magnificent blast of blue-white flames.

'It really isn't your service,' Señor Pons had said, scratching the back of his flabby neck. 'I can't fault what you do, you know that, and I have the greatest of respect for what you have achieved.' He glanced around and shifted in his seat. I looked at him evenly. 'It's the economic climate. I'm sure you understand, we're having to review our entire supply chain. I imagine we aren't the only ones.' My appetite vanished and I put my fork down. 'Between you and me,' he continued, 'our backs are against the wall. We just can't survive without making serious cuts.' His pink face was sweating as he swallowed a large piece of overcooked steak, then wiped a dribble of fat off his chin with his napkin. 'Believe me, we've considered all the options. This wasn't a decision we took lightly, especially after all this time. It's why I wanted to tell you in person.' His eyes darted from one side to the other and then back to his steak as he wiped his brow with the greasy napkin. I imagined the fat from the steak mingling with his sweat and looked away. 'It's the economic climate,' he said again, and I wondered why I came here myself, why I hadn't sent one of the sales team.

My shirt is sticking to my back, and I briefly contemplate taking a taxi to my hotel instead of the train, but decide that I've had enough of the Madrid traffic. I walk into a stuffy, overcrowded café and hurry to a table as a young couple get up to leave, squeezing myself between some business men on one side and a huddle of giggling teenagers on the other. I ignore a business man who I catch making a lewd gesture about me to his colleagues and the resulting explosive laughter. I feel like I'm stuck between two pin-ball machines.

Wedged standing in the clamour and the heat of the metro, I want to scream. After being jostled and bumped for two stops I can stand it no longer, and I leave the train and walk along the busy street in what I hope is the direction of my hotel. I almost enjoy the pain clamping around my temples and the nausea in my stomach, as physical justifications for the anxiety I feel. *It will be okay* I tell myself. But the fact remains. We've lost our biggest client.

Since the meeting, I've been calculating figures in my head but the numbers keep swimming away from me. If only Tristan's new initiative had gone as planned, the loss of the Madrid client would matter less, I think savagely. Or if we had a proper contingency fund. I remind myself that we have the time, that we can count on their business until their current contract expires. But what then? I want to get back to the office as soon as possible, to work out what we need to do in order to compensate for this loss. But it's Friday and I have a weekend to get through first.

I'll get an outline strategy in place by Monday I tell myself. I need to talk with Jean but remember that it's his anniversary and he and his wife are in Venice for the weekend. As I jostle my way through the crowd, everything, the bars, the shops, the people all seem pallid and superficial and I dismiss the designer clothes and handbags as pointless and facile. I stop by a café and look inside. A row of men in business suits are drinking at the bar. I contemplate going inside and ordering a gin but I keep on walking.

In my hotel room, I stand at the window, scrubbed and glowing in a white hotel robe, a towel tied around my head, turban style. The glass of overpriced room-service wine has hit my stomach and I'm grateful for the dull calm it's beginning to induce. I watch the people below walking together or alone through the busy Madrid square. Pigeons flap up towards windows and chase each other around statues. Three young women with back-packs interest me for some moments before disappearing down a side street. A woman in a business-suit shouts at someone on the other side of the square, and begins dodging traffic to cross it. A bus goes past with a Hollywood advert plastered to its side flaunting love and happy endings. A homeless man rifles through a bin for scraps of food.

The dynamic but orderly flow of movement in the street calms me. There is, I think, a predictability in this motion that is interesting but not surprising. Every person I can see probably thinks they are unique. Maybe they are, on the inside. They make me want to lean out and yell at them *'What are you doing?!'* but instead I just watch and sip my wine. I think, as I gaze out, that we almost never inhabit what we are right now, but focus instead on some projection of ourselves into the future, some image of what we would like to become. Well-travelled; together; loved; less hungry. *'I think, Father, that we are always becoming, and never just being,'* I say out loud.

183

The value of the lost business reappears in my mind and I suddenly remember the dream I'd had last night. I was at my childhood home for some kind of gathering but the mood was sombre. A woman with a shadowy face was saying she couldn't understand women who didn't have children. She kept saying it and eventually I yelled at her to shut up. An old man who in the dream was both my father and François, started beating me. I shouted to the woman for help but she had disappeared. I heard a man's voice saying, 'You'll learn, soon enough.' I'd woken up in a sweat, thinking about TKG Associates.

I gulp down a large slug of wine and turn from the window to sit on the bed. I remember Ardash once quoting a Greek philosopher who said, 'There are only a few things in life that are important, and nothing that is very important.' I think about having to tell the board on Monday that we've lost our biggest client. I decide to stay in Spain for the weekend, to hire a car and to visit Toledo.

Toledo

There are small flowers along the bank of the river. Daisies and vetch shiver in the breeze as I stand by the window sipping my coffee. The two pain-killers I swallowed earlier haven't touched my aching head, and I rub my eyes and my temples with my free hand. The grey houses stand quiet and proud in the town beyond. Toledo looked beautiful last night, lit up on the hill. It still looks beautiful now in the late morning sunshine, the buildings standing tall, rising from behind the River Tajo. I wish I could fix myself into the serenity of this scene and feel only its stillness. I close my eyes and will myself not to think about last night.

Changing my flight and arranging a hire-car had been straight-forward enough, and the Madrid hotel had made the booking with their sister hotel just outside Toledo, on my behalf. The drive had taken little more than an hour and a half even with a stop for coffee at Ilescas, and with the aid of the sat-nav I arrived at the hotel at around 6.45 with a sense of achievement, if not contentment. I decided not to go into the town yet but to spend the evening at the hotel and to explore Toledo in the morning.

After taking my clothes out of my overnight case and shaking them out, I ran a deep bath, emptying the entire contents of the little bottle of bubble-bath into the steaming water. The scent of lavender filled the room and while the bath was running, I undressed and took a long look at myself in the mirror. The dark shadows under my eyes were a testimony not only to my sleepless nights but also to the implications of the meeting. I swept my hair behind my ears and, wiping steam from the mirror, turned my head from side to side. *My god, I look old*, I thought, pulling the skin on my face taut.

Turning from the mirror, I stepped gingerly into the bath, enjoying the feel of the hot water as it enveloped and soothed my body. Letting out an audible sigh, I closed my eyes and let my head fall back, trying hard to retain the sense of the present moment. But, like stretched elastic, my mind constantly snapped back to Señor Pons.

'I'm so sorry,' he'd said. 'We're just not in a position to renew our contract.' Sorry didn't come anywhere close to what I felt.

They've got to be told. I picked up the soap and started to take it out of its wrapper, trying to remember what the rest of the board were doing on Monday. I vaguely remembered Tristan saying he had a supplier meeting in Reims. There was an interim board meeting on Tuesday. *'Perhaps, Father, I ought to break the news then?'* That would allow me to do some number crunching with Jean on Monday. *Dammit, why wasn't I stronger?* Thoughts of the meeting where my contingency plan had been out-voted taunted me, and later, Tristan's voice, flippant and dismissive, telling us his new initiative needed more time before making any money. I could picture his sneer as I broke the news about the lost business. *This is intolerable!* Tears prickled behind my eyes and I sniffed them back savagely, wondering what advice my father would have given me. He would have told me to forget about it until the morning, to get a good night's sleep. 'Everything seems worse when you're tired, girl.' *You're right, Father.* I closed my eyes and resolved to think seriously about the situation tomorrow.

Turning on the hot tap again, my thoughts turned to Ardash. Ardash in London, certainly with a woman. I wondered, as the temperature of the water rose, what they were doing right now. Were they sharing a bath together? Perhaps Ardash was this very moment smoothing soap over her shoulders, moving his hands down her arms, over her stomach, her breasts...? Or was he undressing her as she stepped out of her shoes and turned for him to undo her zip? Perhaps her dress was already lying abandoned on the carpet as they tumbled together onto the bed... I closed my eyes. *I bet she's beautiful, intriguing...* The thoughts were like poisonous flies buzzing around my head and as much as I tried swatting each one away they returned to taunt me.

I turned the tap off with my toe and lay back in the hot water. Smoothing soap over my stomach and breasts, I wondered whether this woman thought about me when Ardash was in Paris, whether she jealously imagined what we might be doing together. I wanted to hate her but reminded myself that it would make more sense to hate him. *'Although that doesn't make sense either, Father, since he isn't deceiving me.'* Saying the words out loud didn't help and perversely, the fact that I knew Ardash was with another woman made me want him even more. *Just what is this freedom?* I felt tempted to phone him, and stared for a long moment at my mobile on the vanity stand by the bath. *Are you really that weak?* I decided to call Theo-Paul instead.

'I seem to be attracted to inaccessible men.'

'Christ, what an opener,' Theo-Paul exclaimed. 'Are you talking about me?' He hesitated. 'You're not going to get all deep and meaningful are you...?' I shook my head and smiled.

'Don't worry Theo-Paul,' I said. 'I know better than to inflict that on you.'

'Good. You know I'm no psychologist. Where are you?'

'I'm in Toledo.'

'Toledo? Toledo Spain? What the blazes are you doing there?'

I thought about telling him about the lost client but I didn't want to discuss it.

'I have no idea,' I replied. 'It was an impulse thing.'

'An impulse thing! You're crazy, you know that don't you?' he said. 'I went to Toledo once with Marine years ago, beautiful place. Make sure you visit the Cathedral. So come on, I want to know, this inaccessible man, it's me isn't it?'

'Don't worry,' I said. 'It isn't a trap, just an observation. I don't need you to be any more accessible than you are now.'

'I'm not sure how to take that,' he replied.

I took my time getting dressed and made-up, and, turning around in front of the wardrobe mirror, wasn't displeased with the result. The make-up had smoothed away the tiredness around my eyes and the smoky eyeshadow accentuated them. I adjusted the neckline of my dress. *Sexy but not obvious.* I wondered why I cared, but didn't care to answer and turned to pick up my room key and purse. I glanced at my novel lying by the bed and hesitated for a moment before heading down to the hotel bar without it.

The place was quiet apart from a few couples sitting at tables by the window. A barman was polishing a glass at the end of the bar, and he put it away and walked over to me as I sat on a bar stool.

'Gin and tonic por favour,' I said. 'Grande.' I watched as he measured out the gin and opened a little bottle of tonic, popping a slice of lemon into the glass. I indicated no ice. He brought it to me with a little dish of olives and I smiled my thanks at him.

As I sat nursing my drink and picking absently at the olives, more people began to trickle in, mostly couples, but also a few lone men. I assessed each one as he walked up to the bar and ordered his drink. Too fat. Too bald. Too old. *Everyone is too something.* I forced myself to find an interesting feature in each of the men. This one, yes he's bald, but doesn't that give him an air of wisdom? And this one, he's old enough to be my father, but he isn't bad-looking. *Christ, would you listen to yourself!* I took a large slug of gin and wondered whether I'd still be objectifying these men if Ardash were here. Perhaps if Ardash and I were exclusive, I would simply have brought something to read with me and not noticed them at all. Or maybe Ardash was right, I'd assess each of them, but wouldn't admit it, possibly not even to myself.

Soon, the bar was full and a second barman appeared and starting taking orders. I raised my hand and motioned for another gin and tonic. Some jazz music began to play and as I was trying to identify the singer, something made me look round, at a man wearing a dark grey business suit who had entered the bar alone. As he walked, he glanced around, taking in the couples at the tables and the lone drinkers at the bar. He looked at me, his eyes sweeping up and down my body before walking up to the seat next to me. I, in turn looked him up and down and noted his slim build, his formal tie and well pressed shirt beneath his jacket. He was perhaps in his mid-forties, not unattractive. *Too pink* I thought, stifling a laugh as I noted that flushed complexion which often suggests a fondness for more alcohol than is healthy. I turned away without acknowledging him.

One of the barmen hurried over and I listened as the man ordered a martini in Spanish. I continued to sip my gin, aware of his presence by my side. After some long moments I flicked a sideways glance at him, and then turned slightly in his direction. The man looked at me for some seconds before nodding at me. I nodded back. He said something to me in Spanish.

'I'm sorry,' I said. 'No hablo Español.'

'Ah,' he said. 'English?'

'Actually I'm French, but English will do.'

The man's martini arrived and I turned away, continuing to sip my gin.

After a while the man said, 'Are you waiting for someone?'

Sighing, I contemplated the question. I thought about Theo-Paul making ribald jokes and openly ogling other women, about Ardash and his lover laughing and talking in some London bar, his hand stroking the back of her neck, her hand on his thigh...

'No,' I said. Downing what remained in my glass, I turned to fully face the man. 'I'm not waiting for anyone.'

'Well then,' the man said, 'in that case, may I buy you a drink? I'm Jorge.'

Achille De Quincy—Before my death

...Pauline. She wasn't perfect and I won't let her become so in death, she was a woman not a saint, damn it. If she was aggrieved, she had a mood about her fit to set anyone cowering. Not a loud, flash and burn temper, but smouldering, quiet; not sulky, it never lasted but while it did, she'd lash you with her stare and a tongue that silenced you flat with a word. Standards, she had, principles and it wasn't enough for her to live them, she needed us who were close to live them with her. Sincerity. Optimism. Integrity. She didn't demand perfection but there were certain qualities, certain ways of behaving that were non-negotiable for Pauline. And so for the girl and me too.

I remember late one Saturday afternoon, the girl must have crept into our bedroom. Took a bottle of perfume from her mother's dressing table, she did, sprayed the whole lot all over herself, fit to set her and everyone else sneezing and coughing something terrible. Only about three years old she was. Comes sidling into the salon all furtive giggles and sneakiness. I swear you could have smelt that perfume from the road downstairs. I look up from my paper to see what Pauline will do and she's staring at the girl, all raised eyebrows and silence. The girl grins.

'You've used my perfume without asking,' Pauline says to her, plain as that. The girl is sucking a long dark curl and tries to edge behind the sofa.

'No I haven't,' says she, as nonchalant as a three year old can get.

'Young lady,' says her mother. 'You come here right now.' I know what's coming and make like I'm absorbed in my newspaper. 'Do you know what a lie is?' The girl isn't giggling any more, stands silent in front of her mother, looks down at her feet. 'Well?' asks her mother, all quiet-

191

voiced and stern. 'Yes,' mutters the girl. 'Speak up,' says her mother.

'It's when you tell something that isn't the truth,' says the girl, clear voiced and wary in her guilt.

'Good,' says her mother. 'And not telling the truth is a bad thing. It makes you a liar. A liar is a bad person. Do you want to be a liar?' The girl shakes her head hard and curls bounce all round her face.

'Then don't be,' says Pauline. Then she takes the girl into her arms and hugs her fit to bursting.

Toledo

I decide to leave my car at the hotel and walk the short distance into Toledo. I don't care that I'm too late for breakfast but hope, as I hurry through the reception and out of the hotel that I don't bump into Jorge. Nausea threatens to overcome me and I clutch at the hotel door for a second or two, swaying as I adjust to the light. In spite of my dark glasses, the bright sunshine hurts my eyes. I take a deep breath. *Be resolute!*

My head is still throbbing and my legs are shaky but in spite of my tiredness, I force myself to keep a steady pace. Queasiness forces me to stop on the Paseo Cristo de la Vega and I stare for a weary moment at the town ahead of me, before pushing on up the steep road into town. I don't stop, fearing that I won't find the strength to continue, turning instead into a narrow cobbled thoroughfare and continuing slowly up the hill. Only at the top do I pause to catch my breath. I glance around at the pretty little gift shops, their rows of porcelain Madonnas and wooden rosary beads tempting the tourists, but the enthusiasm to be interested eludes me. My breathing slowed, I wander down the street, feeling a little more soothed, enjoying the feeling of being anonymous in a foreign town. This thought takes me crashing back to last night and my momentary calm is shattered. *Oh God.* I decide to visit the Cathedral.

Catedral Primada Santa María de Toledo is big and dark and impressive, and I take in its thirteenth century high gothic excess as I wander slowly, my heels echoing around the vaulted expanse. Carved and chiselled mythological figures and illuminated saints glare down at me in concert, and as I look up at one stern face after another, I get the feeling they are judging me. I stand in front of a statue of the Virgin Mary, and wonder whether to light a candle. *Can you redeem me?* I ask her. I hear the clack and echo of someone else's footsteps and I turn to see a man in a brown tweed jacket hurrying up the nave towards a small organ, not the grand, ornate one on the other side of the Cathedral, but a modest wooden one. I watch as he takes some sheet music out of his leather satchel, taking his time to arrange it in front of him. He stands up and sits down a few times, adjusting his position and once finally seated, briefly closes his eyes and rubs his hands together before starting to play a baroque requiem. I turn away from the Virgin Mary without lighting a candle, walk over to a pew and sit down to listen. As the rich, doleful notes begin to fill the dim space, I am appalled to find that I'm on the verge of tears.

'A drink would be lovely, thank you,' I'd said, and smiled at him. 'Perhaps you can recommend a good Rioja?'

Jorge hailed the barman. 'Una botella de Torre Ercilla Reserva, favor.'

'A bottle?' I raised an eyebrow.

'Are you in any hurry?' Jorge replied, moving his stool closer to mine. I wondered whether to feel affronted by this presumptuousness but my thoughts flicked to Ardash and his lover and I decided that sharing a bottle of wine with a vaguely attractive Spanish man wasn't a completely unappealing prospect.

Jorge told me in perfect English but with a heavy Spanish accent that he worked for a medical drugs company and that he spent most of his time on the road visiting hospitals and doctors' surgeries.

'I don't get home very often,' he said.

'Where is home?' I asked, more to keep the game going than out of actual interest.

'Oh, in the south,' Jorge replied vaguely.

He'd had a number of appointments around Madrid and Toledo this week, he told me, and was leaving for Valencia in the morning.

'But really, I don't want to talk about work,' he said. The barman arrived with a bottle and held it out for Jorge to inspect. Jorge glanced at the label and nodded his acceptance.

'Tell me about yourself,' he said, as the barman began to work the cork.

I wondered what to tell him. I too had no urge to talk about work and I certainly didn't want to talk about Ardash. The barman uncorked the bottle with a satisfying pop.

'I'm a prison psychologist,' I said without breaking eye-contact.

The lie was thrilling and I waited for Jorge's response as he tasted the wine. He nodded at the barman.

'I work in a high security prison with long-term recidivists,' I continued as the barman poured our wine. 'Drug offenders mainly, and violent criminals with anger problems.'

I savoured the rush of excitement as I embraced the feeling of being able to be whoever I decided with this man. Jorge raised his glass.

'To getting to know you,' he said. I smiled and clinked his glass with my own.

We dined at the hotel restaurant which turned out to be surprisingly good. I ordered Patatas Bravas and Gazpacho Manchego and a bottle of 2005 El Pecado, and wondered who would be paying the bill.

'Your work must be very interesting,' Jorge said as we were eating. I smiled and nodded.

'Oh it is,' I replied. 'You wouldn't believe some of the cases I have to deal with. Of course I can't go into specific detail.'

'No, of course not,' Jorge said. 'But what a fascinating job, you must never be bored with it.'

I looked at him through the flickering light of the artificial candle and nodded and smiled again.

'Have you done this kind of work for long?' Jorge asked.

'Yes, for many years,' I said. 'I work in Fleury-Mérogis. It's the biggest prison in Paris. Have you heard of it?'

Jorge shook his head. 'No I haven't,' he replied, picking up the bottle and filling our glasses. I thought for an instant that perhaps I was drinking too much and too fast, but decided that I didn't care and, picking up my wine, looked at Jorge for a long moment.

'My husband is the Prison Governor,' I said. 'That's how we met.'

Jorge's eyes widened. 'Husband?' he said. 'You don't wear a wedding ring.'

'No, I lost it,' I replied. 'But yes I have a husband. Don't worry though, we have an open marriage.'

'An open marriage?' His eyes widened even more. A waiter arrived at Jorge's elbow with a basket, making him jump. He took a piece of bread quickly and tore it open.

'Oh yes,' I said, shaking my head at the waiter. 'Jacques —that's my husband—he's with one of his lovers right now. He phoned just before to tell me how his evening was going. Well by all accounts, they're having dinner. I bet it won't take them long to get to his room though! We have a completely honest approach to our marriage and we don't try to restrict each other at all.'

Jorge's eyes bulged. 'Really?' He sat back in his seat and regarded me for a few moments, a half-eaten piece of bread in one hand, his wine glass in the other. He recovered himself and took a long sip. I fought not to laugh.

'How long have you been married for?' he asked eventually.

'Oh, ten years now,' I answered. I sipped my own wine and met Jorge's eyes over the top of the glass.

'And it was an... open marriage from the start?' Jorge sounded incredulous now and I had to take a large gulp of wine in order not to laugh.

'Yes, we discussed it all before we got married,' I said.

'And are you ... you're happy in that kind of marriage?' I wondered whether a tinge of judgement had crept into Jorge's voice. I watched him intently as he placed his glass on the table and started to cut into his meat.

'We're grown-ups,' I said. 'We're responsible for our own happiness, not each other's. It's rather unrealistic, don't you think, to expect that one person can provide for all our needs, all our lives?'

'Well...' Jorge faltered. 'Possibly. But I'm not sure I'd be happy with that kind of marriage.'

'What part wouldn't you be happy with?' I asked. 'Being honest about your own behaviour, or knowing for certain that your wife is sleeping with other men?'

'What makes you think I have a wife?' Jorge replied defensively.

'Haven't you?' I asked. He hesitated, his glass half way to his lips. 'Of course you have,' I said, eyeing the pale patch on his ring finger. 'I expect your wedding ring is in your hotel room inside your wash bag where you won't lose it.' I watched him flush a deep red. 'My point is this,' I said. 'My husband and I don't need to be deceptive about our desires and how we act on them. We don't need to keep secrets from each other. We can spend an evening or a *night...*' I paused for the briefest of moments '...with whomever we please and it won't harm our marriage.' I took a long, slow sip of wine. 'I suspect that you on the other hand keep a few carefully hidden secrets from your wife.' I felt as though I'd scored a victory and I looked at Jorge with something of a challenge in my eyes.

'Well, I can see your point I suppose,' he mumbled, not sounding in the least convinced. He drained his glass and looked around him as though planning his escape. I wondered whether he was beginning to regret approaching me in the bar and once again I fought the urge to laugh. I decided to throw him a life belt. I leaned forward slowly, ensuring that Jorge got a good glimpse of cleavage. His mouth twitched and he shifted in his seat.

'You know, Jorge,' I said, lowering my voice and holding his gaze. 'Whatever happens tonight is okay.' I didn't break eye contact with him and his lips moved into a slow smile. I sat back in my seat. 'Have you ever heard of Pascal Payet?' I asked lightly.

'Er, no I haven't.'

'He's one of the most notorious criminals in France. He's very violent and is famous because he's always escaping from prison.'

'Oh?' Jorge sounded relieved to retreat to the safer territory of the violent criminal underworld rather than remain in the dark and dangerous realms of truth and honesty in marriage. 'And in your work, have you ever had to deal with him?'

I drained the last of my wine and replaced my glass on the table before saying in a hushed voice:

'I'm his psychologist. He tells me all his secrets. Even the most intimate.' I paused and looked Jorge in the eye. 'Secrets,' I whispered, 'can sometimes be fun, don't you think?' I arched my back and pushed my breasts forward. The hand on my thigh and Jorge's lecherous smile told me I'd scored a further victory.

'Indeed,' he replied, hailing a waiter. His hand crept higher. 'Let's order some Cognac shall we, and you can tell me all your intimate secrets.'

Ardash, I thought, you can do what you like tonight, and so will I.

As the organist's notes continue to fill the incense-scented air, I wipe my face and make a supreme effort to suppress my tears. I stand up and hurry between the pews and into the aisle, past the praying old ladies and dawdling tourists. Outside, the bright sunlight hits me like a blow and I stand in front of the Cathedral, squinting and blinking into the light. *I don't want to be in this town anymore. I want to go home.* I start to make my way quickly down through the winding cobbled streets. A young couple brushes past me holding hands and laughing, and I suddenly recollect my strange dream. I dreamt that versions of myself were being streamed into the world, like multi-dimensional, multiplying fractals, that every moment contained infinite possibilities and that at every instant, a new version of myself was splitting off into infinite different futures. I remember feeling liberated, as though all I had to do was to create myself anew in whichever life I chose.

But now, as I make my way down the hill towards the bridge, I sigh and pick up my pace. I know that whichever version of myself I would like to be here in this bright, pretty, town, whichever version I weave in order to seduce attractive, foreign men, on Monday I will step back into my own life, knowing what I have to do.

Paris—Montparnasse Tower

'Christ almighty! The whole contract?'

I clench my teeth and will myself not to look at Tristan's reddening face, fearing I'll either yell or laugh.

'Yes, the whole contract.' I curse the fact that my forced even tone sounds false, rather than authoritative, but continue. 'Of course I offered a number of incentives and compromises but it was clear the decision had been taken before I met with Valentino. He was apologetic but completely resolute.'

'Well, that's just fabulous!' Tristan flings his pen down on the table in front of him. 'What are they worth?' He makes a show of calculating the revenue the Madrid client brings in. 'Christ!' he says again. 'Tell me you're joking!'

'Obviously I am not,' I reply, sliding his pen back to him.

The meeting had begun like any other with the usual shuffling of seats and papers, last glances at smart phones, pens taken out in readiness, laptops opened. Closing the Venetian blinds around the glass walls of the board-room, I chose not to think about the discussion to come.

'Would anyone like coffee before we begin?' Marine asked. I looked at her, eyebrows raised but she merely shrugged before going off to the kitchen. It was Tristan's turn to make the drinks, but I couldn't be bothered to argue.

I'd been tempted to talk the situation through with Theo-Paul the night I got back from Spain, but I changed my mind and instead, took out a sheet of paper and sat at the table in my salon weighing up the possible ways forward. There were only two workable solutions I could think of. I wrote them down and stared at them in turn. The positives and negatives of each were clear. I sighed and turned to gaze out of my open terrace doors. There was no light in the apartment opposite and the geraniums on the balcony looked black in the darkness of the late evening. I screwed my sheet of paper into a ball and threw it across the table.

'Okay,' I began once the meeting had opened and we were all seated with our coffee. 'Marine is taking the minutes today. I want to get the routine matters out of the way first as there is a much more pressing issue that will need our careful consideration.' Jean nodded slightly. 'The quarterly profit is slightly down on the last but is nothing that wasn't expected. As Jean will explain, this is owing to a large invoice payment that we'd been accruing for. Core business sales have been pretty consistent, although we still haven't invoiced anything at all for the new service.' I glanced at Tristan who didn't look up from his notes. 'First, Jean, perhaps you'd take us through last month's management accounts?'

Jean clicked a few keys on his laptop and straightened the papers in front of him.

'It's all pretty straightforward for now,' he said, glancing at me. 'The software licensing invoice finally arrived three months late and was more than expected but nothing to worry about. The VAT payment went through as expected ...' He continued down the spreadsheet in front of him, outlining the spend in each line before looking up from his screen. 'Any questions?' he asked.

Tristan looked as though he might have something to say but remained silent. I took a deep breath and looked at Jean for a second.

'Okay, thanks, Jean,' I said. 'Now, I want to come to a serious matter that I'm going to need your considered input to resolve.'

Tristan leant back in his seat and folded his arms. Outside two pigeons flapped silently past the window. For a fraction of a second, I envied their freedom.

'At least one of you is aware of what transpired last week.' Jean nodded. 'As you are all aware, I met with our Madrid client on Friday. I'm afraid the result of that meeting is not good news. Once their current contract is up, they're not renewing. They're ending their relationship with us.'

Silence. I didn't break it, but watched Marine and Tristan's faces crease to frowns as the news sank in. Jean looked down at the table.

'What do you mean ending their relationship with us?'

'I mean, Tristan, we've lost them.'

I sit here now, at the head of the table and regard each of them in turn. Marine and Jean are glancing between Tristan and me. Tristan's face is mottling and perspiration is beading his forehead. In spite of his outburst, something in his smirk suggests he's almost pleased. I've never wanted to punch someone more.

'Our biggest client!' he's saying. 'I mean what the…'

'Look,' Marine interjects. 'This isn't helping. We need to discuss this sensibly, not bicker.'

'Agreed,' I say, thinking about François' insistence on selling. 'TKG are still a possibility and we can't afford to frighten them off. We need to take control of this.'

'I've been looking at the figures,' says Jean. 'This isn't going to affect us for some months yet. We're not going to be able to ride this out by doing nothing, but we do have a small window.' Jean looks at his hands. 'Where we can… take steps.'

'Exactly,' I say. 'Clearly we have a serious situation here. We don't have a contingency fund big enough to cover this loss this early on in the financial year.' I make eye contact with Tristan who's still looking incredulous. 'And it seems we can't count on revenue from the Luxembourg service which we'd factored into the budget.'

Tristan looks as though he wants to hit me. Marine holds up her hand and quickly intervenes.

'Are you thinking of postponing the Mumbai project?' she asks.

'It's certainly one of the options,' I say. 'I don't want to, but the set-up costs will be considerable. We may have no choice but to push it back to next year.'

'Out of the question!' Tristan explodes.

'Tristan,' I say, 'nothing is out of the question. We need to consider every option here.'

'Well, what about Claude?' he says. 'Claude works almost exclusively on the Madrid account. Part of the solution surely involves getting rid of *him*.'

'Tristan!' Marine fires back. 'That's our last option. Claude has worked here for longer than you or me. He still has kids at home for goodness sake. Surely we ought to look at every other possibility before that?' I make eye contact with her and nod my agreement.

'Not an ounce of ambition,' Tristan says. 'I knew his father. Lived in the same house all his life. Claude is just the same. We wouldn't miss him.'

I go to speak, but Marine gets there first. 'Look, Claude is good at his job and is happy to do it. Why is that a bad thing?'

'No ambition whatsoever,' Tristan repeats.

'In any case,' Jean cuts in, 'Claude's ambition or lack of it isn't the issue. Getting rid of him would only be part of the solution. Although I for one don't see how that's avoidable. Even if we do postpone the Mumbai project, what do we do with him? Claude works almost wholly with Madrid.'

'He's got to go,' Tristan says. Sweat is trickling down his pink face. 'And while we're at it, I can think of one or two others we can afford to lose. What does Solange do all day for example?'

'Calm down Tristan.' Marine's voice is icy.

'I will not calm down!' Tristan explodes. 'We've lost our biggest client. The question has to be asked, would they be leaving if the account had been handled well? I mean for Christ's sake, why didn't we know about this months ago? What's Claude been doing all this time? Who's been supervising him?' He turns to me, his face bright red now. 'Heads have got to roll! *You* must have known about this!'

He's practically shouting and he's jabbing a finger at me. Marine glances at the door.

'Do control yourself,' she says. 'We have the staff outside to consider.' Tristan snorts at her and doesn't reply.

God, how I wish I could fire that man! I feel as though I'm slipping down a fairground-slide. *Come on*, I tell myself, *take control.*

'Tristan,' I say, working hard to keep my voice level. 'I will not have talk of 'heads rolling'. We are not that kind of company. And at this stage there is nothing to suggest that this is a service issue. Valentino is willing to put that in writing, and to provide an excellent testimonial for us as a company and indeed for Claude himself. They've told us that it's a matter of economic necessity. Valentino was at pains to make that very clear.'

I pause. Tristan has his arms crossed again and is leaning back in his seat, shaking his head. Jean is looking down at his spreadsheet, elbows on the table, hands on his forehead. Only Marine looks calm, sitting up in her chair, her face impassive.

'I don't know why they didn't tell us sooner,' I continue. 'And of course there will be a thorough investigation of the handling of the account. But I'm not willing to leap to conclusions or solutions without carefully considering all the possibilities. We all know how important TKG are. I'm well aware that whatever solution we come up with needs to preserve their interest in us. But I will not have a scapegoat. Let me make it perfectly clear, we will do the right thing here, not necessarily the easiest thing.'

Everyone is silent, and I make eye-contact with each of them, ending with Tristan. The sun is streaming in through the plate glass window and, as Tristan looks away, I look out at the Eiffel Tower, tall and erect in the middle distance. I feel a sudden wave of tiredness and my head begins to ache.

'I want us all to give serious thought to this over the coming week,' I say. 'I'm scheduling a meeting for next Friday and I'd like fully-costed proposals on my desk by close of business Thursday please.' I feel no relief at having concluded the meeting. 'Jean,' I say, 'will you ask Claude to come to my office in half an hour's time please. And Tristan...?' He flicks me a nasty look. 'My office. Now.'

Insomnia

2.10 I return from the kitchen with a glass of water. Why did I not get sleeping tablets? Perhaps I should read. That would just wake me up further. Perhaps I should work. I wouldn't be able to concentrate.

3.00 Biggest client, lost, pathetic contingency fund, no revenue from the Luxembourg service, paid ourselves too much in dividends, irresponsible decision making, why did I listen to them, failed to future-proof the company, how to avoid redundancies, bigger shareholders too powerful, François won't let go, selling off the business, TKG Associates, precarious economy, lack of autonomy, Theo-Paul, Ardash, Father! Father! I grab the glass from the bed-table, hurl it at the wall; TRISTAN FUCKING PLOUM!

Paris—Ile Saint Louis

Dear Ardash
Too formal.

Hi Ardash
Too chatty.

Ardash
Too cold.

I breathe out through pursed lips while looking up at the ceiling, noting with annoyance a cobweb nestling in a corner. It's Saturday morning and since coming back from Toledo my anxiety about whether or not to tell Ardash about Jorge and that disgraceful night has been mounting to a point where unless I purge it, it will erupt into a surge of chaotic emotion.

We haven't spoken since before I went to Spain and I sit here now in my apartment, a cup of coffee cooling beside me, trying to compose an email. I hate the fact of how I feel, but our honesty seems false unless we are—or perhaps unless I am—completely open.

Hesitating at the screen, I tell myself that in spite of his questions Ardash isn't interested in my lovers. Lovers! The word is hardly appropriate for what happened with Jorge. I feel my face colouring as fractured images flit through my mind; scrambling out of clothes, the smell of unfamiliar sweat, his naked body on mine...

The blank email in front of me is defying me to practise too shameful an honesty. Maybe I should forget the night ever happened and never think of it again? And certainly never speak of it. But that won't cure my feeling of having been deceptive. *This is intolerable.* I put down my cup and try again.

Bonjour, Ardash

I know you probably don't want to know, but there is something I feel I must tell you.

I pause, my fingers over the keys. This isn't the kind of thing you should tell someone you care about in an email. If I'm to tell him at all, I should do the right thing and tell him in person. He'll certainly get angry. 'That I can handle,' I say out loud, my lips moving to a half smile as I think back to the frenzied night of love-making we'd had after I'd told him I was going to Stockholm with Theo-Paul. No, his anger isn't the point.

I wonder as I stand and open the balcony doors to a rush of traffic noise, whether his London lover has lovers of her own. A fresh breeze stirs the curtains, and as I stare up at the puffs of cloud scudding across the sky, I imagine her, calm, in control, without the need to confess. Part of me would like to meet her, this mysterious woman who has the ability to captivate Ardash. Walking back to my desk, I wonder what he'd think if he arrived at her place in London to find both of us there waiting for him. I smile. He'd probably love it. I entertain a brief fantasy where Ardash, having let himself into her apartment, finds us there on the couch, comes and sits between us, smiles his sexy smile at each of us while starting to stoke us both on the backs of our necks... I raise my eyebrows and snort out loud.

I sit down, look back at my aborted email, and start to type:

Ardash, you rip the clothes from my defences, you are the fire that brings darkness into my life, you are the night that colours my days red.

Well, it's certainly poetic! In spite of my frustration at his contradictions, in spite of what seems like his hypocrisy, the sense of undefined danger I feel in relation to Ardash, the carnage that he wreaks in my tranquillity, the way I start to sweat when I think of him in her bed, or in mine, undoes me; demands abandon, passion, and devotion.

'I'm sorry, Father,' I say. 'This isn't a dilemma you could have helped with.'

I snort once more, this time at the idea of asking Theo-Paul for his opinion. I look for a long moment at the phone lying by my laptop. I remember Marine telling me that she's a good listener. 'Oh, for God's sake,' I say out loud. 'Grow up!' I get up from the table, grab my coffee and return to the balcony.

The breeze is flicking the water of the Seine into tiny white peaks and the air feels clear and fresh against my hot face. I inhale deeply and stretch my back and shoulders, glancing across at the geraniums opposite. They look garish and brash in the bright morning sunshine and I have the strange sense that they're mocking me. I don't know whether I can live like this. Perhaps I won't go to Stockholm after all. I feel a sudden wave of anger at both Ardash and Theo-Paul. *I have more to worry about than these two idiots.*

I turn away from the geraniums and look instead across the bridge. People are hurrying about their day. I watch two young women chatting as they stroll, their well-dressed babies content in their smart, modern pushchairs. An old couple in matching yellow shirts smile at the babies as they walk hand in hand towards the bridge. A homeless man in ancient khaki trousers folds his sleeping bag, places it neatly in front of him, and turns to gaze out across the river. *Is it just me who can't get a handle on what on earth it is they're doing with their life?*

This is ridiculous; I'm an intelligent, professional woman. I won't be made a hostage by my inability to organise my love life. I need to treat this like a business problem. What I need, I tell myself, is a strategy that will cause the least immediate damage and have the most beneficial long term effect. I flick a proud glance at the geraniums before going back inside.

At the table, I set down my empty coffee cup and nodding, delete my unfinished email with a decisive click. I will stick with my plan and go to Stockholm. I won't tell Ardash anything before I go. When I return I'll decide how I feel about him and how I feel about Theo-Paul. And then I'll consider whether or not I can continue in this way. Good, I think, opening a spreadsheet on my laptop. Now I can do the adult thing and concentrate on my work.

Achille De Quincy—Before my death

…Pauline…yes, she had an intimidating streak in her; you generally wouldn't want to cross her. But she had a powerful sense of fun to match, soft, playful, you might even say. It damned near undid me at times. On our best days, the three of us, Pauline, me and the girl would fit so well, you'd think we were parts of a three piece jigsaw, we only made sense when we were together. Even on our worst days, passionate she was and fully human, all lioness strength, fierce love...

Well, there's an end to it. I'm not going to say any more about Pauline than that. God knows it's more than I've said since she … Since she died. Other than it's a terrible thing to lose a wife and a terrible thing to lose a mother that way…

It changed our girl. There, I've said it, it was that which changed her. How could it not? When it comes for a woman that young, death wears hob-nailed boots and it doesn't tread lightly.

As for the girl… Well, it was as though her mother walked off hand in hand with death taking the joyful part of our daughter with her.

Stockholm

Gamla Stan looks washed and clean in the late morning sunshine and I'm forcing myself to enjoy watching the swans glide about on the chilly Baltic Sea. I remember being here one February a few years ago when the sea was frozen, and the swans skidded and flopped about on top of the ice. It's mild here now, the early autumn breeze not yet giving up its summer warmth, but still, the two braziers are burning cosily either side of the café door.

Theo-Paul has gone to Skansen on his bicycle. Mine rests on the wall of the Blomlåda Café where I'm drinking black coffee and eating a Lussekatt, noticing absently that the pastry's shape is reminiscent of the swans' curved necks. It begins to rain, a fine, delicate rain which mists the channel between here and Djurgarten and settles in the hair of passers-by like spider-webs. I feel lonely.

...

The Gylden Freden restaurant on Gamla Stan tinkled with conversation and I'd been pleased and surprised to get a table without a reservation.

'Have you been here before?' an American woman had asked as we were finishing our meal, her loud voice easily filling the space between our two tables.

'Yes, a few times,' Theo-Paul answered her. 'Stockholm is one of my favourite cities. How about you? Is this your first time here?'

'It's our first time in Sweden, and so far we love it. Can't say a god-damned word though. I mean, how the heck do you pronounce the name of this restaurant for instance?' The woman turned her chair the better to talk with Theo-Paul.

'Den *Gyl*-dene *Fre*-den,' her companion said glancing up from his meatballs. It was the first we'd heard him speak. 'It means golden peace.' The woman ignored him.

'How long are you guys here for?

'Just for the weekend,' Theo-Paul answered. 'We're off home to Paris tomorrow night. How about you?'

'You guys are so lucky being able to flit about to so many different countries for the weekend,' the woman answered. 'I'm Rita by the way.' She thrust her hand out to Theo-Paul. 'And this here is Greg, my husband.'

We all shook hands and exchanged our names.

'Pleased to meet you both,' I said. Greg went back to eating his meatballs.

'Do you want coffee?' I asked Theo-Paul. He didn't, so I motioned to the waiter for our bill.

'Where in America are you from?' Theo-Paul turned back to the couple.

'LA?' Rita pronounced her anwer like a question which grated on my nerves.

'LA, great,' said Theo-Paul. 'I love it there, one of my favourite American cities.'

'Oh really, wow. Yeah it's a great city,' the woman replied. 'We're in Hollywood.'

'Wow,' said Theo-Paul.' I glanced up at him with a quizzical look—it was the first time I'd ever heard him use the word 'wow'. He ignored my smile.

'Well, I think we're about ready to go,' I said, having punched my code into the card-machine the waiter had proffered. 'Nice to meet you both.' I moved my chair back to stand up. 'Enjoy the rest of your trip.'

'Hey,' said Rita to Theo-Paul, ignoring me. 'Have you been to Kvarnen? It's a bar over on Sodermalm.'

'I don't know it,' said Theo-Paul. 'Why, are you two planning on heading there?

'Sure thing,' said Rita. 'Wanna come along?'

*

213

Kvarnen was crowded with people, mostly twenty-somethings, but with a few older men leaning against the bar. Jorge flashed into my mind, and I shoved him resolutely out. After pushing our way through the crowd, we were lucky enough to grab a table by the window, as a loud group of youngsters got up to leave. I slid in next to Rita while Theo-Paul and Greg sat opposite. A waitress arrived almost immediately and Theo-Paul, Rita and Greg ordered beers. I ordered a glass of 2009 Interkardinal and hoped I wouldn't regret it. I slipped off my jacket.

'What do you do Rita?' I asked over the hubbub of conversation.

'Actually, I'm in the movie business,' she answered, taking off her own jacket.

'Wow!' said Theo-Paul. I raised an eyebrow at him. 'Really? Are you an actress?'

'I sure am,' Rita answered, turning to Theo-Paul. 'Mainly small parts for now, but I'm getting a few bigger roles?' Again her statement was spoken like a question and I cringed inwardly. Our drinks arrived and we clinked our glasses. 'Cheers,' Theo-Paul said and we all took a sip. My wine was surprisingly good. Greg was staring out of the window into the dark street.

'And what about you Greg?' I asked. He looked startled.

'Me? Oh, I'm an engineer,' he said turning to face us. Theo-Paul looked at him, clearly intrigued.

'Really, that's interesting,' I said. 'What industry do you work in?'

'Yeah,' said Rita, before Greg could answer. 'He designs metal parts for alarm systems at my dad's electronics company. My dad gave him the job. Greg was bumming around before that, wondering what to do with his expensive college education weren't you Greg, honey?' Greg took a swig of his beer.

'How long have you been in engineering?' Theo-Paul asked him. He was having to raise his voice to be heard above the music.

I could see that Rita was about to cut in again, and I put my hand lightly on her arm.

'Rita, do you do a lot of travelling?' I asked her as Theo-Paul continued to talk with Greg.

Her response was a series of staccato sentences articulated like questions and as she spoke, she repeatedly glanced across the table to Theo-Paul.

'Isn't this place great?' she said to him the instant Greg finished his sentence.

'It really is,' Theo-Paul replied. He was looking around at the youngsters, laughing and talking at tables and along the central bar. I followed his gaze, wondering what on earth I was doing here.

Rita stretched her hands above her head and pushed her ample breasts forward in Theo-Paul's direction. Greg turned to stare out of the window. Theo-Paul gawped.

'Wow,' he said.

Sitting outside the Blomlåda Café, I sip the last of my coffee and think about what to do with my day. I look past the swans and the little boats, across the channel to the green slopes of Djurgarten and think of Theo-Paul on his bicycle at Skansen. I'm glad I didn't change my mind and go with him. The rain is coming down steadily now and I am not inclined to leave the café. As cars swish past I watch the spray from their wheels shimmering in the morning sunlight and wonder whether to go inside. But glancing up at the grey-blue sky I decide to stay where I am, warm and dry under the canopy by the brazier. I hope, as I spot the waitress and motion to her, that the rain will stop soon so that I can go for a ride around Sodermalm. I order another coffee and smile to myself as I think of Theo-Paul getting wet on his bicycle.

215

An old woman arrives and she shakes out her umbrella and seats herself at a table near mine. I watch with vague interest as she takes off her lavender scarf, folds it carefully and makes herself comfortable by the other brazier. I prepare to nod and smile at her but she doesn't look at me, instead settling her gnarled hands on the table and gazing out across the water. The waitress arrives with my coffee and takes the old woman's order which she gives without making eye contact. I study her surreptitiously as I sip. Her grey hair is pulled back into a loose bun, her rheumy blue eyes staring out of a face that seems to have the lines and creases of her whole history etched into her powder-pink skin. She doesn't look around or glance at her watch and it's clear that she isn't waiting for anyone. As she stares steadily ahead, her expression is one of vacant peace, as though she inhabits her aloneness so closely, so intimately that she's not even aware of it. I follow the woman's gaze out to the misty grey of the Baltic and I feel my aloneness intensified by the fact that she doesn't feel hers. I need to speak with Ardash.

'What's your problem?' Theo-Paul had said, 'we weren't away for that long.'

'Long enough for Greg and I to finish two more drinks and for me to listen to the entire story of his failing marriage,' I barked.

Katarinavägen was deserted and the sound of my shoes echoed into the night as we walked back from Sodermalm to our hotel on Gamla Stan. We were both a little drunk and I wished we weren't.

'The point is, Theo-Paul,' I said. 'I came here with you in order to spend some time together. I didn't expect to be left in some bar with a stranger while you pursue his wife.'

'Oh come on,' Theo-Paul drawled, 'I wasn't pursuing her.'

I shook my head. 'Seriously Theo-Paul,' I said, 'what did you think you were doing, going off with her like that?'

'We were talking, that's all.'

'Then why didn't you come back to the table so we could all talk together?' Theo-Paul shrugged.

'Why didn't you come and talk to us?' he said.

'Because I was at our table with her husband!' I exclaimed. I was aware of the shrillness of my voice in the silence of the empty street but I didn't care. Neither of us spoke for a while as we walked.

'You know, Theo-Paul,' I said, 'I'm not sure what you and I are about. Did you invite me here as a friend or as a lover?'

I knew it was the wrong time to have this conversation but my anger and the fact that I was drunk spurred me on. Theo-Paul didn't answer straight away.

'I don't understand you,' he said eventually, stopping and turning to face me. 'You're distant one day and possessive the next. One minute you make a great show of asserting your freedom and your independence which are so damned important to you, as you often remind me, but then you expect me to behave as though we're a goddamned couple. I just don't get you.'

I almost laughed at the irony of what he'd said.

'Rita does that kind of thing all the time,' I said meanly.

'What kind of thing?' Theo-Paul sounded sulky.

'Going off with strange men in bars. Greg told me.'

'Oh, did he.' It was a statement rather than a question.

'I asked him what he thought about her going off with you and not coming back. He said he's used to it.' Theo-Paul didn't respond. 'He asked me what I thought. I told him it was none of my business because you and I are both single. He told me to stay that way. That marriage is over-rated. And you know what? If that's how marriage ends up, I'm inclined to agree.'

His phone rings for a long time and I'm about to give in to despondency and press 'end call' when Ardash answers.

217

'I need to be with you,' I say.

'Then why aren't you?'

'You know why.'

Silence. I wonder whether the old woman can understand our conversation, but she's staring resolutely out across the channel. Rain is still misting the view and I can only just make out the blurred shapes of the trees on Djurgarten.

'Ardash...' I say, pulling my jacket more tightly around my shoulders. 'I want to talk with you. Properly talk I mean, not on the phone.'

'Don't we always talk properly?' I can't tell his mood from his voice.

'I'd like to talk about us,' I say. 'About you and me—our relationship.'

'Be careful,' he replies.

'Look, I don't want to play games,' I sigh. 'There are things I want to say to you. And things I want to ask. Let's plan some time together. Soon.'

Paris, Ile Saint Louis and Les Halles

But we don't manage to get any time together. Ardash is working on securing an important new contract and has a lot of work to do before going back to Mumbai to finalise the detail. I wonder whether he'll find the time to see his other lover first, but of course, I don't ask. I still can't decide whether our relationship is over or just beginning. All I know for now is that things can't stay as they are. He'd phoned to tell me about his trip to Mumbai.

'It's potentially a major contract,' he said. 'I've been asked to work on certain aspects of my proposal and then to go back to Mumbai next week and hopefully seal the deal. I'm going to be tied up until I get back.'

For some reason, at that very point the fragile membrane that had been barely covering my emotional state ruptured and released a wave of pent up anguish.

'Ardash,' I whispered, biting back the tears, 'I so want to be with you.'

There it was; a simple, undeniable truth. The words were shocking, both because I'd voiced them, and because I realised what they meant.

'You were right,' Ardash said quietly. 'We need to talk.'

I took a deep breath and paused to recover my composure, holding the phone away from my ear with one hand and flicking tears from my cheeks with the other.

'You know Ardash,' I said, bringing the phone back and struggling to keep my voice even. 'I think it's a good thing I won't be seeing you for a while. I… I want you too much. I know that isn't good for either of us. So many things have happened recently, not just Stockholm…' I paused, thinking about what happened with Jorge in Toledo. Ardash too, remained silent.

'I don't want this… this needy part to dictate to me,' I said eventually. 'I want to be clear and sure about what it is that I want. And what I don't want.'

'We'll talk,' Ardash replied. 'As soon as I'm back from Mumbai.'

My own work is consuming me. All week before I went to Stockholm, I worked late in the office.

'You know, with this Madrid situation… we'll have a fight on our hands if we want to avoid redundancies,' Marine had said. 'Tristan will never go for postponing the Mumbai expansion. I think he sees it as a way to redeem himself over the fact that his last project hasn't been the roaring success he predicted.'

And to secure TKG's interest in him, I thought grimly. I had to speak to François.

'I tell you what,' he said on the phone, 'I need to come into town to collect my new glasses. Why don't we meet at the Les Halles Novotel tomorrow, late afternoon? They know how to mix a proper gin and tonic there.'

I leave the office early and decide to walk the forty minutes to the hotel. I walk fast, enjoying the clack of my heels on the pavement and the autumn breeze, fresh against my face. As I negotiate the busy street, I try to bolster myself for the meeting. I think about that other time I met François at the Les Halles Novotel, three years ago. I'd felt a similar sense of anticipation, but for a very different reason, and that time I'd left with a job offer and an exciting opportunity to consider. Now, all I have is bad news and a growing sense of failure.

As I round the bend into Boulevard St Michel, I see a beggar sitting in front of a souvenir shop, his head down and his hand outstretched. People are hurrying past, pretending they don't see him, their eyes resolutely averted. As I near the man I see he has a sign in front of him: 'Will work for food.' He is no more than about forty five and he doesn't look too dishevelled. I note his reasonable shoes, his clean jacket and neat hair. He can't have been begging for long I think, as I rummage in my handbag for my purse. I place a few Euros into his hand and the man looks up, his expression so surprised, so grateful, as though I'd handed him not a few coins but a thousand. Even so, the shadows beneath his eyes are dark with defeat and I think, as I hurry on, of how he must have agonised over his situation, how he must have gone through every possible option, over and again before it finally dawned on him that begging was his only remaining choice. I imagine his shame the first time he took to the street with his hand outstretched, offering up his humiliation and degradation like a penance. I hasten my pace to my meeting.

I arrive at the hotel before François, hot and perspiring and as I mount the steps to the raised bar area, I feel glad that I'll have some moments alone to freshen up and compose myself. I pause at the restroom and after fixing my hair, I stare at myself in the brightly lit mirror. I don't like what I see. My cheekbones are beginning to protrude, making me look gaunter than I used to, and there are dark shadows under my eyes, despite my fresh makeup. My mind flicks back to the beggar. I look away and leave the room.

I take a seat as far away from the piano as I can and hope that no one will come to play it. François arrives shortly after and I watch him walking, slightly hunched across the lobby. He looks old, and I feel sorry for the bad news I have. *He doesn't deserve this.* We kiss each other on the cheeks and François looks around and hails a waiter.

'Good to see you,' he says. 'Although I'm guessing you don't have good news for me.' He sounds guarded and there's a hard look on his face as he takes off his coat and sits down. *Tristan*, I think.

'Coffee,' he says curtly to the waiter who has hurried over. I nod my agreement. François glances at his watch. 'Let's start shall we, I don't have long.'

I begin to outline the Madrid situation.

'We need to act,' I say, 'The contingency fund won't cover the loss. And Tristan's project has yet to realise any significant income. He's unable to say when it will. As you know, that was to be an important revenue stream for us.'

The waiter arrives with our coffee and a little dish of biscuits which François pushes away. I continue.

'The only two ways forward are either postponing the Mumbai project, or redundancies,' I say. 'As much as I want to expand into India, it seems to me that we have no choice but to put it back.'

François picks up his coffee and shakes his head.

'Tristan told me that was your plan,' he says. 'And he's right. We can't possibly postpone Mumbai. It would screw up the acquisition; you said it yourself, it's one of the major reasons for TKG's interest in us.'

I go to speak, but François puts up a hand. 'Tristan has a right to express his views,' he says. 'And not to receive a dressing down for doing so.'

'A dressing down?' I don't bother to hide my anger. 'So he came running to you did he?'

'He gave me an account of the meeting, and of your... little talk with him after.'

My mind flashes back to Tristan, red-faced and silent in my office. 'You will not speak like that in a meeting again,' I'd told him.

Fearing I'll say something I'll regret, I pause. François thinks better of refusing the biscuits, grabs one and places it whole in his mouth.

'Of course Tristan can express his views,' I say at last. 'But respectfully. And I won't have a witch-hunt.'

'Don't you have a meeting with TKG next month?' François says. I can see he doesn't want an argument.

'Yes I do,' I say. 'But the way I see it, selling the business isn't our only consideration here. People's livelihoods are at stake.'

François narrows his eyes and gives me a long, level look.

'I'm surprised at you,' he says at length. 'Surprised and disappointed. Your job is to secure the long term survival of the company. The company I spent more than a decade building. Sometimes that involves taking tough decisions. I shouldn't have to tell you that.'

The injustice of what François has said provokes renewed rage, and I bite down hard on my bottom lip. I want to yell. *The contingency fund?* Instead, I lean back in my seat, fold my arms, then, not wanting to look defensive, unfold them again. I compose my reply carefully.

'François,' I say, after taking a deep breath. 'The situation with Madrid would have been different had Tristan's initiative in Luxembourg brought in his predicted revenue, or even if we had a sensible contingency fund to fall back on. But neither of those being the case, this is my proposal. The loss of Madrid won't hit us until later. We can defer the India expansion, at least until after this financial year, and refocus Tristan on his original project. I plan to shift across Claude and two others and get that revenue stream up and running this quarter. That way, no one loses their job and we're not out on a limb with the Mumbai set-up eating into our profits.' I pause once more. 'Of course,' I continue, 'this would, in all likelihood mean the end of TKG's interest in us.'

François replaces his cup in its saucer and gazes past me. I watch him, the reddish pouches bulging under his eyes and the little purple threads in his nose, realising as he shakes his head that I'm looking at a tired old man.

'You know you've always had my full confidence,' he says at last. 'I appointed you with good reason and you haven't let me down. But I have to say, I don't think what you're proposing is the right thing. I don't want to overrule you, in spite of what Tristan wants. But I'm not willing to go along with any proposal that will interfere with our plans to sell the business. You've got my backing if you can promise me that. And, you'll have to convince the board to accept your plan.' He levels a hard look at me. 'The entire board.'

Achille De Quincy—Before my death

...the girl... I don't know if I'm awake or asleep, remembering or dreaming.

...the girl took a different path towards the woman she would become. An altogether more solitary, more driven path. It was as though at the age of three, she'd looked into the centre of power itself, and had seen herself defenceless against the absurd and illogical hand of fate. Maybe it was my fault, I've considered that, god knows I have. After Pauline...after Pauline died, I barely knew how to manage my own existence, never mind how to care for a three year old who wants to know when her Mummy is coming back.

'But where is she, Papa?' she kept asking. 'Why can't she come home?' She was both too young and too old for her mother's death, and it damn near broke me.

Those were the blackest days. Back then, survival was the best I could do, and I won't deny it, there were days when I knelt there by the grave, the girl's tiny hand in mine and I wished us both into that pit with my poor Pauline. But we remained, the girl and me, together and alone, and there was I, both mother and father now, to this confused and sorrowing little thing. I swore to my Pauline, there and then at her graveside, in the sight of all those hard-faced angels and saints, that no-one, NO-ONE would ever take our girl away from me.

Paris, Ile Saint Louis

'A break? A break from what? It was one silly misunderstanding, I don't know what you're getting all het up about!'

I'd arrived at Lutetia's before him and I chose a quiet table in the corner of the café. The usual waiter was there and he nodded at me as I arrived, with a deferential 'Bonsoir, Madame.' I wondered with a smile at what point I'd graduated from being Mademoiselle to Madame. 'Certainly not recently, Father,' I said silently as I took off my jacket and made myself comfortable.

'And will Monsieur be joining you?' The waiter spoke discreetly and I smiled at him. 'Yes,' I replied, 'but we won't be dining this evening.' He nodded, collected the cutlery from the table and left. Moments later a taxi drew up outside and I watched Theo-Paul heave himself out of the back seat and take out his wallet to pay the driver. A fine rain had begun and I watched him squint up into the sky and frown just as all the street lights flicked on.

'You never walk much, do you?' I said as he arrived at our table and sat down heavily after kissing me on each cheek.

'Walk?' he exclaimed, as though I'd asked him to swim here up the Seine. 'Why on earth would I want to do that?' He picked up the menu and flipped it open at the wine list. 'Pomerol?'

'No,' I answered. 'Just tea for me thanks.'

Below my apartment, the Saturday morning traffic purrs as I sip my coffee and stare at the screen of my lap top. I've been refining my plan, switching between spreadsheets and stabbing the buttons on my calculator for the past hour, and the numbers are beginning to detach themselves from their context. My head hurts and I don't know if I'm

226

making progress or not. I put my elbows on the table and lean my head on my hands. I try and fail as I rub my throbbing temples to remember the last time I had a good night's sleep. I wonder whether I'm becoming addicted to painkillers. Flicking a contemptuous look at the screen, I muse that previously I would have talked through my plan with Theo-Paul but after what happened in Stockholm, I've had no desire to be in his company.

Last week, though, unsettled by how much his behaviour with the American woman affected me, I'd called him.

'We need to talk,' I'd said. 'Meet me at Lutetia's.'

'Theo-Paul, listen, I asked you to meet me here because I have something to say.'

He had capitulated and ordered two cups of tea instead of wine. He picked his up now and eyed me warily as he blew across its surface.

'Alright then,' he said. 'I'm all ears.'

'Okay,' I began. 'The thing is, I didn't like what you did in Stockholm. I made that clear at the time. We both said our piece and I don't want to go over it again any more than you do. But that isn't the point.' I paused and looked at him.

'So what is the point?'

His voice was bordering on sulky, but I ignored it. I put my cup down in its saucer.

'Look. What happened made me think about you and me. It's not the fact that you went off with another woman that bothers me.' He looked like he wanted to cut in but I continued. 'It's more than that. What happened there has made me think about what we are, and what we're not. I think I've come to some kind of impasse. In fact I think our relationship has come to an impasse.'

'Impasse? What impasse?' Theo-Paul slopped tea into his saucer as he put down his cup. 'You and I are great

227

together. You know that!' I saw the waiter flick a look at us, and gestured to Theo-Paul to keep his voice down.

'What I'm saying,' I said quietly. 'is that I'm taking some time alone to think things through.'

Theo-Paul is true to his word and doesn't contact me. I've worked late all week and it's once more the weekend. I'm still working but at last I close the lid of my laptop. There is nothing more I can do with my plan before Monday, so I walk to the kitchen to make a fresh pot of coffee. *Theo-Paul and Ardash*, I think, shaking my head. What a mess. Is it loneliness or relief I wonder, popping a pain-killer out of its bubble, that makes the day seem so much longer? But whatever I feel, I know that taking a break from them both is the right thing to do. *'Father,'* I say, swallowing the tablet with some water, *'I feel like an adolescent.'* I rub my eyes and stretch my back before spooning fresh coffee into the cafetière.

Back in the salon, curled on the sofa with a steaming mug of coffee, the weekend stretches aimlessly. The thought of two days with nothing to punctuate them brings back memories of afternoons with my father.

'I'll be over at four,' he'd call me to say, and I'd smile at the fact that his routine only varied if mine did. I look at my phone on the table and force myself to push away the thought. Instead I think about Ardash. He'll be back from Mumbai soon. He may even be back already. *No*, I say out loud. I grab the remote control, click on the television, and spend the next hour watching a news programme.

When it ends, I yawn widely, stretch out on the sofa and contemplate flicking though the channels to find an old black and white film but the thought doesn't inspire me, and a pang of annoyance bites at my lack of motivation.

'Perhaps, Father,' I say, *'it's time to sort out your affairs.'* Affairs. What an odd word. I think back to after the funeral, when my aunts and cousins had congregated at my father's

apartment to drink tea, eat cake and eye his furniture. 'I've always loved this dresser,' my Aunt Constance had said, running a liver spotted hand over the dark wood. 'You will call dear, won't you, when you decide to clear his things?' *Clear his things.* I know that at some point I'm going to have to do that, as well as deciding what to do about his apartment. 'Not today,' I say out loud, and reach for the TV remote control. But before I press the button, my mobile phone rings, making me jump. I get up and look at the display.

'It's you,' I say.

'It's me,' he replies. 'Have dinner with me this evening. There's a new place on Rue de la Roquette. It has excellent reviews.' I go to speak but he cuts across me. 'It's time to talk. No ifs or buts, I'll be at your place at eight. Wear something nice.' I stand and take the phone out onto the balcony. A fresh breeze is blowing and I can hear the commentary from a tourist boat as it cruises up the Seine towards the Eiffel Tower. Suddenly the weekend has a point to it and I automatically start to think about what I might wear. I go to speak, but glancing up at the geraniums I stop myself, as I catch sight of the woman leaving her balcony.

'Look,' I say, letting just enough resolve into the moment. 'I'm not going to have dinner with you tonight.'

He starts to speak but I cut across before I can change my mind.

'No, just listen.' The woman has left her balcony doors open and I can see her shadow moving around inside. I take a deep breath.

'I wasn't planning on saying this on the phone, but I think it's best. The thing is, I'm not sure whether what we have is good for me—for us. I'm not necessarily saying our relationship is over, but I want you to know that there's a strong possibility of that.'

He makes a sound as though he's breathing out through pursed lips. 'I've been thinking things through as well,' he says quietly.

'Look ...' I begin, but he cuts me off.

'I've listened to you, now please, hear me out. I was going to wait until tonight, but ...well, since you're being as stubborn as ever, here goes. We know each other, warts and all. We're good together. And you're right, what we have is ... I mean, I don't know either, whether we're friends, more than friends. But there's a simple way to fix that.' He pauses for a moment. 'I was going to put the question to you tonight, but ...'

I close my eyes and hold the phone away from my ear. *Why now, Theo-Paul?*

Paris, a Café near Bastille, and the Montparnasse Tower

'I have something to ask you, and you may not want to discuss it, but I'd really appreciate your honesty.'

Afternoon shoppers are darting under the awning to get out of the sudden downpour and thunder rolls and booms in the distance as a flash of lightning momentarily casts the faces of the people around us into sharp relief. I pull my jacket around me and look up warily, wondering what is coming next.

The call had surprised me as I'd been cleaning the fridge, having eaten an early lunch of stale croissant and old cheese. The thought of food shopping was less than appealing and I had a vague plan to eat alone at Lutetia's later on that evening, if I could be bothered to dress. I'd been wondering yet again whether I had the strength to go to my father's apartment and start sorting out his things. I snorted. *'How am I going to manage that, Father'* I said, *'if I can't even manage the shopping?'* I settled instead for another day of lacklustre reading and old black and white films. The fact that I had no plans to see Ardash or Theo-Paul didn't tempt me to interrupt my apathy when the phone rang and I resolutely ignored its incessant buzzing. I waited for a follow-up text and felt relieved when it didn't arrive.

Ten minutes later the phone rang again. I felt ready to switch the damn thing off when a glance at the display told me that it wasn't Theo-Paul or Ardash, but Marine. I hesitated, flicking a look at the TV which at that moment was showing a news item picturing a line of homeless people queuing outside a Paris soup kitchen. I answered my phone. To my surprise, Marine's invitation to meet her for afternoon coffee actually felt like a welcome relief.

'I thought you might like some company,' she said. 'And I'd certainly like to get out of the apartment for a while.'

I actually find myself relaxing into the gentle sway of conversation with her. We've been at the cosy little café off Rue Saint-Antoine for almost an hour, not wanting to venture out into the rain. Marine has been telling me about her son in Troyes who has girlfriend problems.

'You wouldn't believe it, considering how Theo-Paul is, but Marcel is such a sensitive boy. Even though he's in his twenties, I sometimes wonder if it was the right thing for me to move away. I'm going down for a weekend soon. I wonder if François still has that old cottage you used to use?'

I glance up at her sharply at her mention of the cottage, but Marine continues talking about her son, and I relax, listening and nodding and making affirmative sounds every now and then. The rain drums noisily on the awning and I stare into my *allongé*, stirring it absently with a little wooden spatula.

'It's such a worry,' Marine is saying. 'I know you can't solve their problems for them, you have to let them grow up, but it isn't easy, they're always your babies at heart.' She looks at me. 'You never had children,' she says, a statement rather than a question, but I can see that she expects me to respond. I simply shake my head. 'Well,' she continues 'it's good to have someone to talk it through with. Theo-Paul is no good at this kind of thing.'

I look at Marine curiously. Does she think that she and I are friends, I wonder, with a sudden pang of guilt. But then, would it cost me so much to be a bit friendlier with her? I watch two women rush in, laughing companionably as they shake out their umbrellas and take off their wet coats. They sit down at the next table, and one of the women rolls her eyes at us in complicit astonishment at the weather.

'It's an utter deluge out there!' she says, as her friend hands her a menu. I smile at her and feel a little wave of warmth towards Marine.

But now she has something she wants to ask me. 'I'd really appreciate your honesty.' Marine looks at me for a moment and I can't discern from her expression what she is going to say. I really don't want to have any kind of conversation about Theo-Paul and I look back at her warily.

'Okay,' I say hesitantly, 'go on.'

She takes a sip of her coffee before setting the cup down firmly in its saucer.

'Alright,' she says, 'the thing is this: I'm not happy about this potential acquisition by TKG. Redundancies are inevitable now, as far as I can see. I know what you've said in the meetings. But I'd like to know how you really *feel* about it all?'

The previous week, the board had met to decide how we move forward following the loss of the Madrid client. The fact that our only two options remained delaying the Mumbai project or effecting redundancies had been occupying my days and disrupting my nights, and I'd arrived at the meeting exhausted but ready to fight. As it happened, I didn't have to.

'Absolutely not, no way!' Predictably, Tristan's response to delaying the India expansion had been unequivocal.

'Well I'm not going to sit here and allow redundancies,' Marine had countered with equal fervour. 'And let's not forget that you were dead set against Mumbai when it was first suggested!'

Tristan ignored Marine's last statement. 'You're not seeing the bigger picture,' he barked. 'You'd do well to remember it's the future of this company we're talking about and have the guts to do what we have to, to safeguard it!'

233

'The value of this business is more than just the numbers that make up the bottom line,' Marine flung back. 'Redundancies are not our only option.'

I prepared to intervene, but instead decided to see how this played out. I looked at Tristan. Sweat was dripping down his face and Jean looked nervously from him to Marine. Tristan jabbed his finger at her.

'You seem to think we're a god-damned welfare organisation!'

I hated him with a loathing so strong that my fingernails cut crescents into the palms of my hands. They were the same red as Tristan's face and I thought how fitting it would be if they met, hard.

Later, in my office, I sat in front of my laptop, staring at it blankly. Tristan had refused to budge, and even though Jean had eventually been won round, the board was split.

'I've failed, Father,' I said. The screen reflected my pale, blotchy face and I closed my eyes, trying to breathe my way through the pain behind them. My head sank to my hands. A knock startled me and I jerked up in surprise. Marine had put her head round the door.

'Not now Marine,' I snapped. She hesitated momentarily but nodded and left. *Okay*, I said to the screen. I started to compose an email. Half an hour, and three versions later, I read and re-read what I'd written:

Dear François

I want to put on record my concerns about the direction the company is taking. The proposed acquisition by TKG Associates hinges in large part on our expansion into India which, as you know, I would prefer to delay. The reasons for my concerns are our reduced financial stability following the loss of a major client, and the lack of any meaningful revenue from our Luxembourg project. These factors, coupled with the fact that our contingency budget is insufficient, mean that we have only two alternatives; to delay the India project, or to effect redundancies. I am sorry to report that the board was unable to reach a unanimous decision, which since you've insisted on that means redundancies would now be inevitable. However, I want to appeal to you in your capacities as both Chairman and the majority shareholder, to reconsider selling the business at this stage, thereby allowing us to delay the India project in order to avoid redundancies.

I nodded. Hands poised over the keyboard, I hesitated before starting to type once more. *I may as well go for it, Father*, I said. My fingers clacked fast over the keys.

When I accepted the position of CEO, I outlined a vision that put the interests of all our stakeholders, not only our shareholders at the forefront of our mission. I feel strongly that our current situation is an opportunity to test that vision and to challenge ourselves to live up to it. Whilst we still have other options, I cannot support a strategy which will result in the loss of people's livelihoods. Delaying selling the company will enable us to focus on putting the business back on a firm financial footing, retaining the loyalty and trust of our highly skilled staff. As CEO I am recommending that we delay the decision to sell, so that I may pursue my less aggressive strategy. I intend to follow this email up with a business plan that will outline the full financial implications of my proposal.

I pressed 'send'.

How do I feel about it all? Sitting here in the warm little café, our empty coffee cups in front of us, I fold my arms and look away from Marine. The rain has stopped, and fat drips are falling from the awning, plopping onto the wet terrace floor. My gaze comes to rest on a homeless woman cradling a small baby, sitting huddled in a sodden blanket in the doorway of a bank opposite. The after-rain sunshine is glowing vivid and clear, illuminating the woman's face and the stone façade of the building above her. I turn and glance at the two women at the next table. They have their heads bent closely together and are deep in conversation. I look at Marine. Her head is resting in one hand and she's looking back at me expectantly. She leans forward and reaches out to pull a long strand of hair from the shoulder of my blouse, letting it fall to the floor beside us. I watch it drift and land in a neat little curl by my seat. The tenderness and simplicity of the gesture undoes something in me and I unfold my arms, lean back and place my hands together on the table in front of us.

'Would you like a glass of wine?' I say.

'I tell you what,' Marine replies, 'let's share a carafe.'

Paris, the café near Bastille

'It's no good talking to me all the time, girl. You need to talk to someone who can answer you.' As the waiter filled our glasses from the carafe, my father's voice came to me as clear and as palpable as though he were sitting at the table with us and I turned, almost expecting to see him in his tweed jacket and hat, stroking his chin and drinking an *allongé*.

The more Marine talked though, the clearer it became that she shared my reservations about selling the company, and I found myself responding, guardedly at first, like someone learning a new language, confident of the words but hesitant to say them. I decided to share the essence of my email to François with her. She wasn't at all surprised.

'I'm glad,' she said. 'If I'm completely honest with you, I don't think it will change anything, but it is the right thing to do, and it has to come from you. It's a ridiculous situation when the CEO's hands are tied because a powerful shareholder has his own agenda.'

I looked at her intently. What to make of this? I wondered.

'It must be incredibly frustrating for you,' she continued. 'I know it is for me. I'm so sick of fighting.'

So it seemed it was more than just the redundancies that concerned her. And she was right of course. What she said resonated strongly with my own feelings and I was surprised to notice that I felt relieved that someone else shared my frustration.

'You know, Marine, this is actually useful. I really don't think François wants a divided board, and with two of us digging in, I think we have a decent chance of being able to sway him away from selling, at least for now.'

Marine gave me a complex look that lasted a fraction of a second too long. She sighed, and I wondered whether she'd been about to say something else. No matter, I thought. I'd already resolved to spend the next day considering how best to use Marine's support for leverage. Certainly, I would send a follow-up email to François, indicating the inevitability of a split board should he persist with his plan to sell. It will be tricky not letting that sound like a threat, I thought. I'd have to think carefully about the wording. I glanced up as two middle aged men arrived at the café wearing weekend casuals and good shoes. They nodded towards us. 'Bonsoir,' one of them said. He had a pink face and as he removed his jacket I saw that the arms of his shirt were damp with sweat. Tristan's face flashed into my mind. 'Bonsoir,' Marine replied politely but without interest. I looked back at her as the men continued inside.

'I have to admit, it's getting harder and harder for me to deal with Tristan,' I said without thinking, and immediately regretted it. I put my wine glass down. At least I hadn't said how I lay awake at night fantasising about walloping that smug face of his as soon as he began his next self-important diatribe. 'We simply don't share the same values …' I trailed off, aware of how limp that sounded. But Marine seemed to warm to this theme and she nodded emphatically.

'I'm not surprised,' she replied. 'He's fucking insufferable at times. And it's clear to anyone with eyes and ears that you and he simply aren't on the same page.' She looked at me curiously. 'You know…' she hesitated, bringing her two hands up under her chin, 'I've sometimes wondered if it's only work-related differences, or whether there's something more that's caused this … this animosity between you.'

Marine pursed her lips. Troyes flashed into my mind, but I didn't answer. I stared down at my wine and flicked the glass with my finger, relieved when she changed her track.

'In any case,' she continued, 'I'm mightily pleased he didn't get the CEO position. I made Theo-Paul celebrate with me when you got the job. We raised a glass to you!'

238

She lifted her glass to me now. Hearing Theo-Paul's name made me wonder whether I was crawling into a thorny thicket, and as I thought with unease about being questioned about him, or about Tristan and Troyes, I decided it was a good time to leave. I looked around for the waiter to call for the bill. Marine replaced her empty glass on the table and looked at me for some moments as though considering something. The waiter arrived, but before I could speak to him, Marine indicated the empty glasses. 'Yes please,' she said decisively. The waiter flexed his arm out straight before refilling our glasses from the carafe with a flourish. He winked at Marine. I sighed.

'Marine ...' I started to say when he had gone, leaving us with a little dish of peanuts. I intended to tell her that I had somewhere to be but she cut across me.

'Look,' she said, 'I've got something to tell you. Something important.' I cringed inwardly, regretting that I hadn't managed to escape. *One glass of wine, and I'm her confidante!*

'This must go no further than the two of us, at this point,' she said. 'I know I can trust you.' I took a handful of peanuts and resigned myself to hearing what it was she had to confess.

'Of course,' I replied. I hoped she didn't detect the hesitancy in my voice. I imagined what was coming was some sort of romantic admission. *Maybe it's about Theo-Paul!* I felt my face flush and wondered how I'd react.

'Marine, is this about Theo-Paul?' I said, before I could stop myself.

'God, no!' She looked at me curiously. 'You know, I am aware of your...friendship...with him.' I didn't reply.

'No, it's nothing like that,' she continued. 'It's something I've been thinking over for some time. And...' she hesitated. 'And I really do need your trust here. I'm talking to you as a friend, not as my CEO.'

Oh god, I thought, am I about to be placed at the core of some complicated dilemma?

'Look, Marine,' I said, 'Are you quite sure…'

'Don't worry,' she cut across me. 'This doesn't compromise you in any way. But it is about work. And it's only fair I tell you.'

'Okay.' My apprehension turned to intrigue as Marine now hesitated.

'Right then. Well, here it is. I warn you, it's serious…'

Paris, the café near Bastille

My head jerked up and my hand, hovering over the peanuts, froze. My shock struck me silent.

'My God, Marine,' I said eventually. 'Why?'

Marine gazed out of the terrace, into the darkening street. A light rain had begun to fall once more and people were putting up their umbrellas and hurrying along the pavement. The homeless woman across the road was no longer in the doorway of the bank, and I regretted not having given her a few coins.

'I've had a good career here,' she said, turning back to me. 'I've worked for François for a long time and I owe him a lot, I won't deny that. But … I've made up my mind. I'm resigning my position on the board.'

My mind flew around all the possible reasons she could have for such a serious decision.

'But why?' I asked again, my tone betraying my incredulity. 'I thought you liked your job?'

Marine picked up the carafe and topped up our glasses of wine, immediately taking a sip from hers.

'It isn't any one thing.' As she sighed, I realised how tired she sounded. 'I'm going to be honest with you, I owe you that. I had high hopes when you were first appointed as CEO, and you outlined your vision for the company. I thought I could play a part in transforming the business. But …'

I started to speak but Marine reached out and put a hand on my arm.

'Let me finish,' she said gently. 'I've needed to say all this for a long time.' I nodded and sat back in my chair. 'I really bought into your view of how things could be' she continued. 'What you talked about, being about more than just profit-driven, valuing our people, the India expansion, Project Saucha—I thought it was courageous and progressive and I wanted to be a part of it. But I think I was the only one who did. François just wants to sell up, Tristan's agenda has always been Tristan, and Jean… well, Jean will simply go where he thinks the power lies.'

She paused, and as I let what she was saying sink in, I wondered whether Marine was trying to gauge my reaction. When I didn't say anything she continued.

'Don't get me wrong, a lot *has* changed, especially with how we treat our staff.' She shook her head. 'But it isn't enough. It's clear how things work. In order to get anything done, it's a case of either fighting your corner, or playing some clever game. There's no team-work. It's just so…so juvenile.' She paused once more. 'Call me idealistic if you like, but boards don't have to work that way. And what's happening now, with TKG and the redundancies … that sealed it for me.' She looked at me intently for a long moment. 'I've reached my ceiling of hypocrisy.'

We sat in silence. *What on earth do I say to that?* I didn't know whether to feel supported or affronted. But what she had said opened up a gulf between the Marine I thought I knew and the Marine sitting here in front of me, staring into her wine. I studied her intently, realising that before now, I'd never looked beyond the surface of her. Now, I noticed for the first time, the worry-lines around her eyes and the corners of her mouth, the shadows under her eyes. I saw how her knuckles were white from clenching and unclenching her hands, and the fact that her finger-nails were bitten to the quick. I felt how difficult this decision must have been, and wondered if she'd been having sleepless nights of her own.

A sudden memory flickered to life. Marine coming into my office one evening when we were both working late. I remembered her words exactly, as we'd stood by the window: *'The only people working at this time of night, are those interested in 'the dirty gold of the city.''* I'd thought at the time what an odd thing to say, but I hadn't asked her what she meant, and when she tried to talk to me about her concerns, I'd rebuffed her. I thought back to her coming to my office after the last board meeting, when I'd been so angry and upset, snapping at her; *'Not now Marine!'* And all those other times I'd avoided her, or put her off, how less than twenty minutes ago I'd been so keen to leave because I didn't want to hear what she had to say. *'Is it my fault, Father?'* I asked silently. My father didn't answer, but if he had, he might have said that I'd been so wrapped up in my own concerns, I'd failed to see that, far from trying to nudge herself into my life, Marine had been trying to communicate with me.

Insomnia

2.17 Father... Father, you were to me the measure of all things. Nothing separated us. There was nothing to question. The world flowed as naturally between us as rain mingles with the sea. We had no need for heart-to-hearts. It was simple. You had me and I had you. But, Father, you were just a man after all. I see you better now that I am forced to see you from outside your grave. A bereaved husband. A father doing his best. A man.

2.57 Marine is leaving. She has reached her *ceiling of hypocrisy*. She is brave. Am I? I made you a promise, Father. But still, it seems I inhabit my hypocrisy. We shouldn't always have to fight, she said. I, too, am sick of fighting.

3.40 Am I too idealistic? Is real change possible? Is my vision possible? Must I change? Something must.

4.39 Sitting in front of my laptop, a new spreadsheet glowing out at me from the screen. A cold cup of tea beside me. I rub my chin and nod slowly as I consider the numbers on the screen.

5.52 Father, we need to talk.

Paris, mainly Père Lachaise
and a dusty apartment close by

Saturday morning dawned blowy and blustery. I'd finally slept, but fitfully and I'd had one of those dreams that can't be pinned down to a definitive set of images, but gnaws and hunts and leaves you with a feeling of exhausted agitation. I was glad to get up.

Ten minutes later I stood on the balcony wrapped in a winter dressing gown, hands clasped around my morning coffee, my breath mingling with its steam. I stared up at the grey clouds moving across the sky as though they had somewhere important to be. I saw that the balcony doors opposite were open, and I felt momentary surprise that the woman's geraniums were still blooming in spite of the wintry weather. *'She must be really invested in those flowers, Father.'*

I'd been thinking about Marine's revelation all week.

'How long have you been considering this?' I'd asked her.

'It's been some months now,' she'd replied, a sad look on her face. 'You know,' she said quietly, 'I want to do something in life where I feel I'm achieving something worthwhile. I'm not prepared to go on working for an organisation that puts its shareholders first, and everyone else last.' She gave a snorting laugh. 'Even if I am one of those shareholders.' I'd looked at her in astonishment. They could have been my own words.

On my balcony, the wind was beginning to pick up and a light rain was threatening. I was reminded of the day of my father's funeral. I nodded at the geraniums before turning to go inside. *'I'll see you soon, Father,'* I said.

It felt strangely good to wander through the lanes and walkways of Père Lachaise, past the granite busts and the copper statues, the smooth marble of the head and capstones, bearing witness in the stillness of the late morning calm, to lives both known and unknown. It hadn't rained after all and as the wind settled to a light breeze which stirred the late autumn leaves, and the sunshine illuminated the faces of the angels and the saints, I felt an unexpected sense of peace, not simply because the cemetery was quiet, but because I noticed a quietness within myself. I walked on, pausing here and there, enjoying the satisfying crunch of gravel beneath my boots.

I stopped by the graveside of Marcel Proust with its simple, marble top-stone and Grecian urn, so familiar to me from visits with my father. Often on Sunday afternoons we'd stand in front of the graves, mausoleums and monuments, my face upturned, eyes squinting in the sun, the names of Hubertine Auclert, Simone Del Duca and Sophie Blanchard becoming as familiar to me as those of Moliere, Chopin, Balzac, Apollinaire. I would clutch my father's big hand tightly as I stared up at the verdigris faces of crying angels, grieving widows and impassive saints, as he told me about the lives of these men and women he so admired and whom he wanted to act as de-facto role models for me, inspiring and exciting me towards my own great works...

'There's still time,' I said, into the silence of Proust's grave. Someone had placed a bunch of arum lilies on it and I suddenly regretted that I hadn't brought flowers to lay at my father's grave. The strangeness of being here without him hit me as though I'd betrayed him somehow, and I braced myself for tears. But when I looked for that acute sense of abandonment, of bewildered panic that now accompanied me when I did anything associated with him, I realised with surprise that it had been replaced with something softer, gentler, something akin to nostalgia.

As I arrived at the little corner of the cemetery that housed my father's resting place, I saw that some of the trees by the grave were clinging with stubborn determination to a few autumn leaves. Most, however, were bare, and their branches silhouetted starkly against the blue sky created a dramatic effect. I knelt down in front of my father's head-stone and brushed away the leaves that had gathered at its base. As I did so, I felt glad I hadn't brought flowers. *They don't suit the season, Father,* I said. They'd look brash and garish for a few days and then they'd wilt and die and get lost among the fallen leaves. I traced the letters of my father's name on the cold stone, wondering how the shapes bore any relationship to the man. Perhaps they no longer do, I thought, straightening my back and sitting back on my heels. The breeze stirred the leaves and I pulled my jacket closer around my shoulders. *Well, Father,* I said, *here I am.*

I knew without my father having to answer that this wasn't where I needed to be. The walk to his apartment took less than fifteen minutes, along streets and past shops so familiar to me, I could have described them with my eyes closed: Fromagerie Celine, which, years ago had been the talk of the quarter when Celine had run off with her brother-in-law; the Artisan Boulanger where Father would buy me a single macaroon each Saturday morning, a different colour each week; the little news-paper cabin with the old proprietor who was rumoured to be gay and who always saluted his customers... the characters who added the warmth of familiarity to my childhood years.

At the apartment, I climbed the stairs slowly, counting them as I always had. 'You'll never find a flight of stairs in Paris with more than 21 steps,' my father had told me. I never have. I hesitated for a moment at the front door before turning the key in the lock, but as soon as it creaked open, I noticed the smell. Pipe tobacco and coffee. I closed my eyes and entered.

Dust motes stirred in the sudden shift of air, making me sneeze, and in the shy uncertainty of being here, in this apartment, alone in this most familiar of rooms, I sensed a self I only knew with my father. I walked across the salon and sat down in the chair I always sat in, but got quickly up again because the familiar perspective highlighted his absence. Instead, I moved to his chair and looked at the room as he saw it. It wasn't a chair I often sat in, and I gazed around as though for the first time at the huge mahogany bureau, the rosewood piano that had so confounded me as a child, the bookshelves lined with my father's treasured French classics whose names, Balzac, Zola, Baudelaire, Proust were as familiar to me as those of my aunts.

The scent of the room was so quintessentially him that I almost believed it could be possible to slip between the folds of its substance, to a time that hadn't after all disappeared, but had simply glazed over. It was as though, if I opened my eyes, I could steal back the time that separated us and, find my father sitting in his usual chair amid a swirl of tobacco smoke, pipe in hand, an allongé cooling on the end table whilst his glasses slipped down his nose as he read the headlines in Liberation. For surely, I thought, there is only one dimension that stands between him and me? Surely all that we know, all that we think we know about love, about the power of love, can enable us to transcend a lone dimension, a dimension that in any case, bears us along without ever allowing us the privilege of experiencing what lies at its heart.

I had the impression that if I sat there for long enough, some lingering essence of my father might seep into me, might if only I was open enough, porous enough, imbue me with a lifetime of love. If only I could lock myself into this lingering ghost of my father's departed *now*. But the dark centre of *now* seems always eclipsed by the memory or the anticipation of *then*, so that the actual moment, the point where we can say *here I am* melts away no sooner than the words are uttered, even as we clutch after them like a receding dream, and after all, we are left with nothing but pipe-smoke and coffee. Not even pipe smoke and coffee, but their ghosts which although ethereal and ephemeral, are still a comfort because my father has no ghost that I can recognise outside of this combination of fragrances which, whilst not my father, or even his shade, nonetheless presents him to me as powerfully, as profoundly as though he'd been awaiting my arrival in this room.

A volume of Proust's 'Swann's Way' lay open, face down on the side table. I picked it up and read the first line I saw.

"Now are the woods all black, but still the sky is blue."

'Thank you, Father,' I whispered.

Paris, Ile Saint Louis

The next day, I woke early to the sound of irritatingly loud birdsong, but realised with pleasant surprise that I'd actually slept. Not the whole night, I'd been awake until after two, but a solid few hours. I must have slept, I thought, yawning widely and stretching my arms and legs out in the warmth of the bed, because I'd dreamed. I rolled onto my back and tried to grasp at the detail before it faded, but I couldn't make sense of it... something about fire... the scene of some struggle... bridges burning ...

I showered perfunctorily, before knotting my hair into a top-bun and standing in front of the bedroom mirror. I regarded my body with detached interest, noting the way my chin was beginning to sag, the drooping flesh on the backs of my arms, my slack stomach over protruding hipbones. *A woman aging.* Once dressed I walked through to the salon and opened the balcony to let in some air. The smell of freshly baked bread wafted up from the shop below and I decided to buy a baguette.

Outside, the trees swayed in the cool, autumn breeze, sending leaves drifting to the ground. My boots clacked satisfyingly on the cobbles as I walked the short distance to the boulangerie. The baker was pleased to see me. 'Bonjour Madame,' he piped in his reedy voice. He winked at me and popped a little pink macaroon into the bag with my bread.

Back upstairs, in spite of the chilly morning air, I set the table out on the balcony, and sat there enjoying coffee and hunks of soft baguette, butter melting over the sides. I warmed my hands on the cup, and watched two homeless men by the bridge, passing a cigarette from one to the other. When it was finished one of them turned and threw the butt over the wall, into the Seine. For some reason, fragments of my dream came back to me at that moment. I still couldn't make it out...fire...some kind of ritual...and although the images were violent, the dream felt strangely inspiring. I glanced across at the geraniums, remarkably still in flower, and thought about the idea I'd had the other night

I was still thinking about it an hour later, as I sat at the desk, lap-top open at a spreadsheet. *Yes.* Breathing in deeply, I stood and stretched before walking slowly around my salon. Dust had collected on the little side tables and the statues and carvings that adorned them, and I thought about how dust and time are so intimately related. I paused at the Japanese vase, resolutely whole on its little plinth, feeling an odd sense of empathy with it. I picked it up and turned it around in my hands, the porcelain cool beneath my fingers as I touch the painted birds and trees. *I'm glad I didn't smash you.* I replaced it carefully. Walking over to the bookshelf, I ran my eyes along the rows of books, stopping at the one my father had given me: 'One Hundred Things to Do Before You Die.' I took it down from its place on the shelf and, opening it at the first page, read my father's inscription: *'Be sure to live before you die.'* The book still in my hand, I turned to get my phone.

He was clearly surprised to hear from me.

'I won't keep you,' I said, my voice business-like. 'I need to be in Troyes for a meeting next month. It's on a Monday and I'm planning on going down for the weekend. Would you like to meet me there on the Saturday?'

After the call, I sat on the sofa, staring at the book. Flicking through its pages, I glanced at images of young women sky-diving, old people ice-skating, happy-looking couples hiking up mountains. I closed the book and placed it on the table, picking up my phone once more. The outcome of my next call would be less easy to predict. I hesitated before pressing a button and sat listening to the digital purr as it rang once, twice, before being answered.

'I've had what might be either the greatest, or the craziest of ideas,' I said. 'Can we meet?'

Troyes

François' cottage, all rustic browns and oatmeals, should feel soothing and restful, but I feel anything but.

'Yes, of course,' he'd answered in surprise when I'd asked him whether I could use it. 'It's just standing there empty, after all.'

Once unpacked, my clothes neatly arranged in the big oak wardrobe, I walk to the farm-house kitchen. I smile as I set about making a pot of tea, taking in the wood-burning stove, the saucepans hanging from their pot-rail, baskets full of ancient walnuts, all so familiar to me. But I can't help thinking about what happened the last time I was here, and... *Damn it!* knock hot tea all over the counter.

Turning to find a cloth, I wonder about the wisdom of the evening I have planned. My phone rings, making me start, and I leave the spilt tea and run to the lounge where it's vibrating on the table. I look at the display, hoping he isn't calling to cancel, but it's only Marine. I'm not sure whether I feel relieved or disappointed.

'I've just got here,' she says. 'I thought I'd ring to check what time is good for you.'

'Me too,' I answer, balancing my mobile phone between my ear and my shoulder as I go back to cleaning up the tea. 'I need to run into town to pick up a few things for the weekend first, but I should be back at the cottage for 3.00. Does that sound okay?'

'Perfect,' Marine replies. 'I'm meeting my son for dinner tonight, and there are a couple of things I want to do first. Two hours or so should be long enough shouldn't it?'

'Yes two hours will be fine,' I say. 'I've got plans for this evening as well.'

I decide to walk the half hour into Troyes, enjoying the fresh autumn chill against my face as I make my way along the tree-bordered Via Agrippa and into town, along the little cobbled streets, past half-timbered houses huddling together as if for warmth, all so familiar to me. I pause to stare up at the grand, gothic Cathedral of Saint-Pierre-et-Saint-Paul, thinking about what will happen when *he* arrives. I put firmly to one side my creeping concern that my plans are ridiculous, and tell myself to focus instead on the preparations I need to make.

I've decided to make Truffade Aveyron, and stopping at a little epicerie, I buy potatoes, onions, garlic, lettuce, and a block of tome fraiche de l'Aubrac. I reject the fresh olives because they are in plastic containers, and instead buy a jar. At the wine shop next door, I buy two bottles of Sancerre. I'd told him that dinner would be simple. *'The point of the evening is to talk.'* Even so, I hesitate outside, before going back in and buying a bottle of Beaume de Venise. My shopping complete, I decide to take a taxi back to the cottage, and, walking in the direction of the taxi rank, I pass a lingerie shop. Pausing in front of the window, I take in the display of delicate, lacy underwear, filmy negligees and sexy little one piece costumes. I hesitate once again. A headless model in a provocative pose is wearing a deep purple set in what looks like pure silk. Her stockings have purple lace tops. *No*, I tell myself, repeating my mantra that the point of this evening is to talk. I turn and continue along the street.

By 4.00, Marine and I have been discussing our meeting strategy for the last hour and although I'm still not looking forward to it, I'm satisfied that she and I are at one with how we want to handle Monday's meeting. The relief at sharing the burden of my reservations is immense and I wonder again why I'd been so reticent before. I turn over the thought that perhaps I had some odd notion that sharing something of myself would make me a weaker person. Or a weaker leader.

'Okay,' I say, putting my empty tea cup onto the side-table. 'Let's sum this up. Our aim on Monday is to delay

TKG without scaring them off. We introduce the board. We share the basis of our strategy. We talk about our turnover and our margins without providing anything on paper. *We* steer the meeting and *we* ask the questions. If pushed, we talk in the most general terms about the India expansion. We make no promises. We sign nothing but a standard non-disclosure agreement. We give nothing else away, and we get another meeting date at least two months down the road to give us time. Then we'll work on François and the board regarding the redundancies.'

'We're going to have to keep a close watch on Tristan,' Marine says.

'We certainly are,' I agree. 'I met with him yesterday and I've got his agreement to our approach. It's obvious he isn't happy, but he won't mess around with this one. Too much is at stake. Having said that, I'm fully prepared, discreetly of course, to-reign-him-in.' I speak the last words slowly and deliberately, emphasising each one.

'Absolutely,' Marine says with equal conviction. 'I'm one hundred percent with you on that. And I've spoken to Jean as agreed. He's travelling down first thing Monday morning. He's clear about the approach, and I made it perfectly plain that he doesn't deviate from our steer; and that you're in the driving seat. Don't worry, we can count on him.'

'I think briefing him and Tristan separately was a good idea,' I say. 'And I must admit, I'm glad François won't be here. His wife forbade it. Apparently she said that kind of pressure would be too much for him.'

'Well, he needs to think about that, at his age.' Marine looks at me. 'You know,' she says, 'I wish we'd communicated like this before. Things might have been very different.'

Troyes

After I see Marine out, I walk back into the lounge and sit down heavily on the big old sofa. As I cast my eyes around the cosy room, with its over-stuffed armchairs flanking the huge stone fireplace, the timeworn rugs and cushions, the faded tapestries, I try to see how he will later see it. I'm suddenly struck by the thought that a trinity of life-changing choices has opened up before me. Since my father died, Theo-Paul, Ardash and my career have been my three legged stool. What will happen when one, or more, are removed? Rather than feeling panicked by this test of my courage, I feel an unexpected surge of exhilaration knowing that it is *I* who will decide my fate. Solange told me last week that according to the ancient Mayans, the 21st of December will be the end of the world. 'All sorts of transformative events are supposed to happen,' she'd said. *Very fitting,* I think.

There is nothing more I can do now to prepare for Monday's meeting and I snap my laptop shut, relieved that I can now focus on the evening ahead. I glance at my watch. There are two and a half hours before he arrives. I stand and glance around me, plump up the cushions, and clear away my laptop and papers before walking through to the kitchen to begin cooking the Truffade. My anxiety transfers itself to the knife and, *damn!* it slips as I slice the cheese, just missing my finger. Slowing down, I start to peel the potatoes. The salad takes only minutes to prepare, and while the rest is cooking I mix olive oil, white-wine vinegar and Dijon mustard for the dressing, before putting it into the fridge. The two bottles of Sancerre are chilling there and I glance again at my watch, wondering whether it's too early to drink a glass. One can't hurt, I decide and take out a bottle.

Bending to take a wine glass from the cupboard, I finally let myself think back to the last time I was here at the cottage. What happened then set in motion a chain of events that changed my life. Not only mine. *It seems that futures are forged in this place.* I flick the glass, wondering, as it resonates with a purity I don't feel, whether I should, after all, have bought the purple underwear.

Three and a half years ago, almost to the day, I'd gone directly from work to Gare de l'Est with my over-night bag. It was Friday, and as I hurried through the crowded metro, bumping and jostling along with the other commuters, I felt a wave of pleasure at the prospect of spending a weekend at the cottage. Theo-Paul had called the previous evening to ask what my plans were. I told him why I was going to Troyes.

'I'm interviewing candidates for the Finance Director post on Monday,' I said. 'We're narrowing the field down to two for François to meet. Tristan and I did the first interviews. Seriously Theo-Paul, some of them couldn't possibly have been the same people as on their CVs. In any case not what we're looking for at all.' Theo-Paul laughed.

'Always a few like that,' he said. 'Good on paper.' I smiled.

'We've whittled them down to four,' I said. 'Two women and two men, all with solid backgrounds. One of the guys is quite young for a director post, but worth seeing along with the rest. François wants to do the final interviews with us next month in Paris, so I'm going down to Troyes tonight ready for Monday.'

'Perfect!' Theo-Paul exclaimed. 'I have no plans, why don't I join you there? I could visit my son at the same time.'

'I think not Theo-Paul,' I'd laughed. 'I have plans.'

I'd always enjoyed the journey to Troyes, almost never working on the train ride, but instead creating a rare bubble of leisure which spread itself out over the journey and into the weekend beyond. I'd stock my e-reader with novels especially for these weekends. The luxury of having access to the cottage was a welcome contrast to the bustle and noise of Paris, and I thought of the place as my own retreat where I could distance myself from the hard edges of corporate life. It was an illusion of course. The only reason I had for staying at the cottage was if I had a Friday or a Monday meeting at the Troyes office, and in reality I inevitably used part of my weekends there to work. Nonetheless, perhaps because the cottage wasn't actually mine, it had the air of a cosy, country hotel.

As usual the train journey passed too quickly. I'd just reached the climax of my novel when we pulled into the station, and I snapped shut my e-reader tetchily. The taxi ride took fewer than ten minutes, and I was thinking about ordering a Chinese food delivery as I fumbled in my handbag for the key. I was keen to get back to my novel, and begin a peaceful evening of music and reading by the open fire. I was considering the merits of sweet and sour king prawns as I put my key in the lock, but as the door swung open I knew something was wrong.

I stood motionless at the threshold. There was something imperceptibly different that I couldn't quite place; a subtle change in the air, a sense that something was amiss. I realised that I was aware of a strange noise, a constant background sound coming from inside the cottage. The noise sounded so familiar, I must have heard it a thousand times, but standing there in the dark hallway, I couldn't place it at all. Very slowly, very carefully, I placed my overnight bag on the floor and listened. I heard nothing but the strange sound. I closed the front door quietly behind me, then wondered whether I should have left it open.

'*Okay,*' I said silently, my heart thumping in my chest. I took a deep breath and, bracing myself, flicked on the light-switch. Nothing seemed out of place. I positioned my keys in my hand in such a way that I could use them as a weapon if I had to, and took a few steps forward.

'Hello...?' I called, acutely aware of the trembling of my voice. 'Is there anybody here?'

Now, three and a half years later, I leave the kitchen with my glass of Sancerre and walk through to the bedroom. Opening the huge oak wardrobe door, I take out the dress I'm intending to wear and scrutinise it critically.

'You're supposed to be casual and understated,' I mutter to the beige silk folds. I frown, laying the dress on the bed and wonder whether jeans would have been a better idea. The thought makes me smile. After showering and drying my hair long and straight, I stand naked in front of the floor length mirror on the inside of the wardrobe door. I'm even thinner, I think as I run my eyes up and down my body, noting with a curious detachment my bony shoulders and protruding hip bones. My gaze comes to rest on my breasts. They've lost some of their plump roundness and I wonder whether they'd even be functional anymore. Narrowing my eyes, I consider the totality of angles and hollows that have replaced my curves. *I am no longer soft*.

Dressed and made up, I go back to the kitchen to check that everything is ready. Glancing at the clock on the wall, I see that I have only minutes to spare. Perfect, I think, taking the wine from the fridge. Even so, my anxiety at what I'm about to do makes me edgy, and I jump when at exactly 7.30 the doorbell rings. He is carrying two bottles of Argentinean Malbec which I note with a raised eyebrow. I note too, the overnight bag slung over his shoulder, which he sets down in the hallway. My heart begin to race as he kisses me formally on each cheek.

'You can leave your bag here,' I say, pointing him towards the open door of the lounge. I latch the front door behind us.

'It's been a while,' he says, placing the bottles down on the big farmhouse table and glancing around the room. I watch him taking in the big stone fireplace, the oak furniture, the deep sofa with its cosy cushions and throws.

'Beautiful place.' He shrugs off his coat and throws it over an armchair.

'I thought it might be pleasant if we made a fire,' I say, indicating the empty fireplace. 'Before we get settled, why don't you collect some wood from outside while I check on the food?'

He follows me into the kitchen, and without switching on the light, I unlock the back door and indicate a stack of chopped logs at the end of the garden. I remain inside, and move around in the semi-darkness so that I can see him through the window. I watch as, instead of collecting logs from the pile, he picks up an axe and turns it over in his hand, testing its strength and the sharpness of its blade. I stare as he straightens his back, lifts it above his head and brings it down hard into the stump of an old tree. He suddenly looks up at me and I turn away quickly, busying myself with the glasses, as he bends to collect an armful of logs.

Back in the lounge, he applies himself to making the fire.

'An aperitif?' I ask.

'Of course,' he answers without looking up.

I leave him arranging paper and twigs in the grate, and pour a little Beaume de Venise into two red Venetian glasses, setting them down on the side table. I watch him lean in close to the fireplace, his body stretched and taut as he purses his lips and blows steadily on the little flicker inside the nest of kindling. As the flames begin to grow, he feeds them progressively bigger sticks until the fire catches hold of its own life and begins to blaze. He sits back and watches his handiwork for a few moments before dusting

259

off his hands and coming to join me on the sofa. He picks up the two glasses and hands me mine.

'Let's drink to change,' he says.

'To change indeed,' I reply. We both take a long, slow sip.

'Ardash,' I say. 'I expect you'd like to know why I invited you here.'

Troyes

'Hello..?'

I'd held my breath, aware of the growing nausea in the pit of my stomach as I hesitated in the hallway, my keys at the ready, listening to the oddly familiar sound. No one had responded to my call, and I stood there, not knowing what to do next. Abruptly, the sound stopped and all of a sudden, I realised what it was. Running water! Someone had switched off a tap. Emboldened by the domestic innocence of the act, I began to creep towards the lounge, trying to keep my footsteps silent on the parquet floor. All too aware of my heart thumping in my chest, I reached out my hand and gingerly pushed open the door.

'Hello...?' I said again, edging into the lounge, the keys before me. At the same time the kitchen door on the other side of the room swung open, and the two of us came face to face across the room.

...

'I'm grateful you came. It's kind of you to travel all this way...especially since…'

Ardash finishes my sentence. 'Especially since you made it clear that if I came to Troyes, I was to have no expectations.'

We've moved to the oak table to begin our meal. Shadows from the fire make strange shapes on the walls as I serve the Truffade and salad. Ardash pours the wine.

'The distance isn't an issue,' he replies, handing me my glass. 'Do you remember what I told you about what my religion teaches about *Karma Yoga*—the idea of doing something good for its own sake?'

I nod, thinking back to Saucha and his solitary mission. Ardash smiles at me.

'I came because you asked me to,' he says. 'Not because of what I might receive in return.'

We eat in silence as the fire spits and crackles behind us. I take a sip of my wine. Now that he is actually here, my aim seems less tangible than it did when I conceived this idea, and I'm no longer sure exactly what it is that I want to say, or at least how to begin.

...

'Oh my god!'

She was trying desperately to cover herself, but the fact that she was carrying two wine glasses couldn't disguise the fact that she was wearing nothing but stockings and a flimsy black negligee.

'Oh my god,' she said again.

We stood facing each other, my hand still clutching the keys, redundant now that I saw the intruder. Her face looked so familiar, but I just couldn't place her.

'Well,' I said. 'I think you'd better give me those glasses and go and put on some clothes, don't you?'

The woman thrust the glasses at me and rushed towards the bedroom. I went into the kitchen and put one of them down on the kitchen counter next to a bottle of Nuit Saint Georges. Not bad I thought, noting the year. I walked back into the salon and sat down on the sofa. A few moments later the woman came back into the room, red-faced and wearing jeans and a tee-shirt. I took a sip of her wine.

The shock of recognition caught me off guard, as now she was dressed, I realised who she was.

'I think,' I said to her coldly, 'you'd better explain to me exactly what you're doing here.'

...

'I've done a lot of thinking over the last weeks,' I begin, putting down my fork and dabbing the corners of my mouth with my napkin. Ardash nods. 'Such a lot has changed for me. It's less than a year since my father died. And... I've ended a friendship that has been important to me.'

I glance up, expecting Ardash to respond, but he doesn't, and I'm grateful. Regardless of the fact that I'm at peace with my decision to break off with Theo-Paul, I don't want to betray the friendship we had. Ardash lifts a forkful of Truffade to his mouth, and I watch his Adam's apple rise and fall as he swallows. I notice that I'm twisting my napkin between my hands and I put it down beside my plate. We continue the meal in silence.

Once we've eaten all we are going to, Ardash puts down his glass and I rise from my seat. Ardash rises too and follows me to the fireplace where I indicate for him to sit in one of the two armchairs.

'Don't move,' I say. Ardash sits staring into the flames and I go to collect two fresh glasses from the kitchen. When I return, one of the bottles of Malbec is standing by the fireside. Glancing at it, I see that it's called *Fin Del Mundo*: The end of the world.

I take my place in the other armchair. I have a sheet of paper and a pen in my hand. Ardash picks up the wine bottle, and I watch the veins on his forearms bulge as he tightens the corkscrew. His eyes fixed on mine, he slowly withdraws the cork.

Is it my father's voice I hear, as I turn to the flames.

'...tell me what you've learned then, girl...'

Achille De Quincy—Before my death

How much time remains to me, I don't know, certainly very little. The nurses have grown quieter and the doctor no longer comes. I'm being eased into death. You are here almost all the time, and I love you for that. I have tried to articulate to you some of what has been occupying my last lucid moments. When I speak though, the words I need don't come. Aren't the dying supposed to benefit from some kind of wisdom that eludes us until then? Aren't we supposed to know, suddenly and with luminous clarity 'what it's all about'? If so, I'm being cheated. When I can think, when I'm conscious enough, what consumes me is not fear of what lies beyond this life, but the inscrutability of life itself. For all my introspection, the questions that have occupied my final days remain unanswered, unanswerable, and I am left with the thought that, as a father, indeed, I'll say it, as a man, I've never really known what I was doing. I've played the parts of Achille the Doctor, Achille the husband, Achille the father, Achille the brave widower. But now, after these long days and nights of contemplation, after a life-time of contemplation, an undeniable fact persists: the bewilderment I felt when faced with you, newly born and thrust into my arms, never left me. The most honest thing I can say, at the end of it all, is that I remain mystified.

My girl, there can be no doubt, you are a successful woman. But there is a difference between raising a happy person and a successful one. My suspicion is, that people who drive themselves as hard as you do are rarely content. And I have more questions than answers. Will you find one day that work is not enough? What then? Will you be lonely? Will it be my fault? Do I wish you'd married? Had children? Have I equipped you with sufficient courage and character to take to your own dying day?

Is my mind failing me? Not yet I fear, girl. Perhaps when it does, I will finally stop trying to answer the one question behind all those others that could assuage my ultimate disquiet: have I done my best for you? I've run out of time to explore all that could lead me to that final answer. I suspect that if I lay in this bed for a thousand years, there wouldn't be time enough. So what do I do? Confess to you, or to God that I might have done better? Impart to you whatever I can pass off as a dying father's wisdom? Trust that you have the strength to weather your own storms? What else can I do? The only truth I know is that I have loved you. The only hope I have is that this has made you strong.

Troyes

'First, there are some things I'd like to say.'

The two of us sip our wine and stare into the flames, the fire crackling and hissing and shifting in the grate. Ardash leans forward to pick up the poker and gives the wood a nudge, sending a shower of golden specks flying up the chimney.

'I've been thinking about this for some time.'

Ardash nods and I take a deep breath.

'Okay. I want to start by saying that I'm very well aware that I have a good life. I've been successful, and that has been the result of effort and determination as well as a handful of luck. I know my own strength and I'm not scared of hard work… but… but since my father's death …how shall I put this? I've learned something about myself over the past year. I've become more and more conscious of… It's not that I'm passive or submissive…but even so, I've become aware that there's a part of myself that…that's not acting but reacting.'

I pause. It hasn't come out at all the way I'd intended, and to my own ears I sound garbled and incoherent.

Go on girl, I'm listening…

'Go on,' Ardash says.

I don't look up as I speak, but continue to stare into the fire.

'My father wanted me to be successful. When I was a child he would tell me about the lives of great men and women, people who'd achieved great things. I grew up not doubting I could reach the top of whatever I chose to do. In fact, I grew up feeling that I *had* to reach the top. I sensed, even at a young age, something vulnerable in my father. I knew that not to achieve that degree of success would be letting him down. He said he wanted me to marry and to have children. But no man I introduced to him was good enough. I've sometimes wondered whether he sabotaged my relationships. Looking back, I think I did too. He was the man in my life, and while he was alive I didn't need anyone else...'

Saying the words out loud, I suddenly feel childish and, staring at the flames, question why I thought I'd find them so powerful when spoken. I pick up the poker and nudge a fallen log back into place.

It's such a basic struggle, Father!

Perhaps girl, but it's your struggle.

I replace the poker in its stand and stare at the dark shadows behind the flickering flames, before continuing.

'He was a good man. Courageous. My mother died when I was young. She was killed by a car while she was out shopping. I have some hazy memories, but I remember almost nothing of her. I don't think my father ever truly recovered. After her death, he developed a kind of obsessive need for me to be okay, as though it would be a betrayal of my mother if I wasn't. And there's a sense in which I understand that. I have no doubt that he loved me and did his best for me. And he didn't fail. But... but now... this last year... I've come to wonder whether *I'm* betraying *him* by questioning the part of me that was...that was cut from the template of my father's need...'

I will always love you, girl, there's no changing that...

'Ardash, I'm sorry, it must seem like I should have something grand to say here, to justify bringing you all this way. But there's no big reveal. I have no great secret. I'm just a woman, struggling to make sense of her life. My big epiphany is simply my realisation that it's time to free myself from my father's life and my mother's death. I've come to see how that two-pronged grip has kept me in a kind of a lone, Sisyphean determination to prove myself... I want to change that. And I felt of all the people I know, you'd understand...'

As I listen to my words I feel both detached from, and intimate with them. *Like looking into a mirror.* I glance at Ardash to gauge his response. He lifts his chin in encouragement.

'So, the woman at my office was right,' I continue, 'the world ends tonight.'

Ardash has remained quiet, not touching his wine, simply nodding from time to time. Now, he watches as I take up the sheet of paper and the pen; as I write, taking my time over the bold letters. I look up at him, at his face, shadowed to one side, firelight dancing over the other.

'I'm not letting go of my father's legacy,' I say. 'I'm using it to open a new door.'

I fold the sheet and hand it to Ardash. He looks at me questioningly and I nod. He opens the sheet.

'T-P' he reads aloud.

'*The Past*', I say.

A log shifts and we both glance round at the spray of golden sparks. One lands on the rug and Ardash stubs it out with the toe of his shoe. He folds the sheet, kisses it and hands it back to me.

'You know what this means?' I whisper. 'I won't see you again for a long time. Possibly ever.' I watch the flames writhe in his eyes. 'I want to live without T-P first. I want to be certain there are no T-P shadows, influencing my choices.

'I understand.'

Ardash puts out a hand and strokes my cheeks where they are wet with tears. I kiss the folded sheet and throw it into the fire.

'Burn the old to make way for the new.'

Troyes and Versailles

'Please, I can explain,' the now-clothed woman pleaded. She was standing by the lounge door. I scrutinised her closely from where I sat on the sofa. She was about my age, possibly a few years older, although she looked a little younger now that she was dressed and had tied her hair back. *She certainly looks good in a negligée,* I thought.

'Please do,' I replied, 'I'm listening.' The woman opened her mouth and closed it again. She wouldn't make eye contact with me but cast around the room as though something there would come to her rescue. I didn't blame her, her humiliation was clearly excruciating.

'For goodness sake,' I said. 'Sit down.' She walked over to an armchair and perched on the edge. I continued to glare at her. 'Well? Are you going to tell me what you're doing here?'

The woman opened her mouth to speak but at that moment, we both jumped as the front door opened and closed again with a loud bang.

...

'No François,' I'd said, 'I'm sorry to call at the weekend but I don't think this can wait.' François had clearly been irritated.

'Can't you tell me what it is,' he'd grumbled, when I called him from the cottage. 'I'm sure we can talk it through on the phone.' But I'd been adamant.

'I'm sorry,' I repeated. 'But this is something we need to discuss in person.'

'Okay,' he said eventually. 'If it's that serious, you can come to the house tomorrow. Let's say 4.30, I can't make it any earlier.'

...

'I'm here my pumpkin!' sang a man's voice. 'And you'd better be either naked or nearly naked 'cos I've got something big and hard here that isn't taking no for an answer!'

I looked at the woman and raised an eyebrow. Her face crumpled and I thought she was going to cry. Neither of us moved. Instead we stared fixedly at the lounge door. It opened slowly and we watched as a huge baguette poked its way around the door.

'Bet you haven't seen one this big!' said the man's voice. 'And every inch is for you.'

The woman made a whimpering sound.

'Darling?' said the man.

The baguette disappeared and he stepped around the door, coming face to face with the two of us. I gave him an icy smile. He looked from the woman to me and back again, on his face an expression of complete bewilderment, as though he couldn't comprehend what his eyes were telling him.

'Tristan,' I said. 'I can only assume that you thought you'd conduct an extra one-to-one interview prior to Monday.'

...

I'd arrived at François' home at exactly 4.30 as he'd said.

'I can't believe the utter stupidity of the man!' he spluttered once we were seated in the conservatory. It was blustery outside, and Blondine had clicked on a heater having brought us a cup of tea, before backing discreetly out of the double doors.

'Okay, a man is a man, and having a mistress is one thing,' François said. 'Nothing to be proud about, but, well, these things happen, let's not deny that.' I raised an eyebrow but said nothing. 'He must have known that you use the cottage, what on earth was he thinking? And he gave her a key! Clearly she's out of the running for the

Directorship.' He looked intently at me. 'I hope you made that perfectly clear to her.' I nodded and took a sip of tea.

In fact I hadn't had to say very much to the woman at all. Tristan had grabbed their coats and bags and ushered her out of the cottage muttering something about discussing the situation in the morning. He'd slammed the door behind them. I'd sat there on the sofa, feeling shaken at first, and then laughing out loud at the audacity of the man. *I pity his wife*, I thought, wondering whether she had any inkling. But that wasn't my business. What was my business was the fact that he'd tried to get his mistress a position on the board. I'd left a message with the Troyes office to cancel Monday's interviews, and called François. Tristan had phoned the next day to say the woman had withdrawn her candidacy.

'I don't expect to have to discuss the matter any further,' he'd said in a sombre voice.

'He obviously didn't know you were using the cottage for the weekend,' François said.

'Well no,' I replied, 'there was no reason to tell him. I didn't even know he had a key...'

'No reason indeed!' François interjected. I wondered if I sensed in him a hint of admiration for the fact that Tristan was using his cottage for secret trysts with a lover.

A fierce wind had blown up and something in the garden was making a repeated clanging sound. 'François,' I said, ignoring it, 'using the cottage is one thing, and the fact that Tristan has a lover is of no concern to anyone but him and his wife. What I am deeply concerned about is the fact that he put this woman forward for the Finance Director post. Now that I think about it, he was most insistent she was shortlisted.'

'Indeed,' François replied, getting up to close the curtains. 'That does show extremely poor judgement.'

'It shows more than that,' I retorted. 'As a Director, his responsibility is to the company. He should be making the best decisions for the business, not for his...' I paused. 'Not for his private life.'

'Yes, yes, of course you're right,' François said, sitting back down in his seat. 'I mean, who's to say this woman would have known one end of a profit and loss account from another? It clearly wasn't her skill with a spreadsheet that made him put her forward!'

I looked at François. The pouches under his eyes were sagging, his skin greyish and pale, apart from the purple veins threaded across his nose. I noticed his hand shaking almost imperceptibly as he held his cup to his lips. I felt a pang of guilt for burdening him with this. I sipped my tea, wondering whether I'd over-reacted. No, I told myself firmly, bringing this to François was the right thing to do.

'There's a lot to consider here. More than you know, actually.' François put down his cup and looked at me intently as though weighing something up in his mind. 'Now listen to me,' he said, leaning forward. 'This is confidential, you hear? You must tell no one. Even Tristan doesn't know yet.' He continued to glare at me as he spoke. 'The point is, I'm soon to be retiring. Blondine has wanted it for a long time if truth were known. There are still things to be worked out, but the most important question is who succeeds me.' He turned to the curtained windows and stared as though gazing through them to the garden beyond. He shook his head, and standing once more, went to the window and pulled back a curtain. 'I'd already made my decision, but now...' He paused for a long moment and I followed his gazed through the partly obscured window where dusk was falling. A flock of crows burst from a linden tree, their caws breaking the silence as they scattered into the darkening sky. 'The stupid, stupid man...' François spoke almost to himself, still staring out of the window. 'This little escapade has cost Tristan the job of CEO.'

Paris, The Montparnasse Tower and Café La Tour

François was late, but arrived just as I'd picked up the phone to Le Ciel de Paris to ask them to hold our table.

'I'm sorry,' I'd said to him on the phone. 'I'd rather this didn't wait for too long. It's something I need to tell you soon, and in person.'

'Everything is always urgent with you,' François had grumbled. 'Okay, look, if it's that important, why wait? I want to drop by the office anyhow; I have a stack of expenses receipts I've been meaning to give to Solange. What say we meet at 12.00? We can go up to the restaurant, I'm sure I can get us a table. We may as well make a lunch of it.'

I watched him arrive as I had done so many times before, striding through the office, a smile on his face that didn't reach his eyes, patting backs here, shaking hands there. Jean said something to him as he passed, and François laughed and nodded. He shook Claude's hand whilst looking around to see who else was there, and left him without a backward glance. Tristan came to the door of his office and François walked up to him and stepped inside. I watched through the glass wall as they shook hands firmly, François grasping Tristan's shoulder with his free hand. They spoke for some moments and they both laughed. I caught, 'Good man, good man,' as François clapped Tristan on the shoulder a final time before turning to leave his office.

I rose from my seat and went to greet him as François handed Solange a fat brown envelope stuffed with receipts. He bent to murmur something in her ear. Solange took the envelope and nodded, and I ignored, as I was supposed to, the spurious 'expenses' claims.

'We'd better go up straight away,' I said, accepting a kiss on each cheek. 'They're holding our table for us.'

Tristan watched us as we left.

We rode the elevator to the 56th floor where, inside Le Ciel de Paris, we followed a starched and formal waiter past the central bar to our table.

'Good, we're by the window,' François said. 'I never tire of this view.' The waiter took our coats and pulled out two chairs.

'Can I get you something to drink?' he murmured.

'Give us time, man,' François grumbled. 'At least let us catch our breath.' The waiter bowed his head and left, taking our coats with him.

While François studied first the lunch menu, then the wine list, I gazed through the big plate-glass window. I let my eyes move slowly past La Tour Eiffel, the cluster of towers of La Défense competing valiantly behind it. Beneath them, Paris lay stretched out like a recumbent woman. I watched fleeting shadows cast by scudding clouds dance across the buildings towards the hills beyond. Now that the moment was actually here, all the thinking I'd done over the past weeks seemed to melt into this view—so familiar, yet so aloof—taking the words I'd prepared with it. I looked back at François, glasses slipping down his nose, brow furrowed, as he studied the menu.

'Well, steak it is for me,' he said, snapping the menu shut. 'And what about a nice bottle of Chablis?' *Why not?* I thought.

The waiter took our order and returned with the wine, taking his time to uncork the bottle and pour a small amount into François' glass, turning judiciously away while he swirled it a couple of times before taking a deep sniff. He nodded curtly to the waiter who poured us a glass each, placed the wine bottle carefully in its stand and covered it with a neatly folded napkin.

'Well then,' François said, once he was gone. 'I'm far too old to dilly dally. What was so urgent that it couldn't wait?'

...

'Not here,' I'd said to Marine, later that day. 'Let's go out and get a coffee and I'll tell you what happened.'

Seated at a quiet, corner banquet in Café La Tour, I slowly stirred my coffee.

'So?' she said.

'Well, what I'd planned, was to be honest about it, to tell him how I felt,' I replied. 'That because TKG had made it clear that their main interest in us was the expansion into India, I was left with a major dilemma. That since he was still unwilling to budge on delaying the sale, and because I was so resolutely opposed to the redundancies we'd have to make if we went ahead with India, I'd been left in an untenable situation.' Marine nodded. 'But you know what? I suddenly realised, sitting there with him, staring out across Paris, that none of what I'd planned to say was really the point. The problem wasn't the sale of the business. It wasn't the fact that no-one but you took my vision for the business seriously. It wasn't Tristan and the constant fighting—it wasn't even the redundancies.'

Marine kept her eyes fixed on mine, and I paused for a long moment before continuing. 'I suddenly saw that all those things were simply symptoms of the problem. The real issue, the root of all the others, was that I wasn't holding my own reins. François always had control. He never relinquished it, even after he retired. And in spite of not being made CEO, Tristan was still his man. My own ideas for the business, my aspirations, my plans, my vision —none of that was ever going to be anything other than secondary to theirs.'

...

Our meals had arrived and while François made light work of his steak. 'No need to tell Blondine. Worries about my old ticker.' I'd pushed my sea bass around the plate. François looked at me expectantly.

'Let's have it then,' he said, picking up his glass and taking a large sip. 'Not someone else caught in flagrante delicto, I hope!' He chuckled at his own joke.

'François.' I put down my fork and looked at him, his knife in one hand, glass in the other, his red face shining with perspiration. *A man aging.* 'There's no easy way to tell you this, so I'm just going to say it. I'm tendering my resignation.'

Paris, Ile Saint Louis

Five months, that's all it's been. Five months since I burned T-P in the fire in Troyes. Five months since I said goodbye to my two lovers. And since I quit my job. A trinity of changes. Am I nervous? Certainly. Scared? Of course. But fear has never stopped me before, and this time is no different.

This morning I woke early, having slept for a full eight hours and thirty seven minutes. I'd lain there savouring the sleepy warmth of my bed before flinging off the cover and swinging out my legs. Today is not a day for sleeping-in.

The balcony doors are open wide and I plan to pass a pleasant hour reading and enjoying the morning bustle below. Seated at the table outside, a warm croissant and a cup of coffee steaming in front of me, I pause before opening my book, and take in the view. My gaze moves past the Pont Louis-Philippe to the Seine beyond, sparkling restless-silver in the morning sunlight, and I inhale deeply the warmth of the springtime air, thinking how much can change in the course of a year. I see that the patio doors of the apartment opposite are open and I watch the curtains fluttering lightly in the breeze. The geraniums lasted well into the winter, but now, the pots are all bare. *No matter*, I tell myself. I take a sip of my coffee, pick up my book and begin to read: *"Call me Mary Beton, Mary Seton, Mary Carmichael or any other name you please—it is not a matter of importance."*

Later, I begin to prepare lunch—a simple onion quiche with a crisp green salad. I hum to myself as I bustle around the kitchen, placing ready plates, silver-ware, two Champagne flutes. My phone rings and I dash to the salon and grab it from the table, noting with pleasure the name on the caller display.

'Everything okay?' I ask.

'Yes fine, I wanted to let you know, I'm running late but I'm on my way. I stopped off to pick something up.'

'No problem,' I reply, with a glance at my watch. 'Everything's ready. I'm really very excited!'

'Me too. See you soon.'

I return to collect the silver-ware and take it to the balcony where I lay it out on the table. Below, a group of young tourists are capering over the bridge, and I smile as I catch the words 'awesome' and 'stoked' as they disappear off towards the right bank. They pass an old couple who are standing in companionable silence, staring down the Seine towards the Pont au Change. Still smiling, I watch the woman take the man's hand, as the bells of Notre Dame start their twelve o' clock knell, and as the intricate pealing resonates across the Ile Saint Louis, I feel my new future opening out before me.

'Merci, Father,' I whisper.

The buzzer rings, startling me out of my reverie, and I jump up and dart across the salon to pick up the intercom.

'Great, you're here, come on up,' I say, as I press the release button.

I hurry to the kitchen to take the Champagne out of the fridge before returning to the door where I straighten my loose cotton tunic. It feels good to be out of the formal clothes I'd worn for so long, and I look down at my jeans and my bright red toe-nails, my feet bare against the warmth of the parquet, and smile broadly. After some moments I hear the sound of footsteps on the stairs. I listen as they ascend steadily, and once they reach the final staircase, I open the door and step to one side.

What I see first is not at all what I'm expecting and I laugh out loud as an enormous pot of purple geraniums rounds the door and presents itself to me. A smiling face appears from behind the blooms, flushed and panting from the climb, and I receive a warm kiss on each cheek.

'Well, are you ready to celebrate the launch of *'Saucha Events'*?' Marine smiles broadly as she sings the name of our new company. 'These are for you, Isabelle.' She thrusts the geraniums at me. 'I thought they'd be perfect for your balcony.'

The Geranium Woman has been an absorbing and exciting project. I feel strongly that if we want to offer our children and grand-children a sustainable, healthy and egalitarian life, we must consider how we operate our businesses and the effects they have on our world. I am highly impressed by Richard Branson's 'B Team' initiative, and I, like the CEO in this novel, feel that a shift towards a trinity of 'people, planet, profit' is a worthy starting point. My hope is that in writing this book, I have contributed in some small way to that shift.

I am indebted to a whole host of people in the creation of this novel. Not least my full and grateful thanks to Grahame, Norma, Jim, Ksenya, Ruth and the other members of Paris Writers' Working Lunches. I am grateful also to Hilarie Owen, CEO of the Institute for who made space in her busy life to provide insightful comments. Thanks to Shane for his help with all things Indian, and to the unsuspecting business men and women I randomly accosted in the name of research – merci beaucoup for your frank answers to probing questions.

My heartfelt thanks as ever to Jan Fortune, Adam Craig, Elizabeth Porter and all at Cinnamon Press – an excellent example of an ethically-run enterprise – whose unstinting hard work and belief in me as a writer is both humbling and motivating.

Pierre... Des simples mots ne sont pas assez, et pourtant, je vous remercie d'avoir créé avec moi cet espace où mes histoires viennent à la vie....

And Willow... fy merch byth gariadus, ar ei chyfer hi mae fy ngeiriau - diolch cariad.

'She is my arrow, he is my bow.'

Learn about the excellent work the B Team are doing at
www.thebteam.com